MW00653283

Trencher's Bunker

Shane Noble

This is a work of fiction. Names, characters, places, and incidents either are the product of the author's imagination or are used fictitiously. Any resemblance to actual persons, living or dead, events, or locales is entirely coincidental.

Copyright © by Shane Noble 2020

All rights reserved. No part of this book may be reproduced or used in any manner without written permission of the copyright owner except for the use of quotations in a book review.

First paperback edition November 2020

ISBN: 978-1-7360486-0-3 (paperback)
ISBN: 978-1-7360486-1-0 (ebook)

10 9 8 7 6 5 4 3 2 1

To mom. Thank you for being a reader and encouraging me to write.

Chapter One

Henry Plyman had not been home in half a decade. Work had sent him all over the world, but never had it sent him home.

He got the gig through fairly benign nepotism. He told his best friend that he didn't want to work for him, and instead wanted to travel while young. That friend, Marcus Trencher of *Trencher Industries*, wouldn't take no. They compromised, and Henry found himself globetrotting on a team set out to implement Trencher's revolutionary grid technology, city by city, around the world.

With little explanation, Trencher called for Henry to come back to Indiana. He had to show him something, he said.

Despite the years abroad, Henry still knew the backroads. He cruised them incessantly as a teenager. Winding gravel roads cut through the "stripper pits" – used up coal mining lands full of deep gashes the coal companies turned into lakes to appease conservation law.

He was deep in nostalgia, and the middle of nowhere, windows down.

He came across a fence he was sure wasn't there last he was around. It was ten-feet tall, lined with green privacy screening and topped with barbed wire. Whatever Trencher wanted to show him, he didn't want to show others.

Security waved him through without a full stop. He turned the radio down and squinted through the sun's glare.

Popping gravel beneath his tires gave way to a greater noise rumbling from beyond a ridge ahead. He parked and approached on foot.

Marcus Trencher waited at the edge. Henry stepped up next to him, and before he could properly greet his pal, his gaze dipped into the pit below.

"My God, Marcus. What is this?"

180-ton trucks skirted the edges while workers in white helmets busied themselves like ants carrying morsels of food, earth, and eggs. The pit was circular and ringed with switchbacks, like some great amphitheater into the abyss.

"Henry! You're back," Marcus said. "How was Asia?"

"Great. Glad to be back. Seriously, Trench, what the hell is this hole in the ground?"

"If anyone asks, tell them it's a geothermal project."

Henry was only certain it wasn't a coal mine. Trencher's invention, and source of enormous wealth, was the nail in the coffin for the coal industry before it entered the mass market a decade ago.

"Okay. But what is it?"

Marcus sat down on the rubble-strewn ground. Henry joined.

"Not a soul in that pit is a local. Mostly Army Corp of Engineers, CIA, NSA. I talked to a guy earlier who had a PhD, before he got yelled at by a grunt to get back to work."

"You landed a government contract to dig a hole in rural Sherman County using the army?"

"More or less. Nine years ago, right after we wrapped up in Atlanta, I got an invite from the Pentagon. I figured military contracts, right? It ended up being something much crazier."

He tapped a rock onto another in the alluvial washout to fill the pause.

"Henry, this hole is not a geo-thermal-whatever. It is a super bunker."

"A super bunker?"

"Yes. A large-scale bunker capable of sustaining life long-term."

Henry nodded.

He didn't want to give Marcus the satisfaction of getting a rise out of him. It had to be a joke.

Marcus Trencher did have that kind of stupid money. He could throw ten billion in the pit, burn it, and not feel a thing. There were honest-to-God economists calculating how Marcus Trencher could become a trillionaire someday.

The problem was, although Marcus Trencher had stupid money, he was not stupid. He did not do stupid things.

He wouldn't even do unnecessary things.

Was a bunker necessary?

"A bunker, for like, an apocalyptic event?"

"Yes, or a *sub*-apocalyptic event."

Plyman stood and looked down into the pit. "How much did all this cost?"

"Not a dime. It's not about money anymore. It's all about bunker bids. Life is the new currency – not dollars, not gold, not crypto – but life. At least, for those that already know."

Henry didn't know what to believe.

"Sub-apocalyptic. So, like 2020 pandemic, but deadlier?"

Marcus shook his head. "They made it clear that these bunkers were required, and that these bunkers required certain specs. I don't think it's another virus."

"Then what?"

"Think more *Hollywood*."

Henry played visions of cheesy disaster movies. "Oh, c'mon. An asteroid? That isn't even original."

"Not kidding. They refused to say outright, but a catastrophic impact is the only thing that makes sense. Anyway, if I were joking, I'd think of something better." He thumbed to the massive pit. "I also wouldn't dig this hole just to pull one on you."

The giant hole in the earth was convincing. Marcus also wasn't known for his pranks, or general sense of humor, but...the end of the world?

"Where do you come in? You rub shoulders with powerful people, but I don't see how you got involved in something like this."

"Bunkers like this have been built all over the U.S. and allied countries the past eight years. Hundreds that were decommissioned from World War II and the Cold War eras have been refurbished. I designed power systems for the new ones. That is where I came in. In return for my services, I got us a site right here at home that I've been personally overseeing."

Henry tried to absorb the news. A million thoughts shot through his jet-lagged mind.

"Also, the U.S. government chose every city we implemented our grids in. They've essentially run the company all these years. Those projects across China and Europe you oversaw were picked by them."

"Really? Any rhyme or reason they chose where they chose?"

"The funny thing is, they picked exactly where I would have. The pattern optimized the grid like we were going to do anyhow. I don't know if they used us for political capital or what. I can't imagine the infrastructure would survive an impact, but I wasn't in a position to ask questions."

"Wait...you said that first meeting was *nine* years ago?"

Marcus shrugged.

Henry looked out at the scarred horizon. "I've spent the last five years on four different continents training people on how to rebuild their electrical infrastructure with the whole idea of saving the planet from global warming. I've missed friends and family, when you knew all along that an asteroid or whatever was about to make it all pointless?"

"It wasn't pointless," Marcus sighed. "Look, you got to see the world firsthand on a farewell tour where everyone treated you like a rock star. You didn't have to live with this terrible secret. Your friends and family are taken care of. That was priority. It wasn't a waste."

Henry sat back down.

* * *

Marcus had years to connect dots. He tried catching Henry up, starting in space.

After decades of a lackluster space program, private industry put a base on the moon. A manned mission to Mars was a success, and a decade ahead of schedule. On American campuses, "terra-forming" and "biosphere" degrees popped up in course guides.

"Why all the sudden investment in space, right? Not just space, but colonization," Marcus said.

The mainstream media was brought into the fold early on. The press aided and abetted the shit-show of distractions the U.S. Government provided.

It begged the question on whether the President at the onset was purposely as distracting as he was, or if he was truly that absurd.

Marcus wasn't sure of that one.

Detroit began cranking out tunnel-boring machines, TBI's, like Model T's. 15 states had tunnel projects started within the last five years.

"Tunnels are prohibitively expensive and hardly make sense, yet we all started digging."

Marcus himself had been leading the charge of digging a tunnel beneath the I-65 corridor between Indianapolis and Louisville, putting up most of the funding himself.

It was so ludicrous, late show hosts made fun of him for it. *60 Minutes* dug into his past, bringing up his mother's car accident and his well-known phobia of riding in cars, attributing the tunnel project to his trauma-fueled mission to make travel safer.

In reality, it only existed to connect a network of bunkers.

Henry was overseas, but even he had heard it was causing heated debate amongst Hoosiers. Many applauded the infrastructure job creation and defended Marcus's right to waste his money on it. Others were against it because, well, there are always people against everything.

Henry's parents told him the people fighting it were conspiracy whack jobs. Maybe those people were on to something.

"This is an impossible secret to keep," Henry said. "How come I never heard of any leaks?"

"It's easy to make a leak look like fake news. Plus, the social media guys were some of the first the government took in. Shoot, they killed one of them. People stay quiet to keep their bunker bids."

The economics were fabricated by the Fed, Marcus continued. No one objected to buffed-up entitlement programs post-pandemic. The world economy took off. Mankind appeared to be getting things right, finally. It didn't matter that it was all made up.

One tale was legitimate, though, and that was the story of Marcus Trencher: the boy genius who reversed the meter on the world's energy consumption.

Henry knew the story. At age 7, Marcus got ahold of one of his father's engineering textbooks and showed immediate signs of comprehension. By 10, he had exhausted the local school system. His father took his prodigy son to his job at the local power plant and introduced him to electricity and infrastructure. Marcus became obsessed with it.

Marcus stayed in their withering hometown of Sherman, Indiana. Too young yet to jettison off to an east coast Ivy league, he attended Rose-Hulman Institute of Technology, a top-notch engineering school in Terre Haute. He had one goal in mind: to reimagine and rebuild the electrical grid. Ambitious goals for a teenager.

Henry thought Marcus was taking the pandemic quarantine very seriously all those years ago. He was really perfecting his invention twenty hours a day.

The genius in his breakthrough was not only in efficiency, but the sophisticated synergy of all alternatives of power – and the storage of typically wasted energy. His magical little box could track power usage, store power, and coordinate the grid according to demand. And it scaled. It was not entirely new, but he so thoroughly outdid the competition, he became a superstar.

The first round of willing neighbors saw their electric bill plummet, and word spread.

With enough residential windmills and solar panels, the town of Sherman was capable of exporting energy. Marcus gained national attention, and after wiring up the mid-sized city of Terre Haute, everyone was convinced of Trencher's micro grids. He created the first truly regenerative city. Patents were filed, investment poured in.

He founded *Trencher Industries* and began changing the world. He made billions along the way.

* * *

Henry had all he could take for the time being. It was a lot to digest, the end of the world and all.

"Get some sleep, if you can," Marcus said on the walk to Henry's car. "Come over to my place in the morning, I'll cook breakfast. I'm going to put you back to work – real work. We have a lot to do."

"Okay," Henry said, not feeling okay.

Henry made it back to his brand-new home, built for him while overseas. He didn't even know his way around it yet.

He dropped his things on the floor and collapsed on a sofa.

Before he gave into exhaustion, he thought simple, childlike thoughts.

I don't want the world to end.

I don't want to die.

Chapter Two

They sat in Marcus's kitchen on the far side of Marcus's mansion. Henry chomped on bacon.

"Not sure how much longer we'll get to eat meat. Still haven't decided if we'll be taking livestock down with us or not."

Henry shifted. It all hadn't settled with him.

"Seems risky, you know, humans and animals living in close proximity. Ruined more than a few civilizations," Marcus said as he buttered a piece of toast. "Regardless, I have facilities built in if an expert gives the go-ahead. It's not like we'll be eating raw bat or anything."

Henry couldn't muster a laugh. Marcus stopped and looked at him.

"Hasn't sunk in has it?"

Henry shook his head.

"It's real," Marcus said. "Wish it wasn't. But our future is secure. Nothing will take that bunker out."

"Can't believe I haven't asked, but how much time do we have left?"

Marcus stopped his kitchen work and slapped his forehead. "I didn't tell you! They gave us a hard date! Like I said, they did everything except outright say it's an asteroid."

Henry interrupted. "Marcus, the date? How long do we have?"

"Sorry. A year, but not really. The hard date they gave was July 23, 2030. I have to think that is the day of impact. At some point before than they won't be able to hide it anymore. When that news breaks, it would be best if we got underground. There is still much to be done. I've cut it a little too close, honestly."

Henry was beginning to digest the reality, but he had too many questions.

"Something else you should know," Marcus said. "I had to let Timothy go."

"Really? Timothy Spencer? What happened?"

Company gossip seemed so insignificant considering recent revelations, but this was no ordinary employee. Timothy Spencer was like a big brother to Marcus. They met in college when Marcus was a kid. Timothy was the cofounder of *Trencher Industries*. Henry was astonished that the news hadn't reached him.

"There was no announcement and there won't be. We couldn't see eye-to-eye on something. Don't worry about him. He will be fine."

All the hardware and software specifications on Marcus's original prototype were worked out by Spencer. Particularly, the blockchain tech. His greatest contribution, though, was the sleek design of the *Monolith*, the obsidian box that held Marcus's invention. It was comparable in size to an air-conditioning unit and became a status symbol to

11

place in front of suburban homes, like a Mercedes in the driveway.

"I'm sorry to hear that, I know you were close," Henry said. He knew there was more to the story, but he didn't want to set Marcus off. *Not seeing eye-to-eye* was usually all it took.

"Yes, it's a shame, but I am fine. Go to your real home tonight, eat with your parents and pretend nothing is wrong."

My parents. Henry hadn't seen them since a working vacation in Budapest a year prior.

"Remember, Henry, they are safe. Not a word."

* * *

Henry's own good fortune was courtesy of Marcus Trencher. He was more than reminded when he finally had a chance to explore his new home.

There was a workout room, a movie theatre, and a three-car garage with two expensive cars that weren't his. Or were they?

Henry thought it kind of weird that Marcus had all of this built for him, and it would be abandoned soon. Probably all part of the ruse.

He walked out back. There was a pool, which he vaguely remembered requesting. He admired the view of the expanded Lake Sherman.

Marcus's favorite hobby was conservation, which only seemed morbid now. He bought all the discarded coal mining lands and connected many of the stripper pits. He created one of Indiana's largest bodies of water.

Henry realized the move created a better buffer, a moat, essentially, around the bunker site.

Henry felt restless. He had just gotten home, and yet it wasn't home. Not yet. Maybe never. He went back to the garage and hopped into one of the sports cars. Why not?

He backed out and pulled away, making the turns toward town.

Sherman was different – much different. The Square was bustling around the courthouse. There were unique shops, a café, and a Marriott Courtyard. *Runt's Bar* was now a steakhouse with rooftop seating. Downtown Sherman had become a regional shopping destination. Last time he lived in Sherman, most buildings around the Square were burnt out or vacant, a shriveled downtown given way to the box stores out by U.S. 41.

Trencher Industries original headquarters sat on the southeast corner. The company outgrew it and moved into a larger corporate park, but the downtown space was still Marcus's work office, so it remained the official HQ.

The police department had a brand-new two-story building with sleek, reflective glass. Big city stuff. A fine donation from *Trencher Industries*, no doubt.

There was now a movie theatre on what was formerly Section Street (renamed Trencher Street). Sherman County was the second poorest in the state before Marcus hit it big, single-handedly turning it into the wealthiest place to live in Indiana. The population doubled and a place that had nothing now had everything: Shopping, entertainment, jobs, and tourism. There were constant rumors of a Trencher-sponsored universal basic income for county residents. Despite the changes, it held onto its small-town charm.

I miss this.

I am going to miss this.

Every inch of development was designed or approved by Marcus. He had control over Sherman. Most townsfolk loved him, even though he rarely made a public appearance, much less spoke to a local.

Henry doubted that Marcus ever enjoyed anything after he was finished building it. Only the planning and process appealed to him.

He had been gawking and driving slowly. Pedestrians were staring at him and his *Trencher*-money car. He heard a few call out his name. He was himself a local celebrity. He rolled up his windows.

He parked in front of his parent's home on West Washington Street. He knocked at the door, even though he didn't have to.

It flew open. His mother smiled ear to ear, his father looked surprised.

Henry hugged them both and broke down in tears.

I miss them.

Marcus promised they were going to be taken care of.

Thank God I won't have to miss them in the end.

Chapter Three

Henry woke in a better mood. Dinner with his parents was always nice. He promised to do it often now that he wouldn't be globetrotting anymore.

He considered what to do for the day, and texted Marcus. *Need me for anything today?*

An hour later, still no reply. He dialed.

"Did you get my text? I was checking if you need me today."

"Nope. You spent a lot of time on the job without time off. You can play catch-up."

"Cool. I was wondering if you had heard from Robby lately."

"Sure. I pay for all his art projects and bail him out of jail semi frequently. The police drop him off at my house now."

Henry laughed. "Sounds about right. Is he there now?"

"He works in an old warehouse by the city park. It's his art studio."

* * *

"Robby!" Henry shouted over hard music.

Oblivious, Robby Reed was welding a monstrosity of metal with no shirt on. Henry threw a paint brush to get his attention.

Robby turned and his face lit up. "Henry!"

He turned the music off, then came at Henry, arms wide, bear-hugging him against his sweaty body. "What are you doing in town?"

"Had some time off. What is *that*?" He pointed to the giant metallic head in the middle of the room.

"Don't you recognize him?"

"Um, George W. Bush?"

"Damn right! His shoulders in the other room. Pretty badass, isn't it?"

Henry scratched his head. "Exact word I was thinking. Badass."

"It's going to be a memorial statue."

Henry couldn't fathom why Robby was creating a monument for the guy. They were only kids when he was in office. He couldn't remember hearing great things. Plus, Robby didn't know a thing about politics. "Marcus okayed this?"

"Marcus can't tell me what to do. See that stack of bathtubs over there?"

Sure enough, there was a stack of bathtubs.

"They are going to be filled with dirt and they'll all have running water. The tubs will be located on every side. People will create their own mud to sling at the statue. A basin around the bottom will catch all the mud when rain washes it down. Rinse and repeat."

Robby was pacing about, talking with his hands. "I know some people disliked him, so they'll get to

17

throw the mud out of spite. People who liked him will throw it out of admiration. It's, like, symbolic of shaping his legacy."

"That . . . is kind of cool," Henry said. "But I don't know if your fanbase will be too excited. Do you know what party he was in?"

"Party? Uh, Congress? Shit, I don't know. It doesn't matter. The point is both sides have a reason to throw mud. It's *bipartisan*."

Henry shook his head. "Have you ever even voted before?"

Robby cracked a smile. "Shut up. Let's grab a drink."

* * *

They took a booth under a neon beer sign and caught up on lost time. Laughter, country music, and the clack of games of pool made up the audible ambiance.

"Where are you going to put the statue?"

"The park by the lake. Did you see the copper and bronze corn husk on the courthouse lawn? I did that one, too. When the metals oxidize, it'll turn the husk green. I can't wait."

Henry had seen it but wasn't sure what it was. "Yeah, I saw that, pretty cool."

A drunkard at the U-shaped bar took a spill from his stool. The bar erupted in laughter. The man assured his audience he was fine and staggered to the restroom.

"Still plenty of these jackasses around," Robby said. "Dumbass rednecks. Hey, I have an idea." He turned toward the bar. "Angie! Shots! Over here. Don't care what!"

Henry said, "Oh no. No, no, no."

"We're celebrating. Just go with it."

Cheap whiskey scorched Henry's throat. It'd been awhile. His tolerance was pathetic.

It did feel great to unwind, though, to laugh and talk with a friend who truly understood him.

The drinks and merriment put them in their own zone for the better part of two hours.

Robby took a restroom break, and Henry sat alone, surprised he hadn't had to go yet.

The drunken redneck that fell earlier was slurring words with the younger crowd nearby. He was wearing a grass stained neon green shirt and had a circle worn into the back-right pocket of his jeans. The man swiveled his head toward him.

Great.

"Yer Henry Plyman, ain'tcha?"

"Yes sir, I am."

Robby returned from the bathroom just as the drunk said: "Yer . . . yer like a bill-un-air."

Before Henry could explain to the dropout that he was only a billionaire on paper and had not yet cashed in any of his *Trencher* stock, Robby cut in.

"Hey pal, leave him alone."

The drunk looked up to Robby and smirked. "Where'd you go? To call yer faggot friend, Trencher?"

Robby's reaction was fast and succinct. His fist connected with the man's jaw. The yokel sprawled onto the drunk next to him before toppling to the tile floor.

19

Henry expected the gang of rednecks to surround them, but they didn't. Instead, another burst of laughter.

Robby nodded at Henry and they left on foot.

They detoured to the City Park and found a set of swings to sit down on.

"You didn't have to do that. I'm sure he would've wandered off."

"That guy gets that way all the time. Glad I finally got the opportunity. One time I was in there and he asked if Marcus was 'some kind of gay'."

Henry laughed like he hadn't in so long. He lunged off the swing to a nearby tree to relieve himself.

"You know, I've had gallery shows in New York and L.A.," Robby said from his swing. "Marcus helped me in the beginning, and still does, but I've made a name for myself."

"Seriously? He didn't say anything about it." Henry returned to his swing. He hadn't kept up with Robby and felt like a terrible friend.

"Last week I sold a sculpture for $12,000. Took me two days to make. Some company is going to replicate it and sell it and I'll get royalties." They sat in silence for a pause. "I love Marcus, but the dude doesn't give me credit because he has no understanding of art."

"Man, he has big plans. I mean, bigger than what he has already –"

"Stop. I know."

Robby got up from the swing and started across the park toward his studio. Henry followed a few paces behind. Through his drunkenness, he surmised that he might have said something wrong.

When they got to the warehouse, Henry found a couch and passed out.

* * *

He awoke to rude morning light beaming through tall warehouse windows.

He could feel the hangover coming fast.

After a cursory search, Robby was nowhere to be found. Henry stepped outside and promptly threw up on the sidewalk.

He checked his pockets on his way to the car and was relieved to have everything: phone, wallet, credit card. He had a voice mail. He pressed the button to listen. It was Marcus.

"Get cleaned up and make your way out to the site. Rob's already here."

Robby is at the bunker?

The vague memory of the park swing set played back in his mind. He couldn't believe how careless he had been.

He stopped at home to shower, change clothes and drink a bottle of water. He grabbed the remaining bottle of water from a gift basket and left.

* * *

He found Marcus in khakis, a polo shirt, and a shit-eating grin.

"How are you feeling, champ?"

Henry shook his head. "Awful. Robby knew this whole time?"

"Yes, for a while now. Not jealous, are you?"

"Guess not. But why let him know and hold off on telling me until the last moment?"

"He is an idiot, but he is about as trustworthy as they come. If you say, 'Don't tell anyone,' he won't. He is a steel trap."

"With the secret or with alcohol?"

"Both. Put you under the table last night, did he not? Secondly, he is our farmer."

"Our what? I'm not following."

"Robby grew up on a farm and picked up on a few things from his father when the guy wasn't beating on him. He also studied agriculture down at Vincennes, almost enough to get the degree. And while we are in the bunker, we will need food. We'll have a whole system rigged up. He even has experience with hydroponics, before I convinced him to shut down *that* operation."

"I just assumed he studied art. Is he going to be up to the task? I don't want to starve to death because he took a drunken joy ride in a golf cart and ran over some crops."

"I'll control the alcohol down there. Special occasions only. But he knows his stuff. I trust him, one hundred percent."

They walked around a quarter of the crater and past dirt mounds. A series of garden plots were fitted together. Robby was walking through the rows of short green sprouts, shirtless.

Robby stopped and pointed. "These are tomatoes, cucumber over there, corn, lettuce, green peppers, carrot. Watch your step," he yelled.

Marcus smiled. "It keeps Robby from being a starving artist."

"I have to confess, Marcus, I almost let it slip last night. It was just to Robby – I didn't know he already knew – but still."

"I appreciate your honesty," Marcus said as Robby approached. "Don't worry too much about it. We've all slipped. Well, except Robby."

"Yeah, I ain't no snitch," Robby said.

"I wouldn't like you if you weren't tempted to tell one of our best friends. It is all easy going from here. Just avoid drinking."

Henry let this sink in. He was not comfortable being setup, but the truth was, over the years, he had grown used to it.

"You can trust me, is all I'm trying to say." Henry looked back to the dirt mounds. "And I'm not saying I don't trust you, but the bunker doesn't exactly look close to being finished."

"The bunker?" Marcus smiled. "It is already finished, other than a few cosmetics. That hole over there isn't for the bunker. The bunker is hundreds of feet below. We're standing over it. The hole is for construction purposes. It will be filled in soon."

Henry wasn't sure how they could fill that big of a gaping hole "soon," but it would probably be easier than making it.

"Can I see it? The inside of the bunker?"

"Not yet. But if you thought Sherman was impressive, just wait until you see what I did for our new underground hometown."

"Bastard hasn't let me see it either," Robby said.

"I need you to do one last thing," Marcus said. "It is of the utmost importance. It involves a bit of travel."

Henry sighed. He had just gotten back.

"What is it?"

"We need to figure out who all is going to be down there with us. Come to my place tomorrow at noon. We will go over the details then."

Henry shook hands with Robby and Marcus and headed back up the hill. He peeked down into the crater as he passed. A notch in the tiered walls was painted blue with X's here and there. A tube-shape boring machine was being hauled up, or put down, by crane. He turned and waited for a military truck to cross. He swore he saw missile heads uncovered by the draping canvas. He wasn't surprised to see anything anymore.

Chapter Four

Marcus took a seat behind a cedar desk. It was a mighty piece of furniture. Henry wondered how anyone managed to get it into the room.

"Take a seat." Marcus pushed a portfolio across the desk. "We'll go through this together before we send you off."

They opened the folders simultaneously.

"Trencher Industries is the highest paying large-scale employer in the country, and young people think we are cool. People want to work for us. For a few lucky ones, we are hiring."

"And *why* are we hiring?"

"I want the right kind of people down there with us. I'm not living out the rest of my days surrounded by mouth-breathers and knuckle-draggers."

It had been a while since Henry had heard one of Marcus's tirades about stupid people. The board banned Marcus from TV interviews after he was questioned about his lack of charitable donations. *Trencher Industries* was into hiring people, not giving handouts, he told the interviewer.

In the following weeks, the media dug up his investment in a national chain of shops that specialized in tattoo removal and mending stretched earlobes. When pressed on his involvement, Marcus said he was helping poor, uneducated people look worthy of employment.

He stepped down as CEO shortly thereafter.

To the public, he became a recluse. Little did Henry know at the time, but Marcus had already turned his focus to the bunker at that point. Maybe it was more intentional than it appeared.

"Last month we put publicity out about our job fairs. There has been a Golden Ticket frenzy ever since. We are looking for the best and brightest young people in a few very specific fields of knowledge."

"Knowledge that could be useful in a bunker."

"Precisely. On top of all the walk-ins, we've combed through a list of 'valuable persons' provided by the CIA. These people are going to live in a bunker somewhere, we might want them in ours."

Henry skimmed the pages in his binder. Doctor, veterinarian, geneticist, chef, computer scientist. He was going to be busy over the coming weeks.

"As for the walk-ins, I've dedicated a special team to weed out undesirables. Those deemed potentially desirable will be sent your way." Marcus paused. "You have a way of reading people I'll never understand. I need your expertise."

"I interview them purely on personality? I know nothing about medicine or genetics."

Marcus nodded. "They are qualified before they walk in the door. The only question you are looking to answer is whether you can stand living the rest of your life in the same vicinity as the person. If they smile and a single tooth bothers you, don't pick them. If their accent annoys you, don't pick them. Thank them and move on."

This time Henry nodded. He was to interview as if he were swiping on dating apps.

"You'll see impressive people," Marcus said. "Don't jump at the first one. But after you see them all, call your pick that day. Don't wait. We are competing for these people."

Henry scribbled notes as Marcus spoke.

"Ask them their salary, double it, write out a signing bonus, whatever it takes. Promise them the moon. That's what those other asshole billionaires are doing. Literally, they have a base up there."

He wanted to hear more about that, but now wasn't the time.

"Afterward, we will schedule them for an extensive physical. Don't want to bring someone down who has cancer, you know. They also have to be fertile."

"Fertile?"

"Yes, I don't know if I've made this clear, but we might not ever see the light of day again. Hell, our kids' kids might not. People are going to have babies down there. They'll have to."

Henry hadn't thought that far ahead.

"You'll tell them that Trencher Industries wants them for exciting new projects. Once they are convinced, our people will set them up to fly here at the right time. Everything you need to know is in the portfolio. Call if you have questions." Marcus stood, signaling the end of the meeting.

"Sounds good."

"My jet is at the airport. Pack a valise and head out there within the next few hours. Your first interviews will be tomorrow in Seattle."

Henry expected as much.

"Oh, one last thing. More important than anything else I've told you today."

He placed a hand on Henry's shoulder and stared into his eyes as if he were going to tell him the secret of life. Instead, he said:

"Don't you fucking dare pick an ugly girl."

* * *

He arrived at the quaint Sherman Airport and spotted Marcus's Gulfstream G650. His personal pilot, Tom, had set up a lawn chair next to the plane and was reading a book, back to the setting sun.

"Evening, Tom."

"Good evening, Mr. Plyman! I understand Seattle is on the itinerary."

"Yes, it is. Will we arrive before midnight?"

"Certainly. Pacific time zone will see to that."

Tom took the valise and tipped his cap as Henry passed to ascend the jet stairway.

He slept most of the six-hour flight, only coming to when the tires hit the runway at Renton Municipal Airport. A car was waiting, and he was driven through the drizzle of rain to his waterfront hotel.

He tipped the front desk clerk a twenty to get him some aspirin from the gift shop before heading up to his suite. He was routinely upgraded. Every hotel in the country bent over backwards to attract an account with *Trencher Industries,* so Henry was a VIP everywhere he went. The lavish gift basket was no surprise. He would have been surprised if there wasn't one.

He cracked the portfolio open. He skipped the pages Marcus and he went through and found profiles of the scheduled interviewees.

He read the first few in detail.

Jenna Dothmayer, Master's in Genetics, Texas A&M, hometown, Spokane, WA, ran track on scholarship, 800 meters. Marcus had annotated the profiles with comments like, *"Healthy, athletic. This is good"* with an arrow pointing at the track detail. The idea of why they would need a geneticist in the bunker baffled Henry.

After skimming a few more, and reading Marcus's amusing cliff notes, he caught a trend. They were all women. Not a single guy. He wasn't just recruiting highly skilled labor for bunker purposes, he was recruiting potential *mates.* The shallow dating app analogy was apt.

His gut reaction was guilt and discomfort. But there were going to be tons of people down there, he rationalized. What's wrong with handpicking a few pretty ones?

He flipped another page and saw another note scrawled at the bottom in red ink: "No *ugly chicks!"*

* * *

Soothing *muzak* was blasted away when the elevator doors opened to the second-floor meeting space. The job fair was underway, and the nervous energy of thousands of hopeful employees was infectious.

Here we go.

Henry was greeted by his team. He was handed an itinerary as he walked at a brisk pace through the main aisle of booths. He made eye contact with no one, except when he passed *Trenchers'* sprawling display. He felt a buzz around him.

He walked around the booth into a separate meeting space set aside for the interviews. Air walls killed the outside sound. He removed his jacket, sat down at the desk placed in the room just for him, and looked over the itinerary.

It was going to be a long day.

He gave the nod to the assistant. She was sent by Marcus and was likely a transplant from the CIA or some other in-the-know faction. He hoped so, because the hiring practices he was about to use were probably not above board.

"Mr. Plyman, our first candidate is a Jenna Dothmayer."

"Thank you, send her in."

He stood to greet her. He was taken aback by her beauty . . . and height. She was an inch taller than he was, in her heels. She wore grey slacks with a matching grey stretch jacket, a blue undershirt, and silver jewelry. She was tan, blonde, and her eyes were a lighter blue than her shirt.

"Miss Dothmayer, tell me about your work so far in the field of genetics."

"Thank you. I studied chemistry and biology as an undergrad, and I just completed my master's in genetics. In the last two years I've worked in a research lab focused on curing Alzheimer's while completing my degree." She was succinct, and there were no accent issues.

"Top of your class, too. Have you done anything with animals or plants?"

He wondered how dumb he sounded.

"We did labs early on and it is not dissimilar to working with human DNA, if not much simpler. I feel confident with my base knowledge and could adapt to whatever Trencher Industries has in mind." She paused. "If you don't mind me asking, what *do* you guys have in mind? There wasn't much of a job description on the website."

"We are collecting bright young minds to work on Mr. Trencher's next set of big projects. I'm here to find smart people who can get along with other smart people. The projects are top secret. I couldn't say much if I did know. I assure you, though, it will be well worth your time."

He hardly answered her question but moved on.

"Are you married or have a significant other? I only ask because the job would require moving."

"Nope. Left that in Texas." She forced a smile.

He was relieved and it might have shown.

"All right then. It says here that you ran track in college. How has this helped you?"

A softball question to let her talk.

31

He flipped a page for no other reason than to appear thoughtful. He nodded when she finished.

"Are you ready for that random interview question that comes out of nowhere?"

She laughed. "Ready as I'll ever be."

"If you were stuck in a bunker to live out the rest of your days in a colony of doomsday survivors, what would you, as a geneticist, have to offer?"

I can ask that, right? She doesn't know.

She thought for a moment, squinting her eyes and exhaling. "I guess I could prevent inbreeding, you know, a few years down the line." They both laughed. "But seriously, if there were plants down there, I could figure out how to help, even if just picking tomatoes. Same with animals, if they were in this bunker. If neither, I am an able-bodied girl, I could carry my own weight and adapt to different roles." She ended her answer with a shrug.

He smiled and nodded. Not bad. He stood and extended his hand. "That will be all for now. We will contact you either way, perhaps even today, so keep your phone nearby."

"Thank you for the opportunity. I love what your company has done." She smiled, shook his hand, and was out the door.

He sat through three more interviews before lunchtime. Plain Jane, Dull Debby, and Nervous Nancy.

He asked his assistant how many more geneticists he was to interview.

"We have five scheduled, sir, and two potential walk-ins we've plucked from out there."

"Cancel them all. I've made my pick."

Not such a long day after all.

* * *

Instead of the geneticists, he interviews two medical doctors, but found neither worth consideration. Marcus wouldn't want anyone much older than him in the bunker.

He breezed through the last interview before calling the only candidate worth calling.

"Jenna Dothmayer."

"Hi, Henry Plyman from Trencher Industries."

"Yes, hello."

"I have great news. We would love to offer you the position with Trencher Industries. Starting pay at $200,000 per year fair enough?"

"Oh my, um, yes absolutely. I accept!"

"Congratulations. Our people will get with you to set up the physical and start date and get all the paperwork done. Welcome to Trencher Industries."

She thanked him profusely and hung up.

He walked into the convention hall to find his assistant. She would handle it from there with Jenna Dothmayer. He left for his room, satisfied with his trip thus far.

Next stop, Los Angeles.

Chapter Five

With Henry all set to task, Marcus had things to do.

Senator Orlen Muehlbauer arrived in town and wasn't about to tout his presence. He was not popular amongst Marcus's people. The senator dealt in political capital, and there was much to be gained by taking on a wealthy, controversial figure like Marcus Trencher. But not in the town of Sherman. Marcus was their pride and joy.

Marcus's pet project had been momentarily derailed. His train tunnel connecting Louisville-Bloomington-Indianapolis was meeting resistance. Marcus suspected the opposition was artificial and led by Senator Muehlbauer, the wicked politician of southern Indiana. Muehlbauer had a posse of farmers and fringe activists standing up to prevent the rail from crossing their property.

Peasants.

The completion of Marcus's maglev rails in the face of planetary doom was significant for one reason. The entirety of the project was underground. This decision was outrageously more expensive and hardly made sense, but people liked jobs. It put the senator in an awkward position, but Marcus could have proposed a cancer research hospital and the senator would find reason to fight it.

There was one last leg of the route Marcus desperately needed finished: a line to out-of-the-way Sherman, Indiana. It was to connect to his bunker. The timetable was not looking good.

Marcus was done playing around. He set up a meeting, face-to-face, with Senator Muehlbauer. Marcus knew he would bite. Muehlbauer threw childish tantrums until someone important paid him attention.

They met at *Trencher* headquarters, where Marcus kept him waiting long enough to annoy him before having his secretary call him in.

"Welcome to Sherman, Orlen," he said. "The world's finest example of what you can't do as a politician."

The senator was round, bald, and carried a certain rural smugness that got under the skin. He took pride in being an ignorant country bumpkin.

"Mr. Trencher, how generous of you to invite me to your playground. To what do I owe this pleasure?"

"My trains tunnels, senator. I need you to get out of the way."

The senator tilted back, smiling. "I've got to know one thing: Is it true that you are obsessed with these trains because you are afraid of driving? You know, that thing normal Americans do to get around? It must be awful to be paralyzed in this small town, as quaint as it is. It was your mother's accident that did it, right? My condolences."

While what Orlen said was partially true, he did his best to ignore the comment.

"The train is underground, so it doesn't disturb farmland or infrastructure. It creates thousands of jobs. Take credit for them, I don't care. Other than to piss me off, what is your purpose for blocking this?"

"Oh, Mr. Trencher, I mean you no trouble, but I have to look out for the little guy. People are not as fortunate as you. I have constituents, farmers, who cannot afford to give up land even for a season for your little project. Not to mention the sink holes."

The faux-sympathetic politician tone grated Marcus's ears.

"Sink holes? Really? And you know those farmers are compensated well beyond any negligible profit they would lose. The shafts I want to dig on their property would be the biggest blessing in their lives, but you stand in the way of that." He paused. "I need you to *move*."

The senator threw his hands up in the air. "I wish I could help you, Mr. Trencher, I really do. But like I said, I must look out for the common man, not the super-rich. We still don't know what strong magnets underground would do to crops and water tables."

"Nothing. They will do absolutely nothing. The science is clear."

"We better wait for another study to be sure. This isn't something we should rush. I am sure you'll get your way, Mr. Trencher, you always do. It'll just take a little time."

He didn't *have* time.

"We will have a safe, lightning-quick train in southern Indiana." The senator grinned. "Who would've ever thought it?"

Marcus contemplated if his friends at the CIA would be open to assisting an unfortunate accident.

"There are . . . shall we say, 'incentives' that can speed up the inevitable course of events," Orlen said.

Marcus nodded. "I could toss campaign money your way, but I won't. We're done here."

"Good day, Mr. Trencher."

Muehlbauer left the office, having had his fulfill of exercised power.

Marcus picked up the phone.

* * *

Henry was surprised to learn Marcus had a downtown Los Angeles skyrise apartment where he could crash. He wasn't at all surprised to learn that Marcus had never stepped foot in it.

After a quiet evening in the room, and a good night's rest, he made his way to Trencher's west coast offices. They rolled out the proverbial red carpet for him when he arrived.

He shook hands with Nicholas Pratt, the Chief West Coast Executive, mid-forties, looked important.

Henry brought out his corporate lingo to keep up with Pratt during their short walk together. One or two more buzzwords and he thought he might have a stroke. Pratt was dying to know what Marcus had up his sleeve. Inside information made people feel important, and Pratt made a living off being more important than useful.

He dodged the questions but assured him he would know everything soon enough. The hard truth was that Pratt was going to learn along with the rest of the world.

The office set aside for him was Pratt's. It was high up with a view.

His team from Seattle was there to assist him. He realized he hadn't bothered to learn any of their names. He could at least find out who the lady was that showed people in and handed him the itinerary.

Ashley, and he instantly wondered why he bothered. If she wasn't going to be dead in eight months, she was going to be in a bunker far away and he would never see her again. She was another face with a name that would soon be gone. But so was Pratt and most of the interview subjects. If he started thinking this way all the time, he would fall into deep depression.

Ashley escorted in the first interviewee. She was attractive, which checked off one of the criteria. Her brunette hair with auburn highlights was professionally tangled in an intricate bun at the crown of her head. She flashed a dimpled smile and perfect white veneers.

"Kelly Branson is it?"

"Thank you for seeing me."

"Let's see, you graduated from the University of California-Berkeley, and you are now in your fourth year of medical school...appear to be doing well."

"Yes, almost there! One more year, then residency," she said. "I feel like I would be ahead, but they keep me on a track. I got a 40 on the MCAT after all."

Henry didn't know what she was talking about, so he smiled. Her smile never broke, and he wondered if her face would ever tire.

"If Trencher Industries were to get into the medical field, and we put you in charge, what direction would you take us?"

Her smile turned into a thoughtful look, every bit as rehearsed. "Marcus has really big ideas, so it would only be right for him to tackle the biggest problems in medicine: cancer and heart disease."

He was talking about Trencher Industries, she was talking about *Marcus*. There might be something to this.

Please don't be a Marcus worshiper.

"Tell me what you think of Marcus."

She got visibly excited. She sat up straight and her face blushed. "Oh my gosh, he is like my idol."

Here we go.

"I look up to him so much. I read everything about him. He is a genius! Those people who criticize him and talk about his life and how he doesn't ride in cars and stuff are idiots. They don't even know him."

And you do?

"He changed the world, like Mark Zuckerberg or those guys from Google."

He cringed inside.

"And I probably shouldn't say this . . ."

Please don't.

". . . but I think he's pretty handsome too!"

He stood up, his polite smile still pasted on.

"Well Miss Branson, I'll inform you of our decision as soon as we make it."

He shook her hand and was happy to see her go. The last thing he wanted was a groupie in the bunker.

* * *

Ashley came into the office.

"The next we have is a Mariya Ichinose, veterinarian. I must say, she doesn't look like her resume might entail. Buzz us if she is an activist."

She left and returned with an Asian girl in a tank top, shorts, and a pair of dirty work boots.

Henry was not as suspicious as Ashley. He was intrigued.

"Hello, Miss Ichinose. I am Henry Plyman," he said as he shook her hand.

Her thin eyebrows elevated. "Very impressive! I don't think I have ever met anyone who has got my name right first try."

"I spent some time in Asia and picked up on some pronunciations. Please, take a seat."

He sat down and did nothing but look at her for a moment. She had a dark complexion, which spoke of where her family might have come from, but Henry wasn't as curious about her ancestry as he was about her more recent origins. She was dirty and wearing clothes unfit for a job interview.

"I've been doing several interviews as of late, and nobody has come in as sharply dressed as you."

"Oh gosh, I know," she said, as if just noticing her attire. "To be honest, I forgot about it until this morning and I was already digging around the garden. Thank God for the train, or I would have been a no-show."

"Glad you made it. Says here you are a vet. May I ask what you are currently doing?"

"Urban farming in San Francisco. I run a co-op and sell to the restaurant scene. We have a little bit of outdoor space and a decent greenhouse. We even have a fish hatchery and we are in the process of expanding to tending small livestock."

Perfect.

"Are you a vegetarian?"

"Because I'm an animal lover, right? No, as much as I enjoy their company, I am a carnivore. In fact, we kill what we eat. How about that?"

Perfect.

"I don't know if I could do that." He wanted to sign her up right then but had a few more questions. "Forgive me if I am stereotyping, I'm a total Midwesterner, but is your co-op part of some sort of hippie commune?"

She rolled her eyes. "No, not everyone in San Francisco is about peace and love. There are more ruthless capitalists than anything these days."

"Good, I guess," he said. "Are you married or have a significant other? The job would require moving."

She frowned. "Pretty sure you're not supposed to ask that," she laughed. "No, not tied down. Not gay either. I know you Indiana folks are pretty concerned about that kind of thing."

She was teasing him. If she was trying to bomb the interview, she was failing. Henry could hardly figure out why. It was a feeling, an attraction.

"Sorry, we just get so many that refuse to move." He laughed nervously. He'd heard all he needed and wanted to move on from the awkwardness. "I don't normally do this, but I am willing to offer you the job right here and now."

"Um, I don't even know what the job is."

He had a lie prepared this time. "Basically what you are doing now, but on a vertical farm. Trencher Industries will pay for your replacement in your business, we'll start paying you immediately, and you don't have to move or do anything different for at least a couple months. I don't know how much you make, but we will double it."

She leaned back and eyed him suspiciously. "You say a couple months. Any exact date?"

"You will know exactly when we need you."

"You are convincing, Mr. Henry Plyman." She made him wait a moment for her own amusement. "Tell me where to sign."

Chapter Six

Timothy Spencer stood in St. Mary's Catholic Church in Iowa City, going through the motions of Mass. He was not overly active in the Church, but he had great attendance.

His was in the middle of what some call prayer. In his mind, he was only talking to someone trustworthy who did nothing but listen, Jesus it may as well be. He had never done it before, but there weren't many other people in his life at the time that he could talk about what he knew.

Because, *he knew.*

"Doesn't look like the meek are going to inherit the Earth. Looks the opposite. The meek are going to huddle with their families and cease to exist after a bright white flash. Those who'll be left are anything but meek." He automatically did the sign of the Cross, a hesitation behind the rest of the congregation. "I'm sure you have your divine plan, I'm not criticizing. It's just confusing, as always." He sat down.

He liked the Church. Sitting quietly, standing on command, and reciting prayers imbued healthy obedience totally lacking in the public schools he kept his kids from. Plus, tough lessons received on Sundays were lessons he didn't have to teach.

When Mass ended, his youngest, Madeleine, tugged on his cuff link. "Daddy, can we get some ice cream?"

"That sounds like a great idea!"

His wife Shelley gave him a suspect look. "We went last Sunday. They'll expect it every week."

"I know, I know. Just one more. Besides, you know you want a cherry vanilla waffle cone."

He was enjoying his time as a stay-at-home dad. He loved every second with his girls. Retirement at age 37 bothered his wife, but not him. Marcus forcing him out of the company did hurt, but not because of money or status. Marcus was a genuine friend.

What he knew of Trencher's plans, he didn't like. He couldn't live with it. He had to do something.

He knew more than Marcus's friends, Henry and Robby. He needed to get to one of them.

His acrimonious severance prohibited him from getting anywhere near anything *Trencher*. The public knew nothing of it, but Marcus had exiled him. For months, he was followed by Marcus's people. He didn't think that was the case anymore.

He didn't know Robby well enough to approach. Henry was the man he had to see.

* * *

Marcus had trouble keeping his head up. He couldn't recall it ever weighing so much. Robby had struck again. Marcus was thoroughly drunk.

"I can't tell the difference. What bourbon is good and what is bad?" Marcus asked, studying the amber in the glass.

"Shit, I don't know man. Whatever costs the most is probably good."

That made perfect sense. He thought it was the smartest thing Robby had ever said. They had visited many places during their trip to Louisville, but none as enjoyable as the Fleur de Lis Bourbon and Ale House. They sampled over half the menu, food and beverage.

"Bartender," Marcus said. "Do they make this Maker's stuff in barrels? I'd like to buy a couple dozen."

"Yes, and not too far from here. Down near Loretto, in the heart of Kentucky."

Marcus stared. He didn't say anything.

"Would you like a number? I order from there."

"Yes, that would be great. And who owns this joint? I am impressed."

"That would be me. I opened the place two years ago. Brad Farris."

Hands came up and were shook.

"You cook, Bradley?"

"Yes, my specialty. Designed everything on the menu and keep practicing when not bogged down by paperwork and staff drama."

Marcus was thinking hard. He was trying to concentrate the bourbon away.

"How would you like to open another restaurant? And not have to deal with paperwork or staffing?"

Brad's eyebrows raised. "I'd love to. That is a long-term goal of mine, so long as I can convince my wife."

He turned as a woman stepped up next to him.

"This is my wife, Becky. She is a full-time nurse but helps out here when we are desperate."

She had fair skin and fairer hair. She had Kool-Aid red lips, like they were colored on slightly out of the lines. She wore a black tank top and had a bottle opener strapped to her right bicep. She clipped a lid off, slid the beer to a patron next to Robby, and offered her hand.

"Nice to meet you, gentlemen."

Marcus liked that the wife was a nurse.

He glanced around. In his mind, even while filtered with alcohol, he counted the tables and devised an average bill for each table from the menu prices. He multiplied it by a series of variables and coefficients for hours of operation, weekdays, seasonal slowdowns, and the lease. Then, he doubled his made-up number. He took out a checkbook and pen and wrote the figure down and handed it over.

The couple peered at the check and while Brad Farris did a reasonable job of being poker faced, Becky's eyes nearly popped out of her head. She silently mouthed the word "Wow."

"My name is Marcus Trencher. I really like your restaurant."

* * *

Henry didn't yet have a doctor. The bunker needed someone with medical expertise.

From L.A., his next stop was Denver, Colorado, another job fair, located at the downtown convention center. His initial reaction was favorable. The city, air, and people were clean and amicable. It was a pleasant change of pace. California landed him a fine recruit, but he was glad to move on.

He blew through his first few interviews. He was getting better at it.

Next up, Audrey Bruni, another doctor-to-be from the top of her class.

Another beauty. But this one was not traditional. It took a moment to process. Her attraction was complex, not easy to pin down.

She was a gangly thing, and despite her slenderness, still had shape. Her face was kind and elegance obvious. He didn't know what trigger went off, but like the previous two, his mind was made up before any dialogue was exchanged. It was now up to her to live up to his optimistic expectations.

She wanted to be an obstetrician and eventually an OB/GYN. After she explained the difference, his interest in her increased. This was to be one of the surest medical issues to arise in the bunker.

"What got you interested in babies, and not, say, brain surgery?"

"Honestly? A decade less of schooling," she said. "If I spend much more time in academia, I might explode. Everything we do is pragmatic for the field,

but I want to get out *in* the field and earn a living."
She paused. "I also like babies. That is important."

Pragmatic. He liked the word. He wrote it down.
She was looking very pragmatic for the bunker.

"Trencher Industries is getting into the medical
field, at least our charitable half is, and we will need
people with your expertise." He had been honing his
little white lies. They were so much better than *I don't
know why I am interviewing you.*

"Charitable wing? No offense, but you guys have
a reputation for being non-charity."

"Well, Marcus is more into opportunity creation,
but I am sure you've seen how that has gone over. We
are looking to change that. Much of our own personal
wealth is going into these projects."

"Very admirable, I'd love to be a part of it."

"Done. The hospital isn't even built yet, but you
now work there, if you so choose to accept. The best
part? We will start paying you immediately and you
just continue with your schooling."

"Really? Seriously? Yes, I accept!"

Tears welled in her eyes as she tried to keep her
composure.

He was happy for her, even if it was all a lie. He
was saving her life, to his credit.

He walked her to the door, handing her off to
Ashley to take care of the rest.

He checked his watch. He had a moment before
his next interview. He grabbed his phone.

"Marcus. Got us a doctor! She'll be perfect."

"Great. Ashley texted me that it was excellent
choice." The background noise was loud.

"I knew Ashley was one of your spies."

Rising above the racket was Robby, asking: "*Is she hot? Is she hot?*"

"Yes, very pretty, of course. Where are you guys? It sounds like a bar."

"It is, we are in Louisville. They've shut the street down for some market thing. We are walking around getting drunk. There are thousands of people here and only two or three have recognized me, it's great."

"Sounds like fun. Any luck with the chef?"

"Yes! We ate at a great restaurant and I spoke to the owner. Young guy, real go-getter. Robby and I were pretty drunk, but we bought the place and bought the guy. He has tattoos down one of his arms, but I'm working on my open-mindedness."

Were pretty drunk? Henry thought. *Sounds like they still are.*

"His wife was there. We liked her too. She's a nurse. She is coming along as well. A real couple down there might do us some good, you know."

"That's great, but I have a few questions. How many more do I choose? And what professions? I can't think of anything else we need."

"Make it two more. Anything you like. I almost forgot to mention, we took in another recruit named Melonie. She works at the hotel. When you see her, you'll know why Robby threatened to kill me if we didn't take her. Don't worry about any computer stuff, I am going to take one of our guys, Timothy's replacement. The last two are up to you."

"I like it. I'll let you guys get back to your hard work."

* * *

Timothy Spencer assured his wife he'd be back from St. Louis the next day. He hugged his daughters and promised them gifts.

"I know, I am spoiling them," he said, winking at his wife as he walked out the door.

He opted to drive since it was under five hours and a straight shot down US-218. His government minders would also have a harder time tracking him. He had NPR, an audio book, and junk food to accompany him on the trip. He chose a hotel just outside of the city to be safe. He didn't want to run into Henry's security in the lobby.

He checked in at five and had nothing to keep him busy. The Cardinals were playing a night game at the stadium against a tough Pirates team, but he didn't want to deal with the traffic. He tried his hand at writing an encrypted letter, but he thought it was too risky and too encrypted. Instead he stayed in bed and watched HBO.

* * *

The job fair was in full bloom by 10 AM. Timothy missed Henry's entrance but wasn't planning on confronting him with his whole team anyhow. Lunch time would be best if he left the room, or worse case, at the end of the day. In the meantime, he blended in with the crowd a safe distance from the Trencher booth.

He entertained himself by perusing the myriad of booths. The field of robotics was taking off, and every company had a mascot model showing off. His favorite folded laundry.

He ate free samples of 3D-printed food and was thoroughly impressed. He already had a home 3D printer for plastic trinkets, mostly for his daughters, but had never made any real use of it.

He couldn't help but see every job filtered through the context he knew. Terraforming on the moon, biosphere work, advanced hydroponics, nanotechnologies, the graphene explosion, and industries sprung up around asteroid mining and the space elevator. It all seemed so obvious. We were gearing up for an apocalypse, but nobody here knew it except him and Henry.

He had to keep his gaze averted. The man in front of the Trencher booth had on smart glasses. The facial recognition capabilities were keen, and he knew his mug was loaded up with every pore. The pandemic a few years back normalized wearing a mask, so that helped. Still, he kept a brochure up to cover more of his face.

Lunch was delivered, so he knew cornering Henry during a break was out of the question.

Four more hours passed before sudden booth activity indicated Henry was preparing to leave.

He had to get closer.

Timothy merged in with the traffic moving up the aisle toward the booth. He was behind a burly guy, so he knew he was covered. Timing was the concern. He was twenty feet from the booth when he saw the door open. Henry stepped through and spoke to a woman.

He made his move.

The burly guy who led him so close also obstructed his view. As soon as Timothy stepped around the man, he locked eyes with a giant guard on Henry's security detail.

The man showed no interest until a red square beamed from the agent's right eyeglass. He was spotted.

Timothy darted under a velvet rope of the neighboring booth. He stumbled and his shoulder checked the curtain rig separating the booths. He suddenly had everyone's attention in the vicinity.

"Henry! We need to speak!"

The guard got hands on him and tucked his arm uncomfortably up his back.

Henry's eyes lit up with recognition. He waved, directing the security man to let him go. "No, it's okay, I know him."

But Henry was held back by a woman and another guard. Someone was going to prevent them from talking, and Timothy was losing ground. Based on the expression Henry had, he was realizing it too.

In desperation, Tim began yelling. Henry *had* to know.

"*Ask him how many! How many people! Make him answer you! Ask h–*"

The guard lifted and moved Timothy away. He did not stop until outside of the convention space. He didn't stop in the foyer, or at the door behind the information desk. Timothy was pushed through the employee area of the building until he reached a security station. He was placed in a holding room.

"Don't move," the guard said as he pulled a phone out of his pocket.

Timothy Spencer knew very well who he was calling.

Chapter Seven

Marcus spent most of his first day home in bed, cursing himself for drinking so much, and cursing the human race for still having not invented a hangover cure.

His phone rang, adding to his cursing. "What?"

The security guard from Henry's job fair told him there was an incident with a Timothy Spencer.

"Put him on," Marcus said, wondering what soap opera was going on in St. Louis.

A pause as the phone was shuffled. He quickly skimmed a text from Ashley.

"Timothy, what would possess you to run into a crowded job fair and shout out about things you know need not be shouted?"

"I can't let you do it, Marcus. You have room for hundreds of people down there—"

"Save it. We've been over this. I've made my decision." He sighed. "Look, I was going to call anyway. I've got bunker bids for you and Shelley and the kids."

"I've already got bids. That's not why I did this."

"I can get you in a better bunker. Some are better than others. Come to Sherman with the family before the public announcement. We can't hold this grudge."

Timothy exhaled through his nostrils. "When?"

"January 23. Three months."

"I'll consider."

"Good luck, Timothy. I hope to see you there. I really mean it."

"Can you tell this meathead to let me go now?"

* * *

Timothy walked out of the holding cell, wandering the maze of hallways until he found an exit. When he got outside, he was surprised to find it was dark. The fall air was starting to chill. He flagged down a driverless taxi to get back to his hotel.

As much as he cared about saving as many people as possible, Timothy Spencer couldn't deny worrying about his family. It was human nature. He didn't want to live in a "crowded subterranean ghetto," as Marcus put it. As wrong as he felt Marcus was, the offer was enticing.

Timothy had already cast a line against Marcus's interest – the divulgence of his mini-nuclear reactor designs. Timothy knew Marcus was going to be upset when he found out they were leaked. Marcus would connect the dots back to him. But if all went well, the government would inspect Marcus's bunker and force him to take in more people. That was the goal.

The taxi dropped him off at the hotel and he headed to his room. He struggled to sleep. The ultimatum weighed on him.

He reluctantly turned on the TV and flipped channels. The local news came on and the top story was not what Tim had expected.

A Senator was gruesomely murdered in his southern Indiana home. It was Orlen Muehlbauer.

Marcus's political nemesis.

* * *

Henry was irked that after the Timothy Spencer incident in St. Louis, Marcus wouldn't return his calls. Security wouldn't tell him anything. Ashley said they couldn't talk. Those were orders.

Timothy and Marcus might have had a falling out, but Henry still considered Timothy a friend. It was wrong for Marcus to keep him away without explanation.

Henry decided not to go to Atlanta. Instead, he was going back to Sherman, Indiana. To Marcus's mansion. He texted Marcus with a heads-up. Whether he read it or not would remain a mystery until he arrived.

Ashley and the team went on to Atlanta via Marcus's private jet. Henry drove a rental car to Sherman.

The Trencher estate was as pristine as ever. He was waved through security.

He walked into the foyer and wasn't sure where to go. If he wandered around, it might take him two days to find him. Fortunately, Marcus's voice came through a hidden speaker.

"I am in my office."

Henry remembered the directions well enough to only take one wrong turn along the way. He was about to face Marcus with questions he was avoiding.

Henry needed to know.

Marcus was at his desk, paintings were down from the wall, and books were off the shelf and sorted into stacks.

"What brings you here and not Atlanta where you are supposed to be?"

Henry took a deep breath. "I need to know why Timothy was prevented from seeing me. You two had your differences, and I stayed out of it, but there is something else that you're not telling me."

Marcus was annoyed. "Timothy is a disgruntled employee of high profile. It was protocol. I've handled it. I got Timothy and his whole family bunker bids. He is well taken care of."

"I don't doubt that, but he was trying to tell me something and the security team ignored my commands. You gave them those orders."

"Did they tell you that?"

Henry felt caution was necessary. Throwing one of them under the bus would be throwing them out of a bunker and to their eventual death.

"They wouldn't talk. I came to that conclusion."

Marcus gave a dismissive laugh.

"How many people, Marcus?"

"How do you mean?"

"The bunker. How many people are we taking down with us? A thousand? A few hundred? How many?"

"Twelve."

"Thousand? Twelve hundred? Which?"

"Twelve. A dozen. That is it."

Henry tried wrapping his head around this tiny number. His limbs weakened, but he didn't want to sit.

"*Twelve?* Marcus, that's it? What the hell? What about my family? Yours?"

"Your family has a bid for the Bloomington bunker. They're good. My dad and stepmom will be in Texas or Oklahoma. I am not concerned about them.

"I am not living out the rest of my days under parental supervision," Marcus said. "I am an adult. I've put in my time under my dad's watch until he ran off to Florida after mom died. I absolve myself from those responsibilities. I am going to live for myself and my friends from here on out. Is that so wrong?"

"Yes, it is. I love my parents and I'd like to see them over the next few decades."

"You will. With the unfortunate death of Orlen Muehlbauer, I can now push through my maglev trains. Our bunker will connect to Bloomington. You'll be able to visit anytime you like."

"What about the thousands of people you *could* save? What about them?"

Marcus turned the desk lamp so Henry could see his face clearly.

"I've been dealing with that bullshit since my first paycheck. There are always people asking for more, telling me what to do with what I earned. I am cutting that fucking entitlement cord. Do you really think in a scenario where, at best, one percent of the world population is going to live, the fast food worker deserves a bunker bid? How about that dumbass kid that dropped out of high school and only disrupted every class he was in? Those degenerates down at Dan-O's? I am done with them! I sure as hell am not living out my days surrounded by *those* people. Some people are hopeless and inferior."

"Who are you? Hitler? You think this cosmic Holocaust is a good thing?"

"Don't feed me your liberal studies bullshit. I am being a realist. Assess the situation. If there are a finite number of lives that can be saved, we have to save the lives worth the most. Intelligent, healthy people. And don't kid yourself – some lives *are* worth more than others."

"I can deal with that. But twelve is a horrific number. You can do better, and you know it."

"I could and I have! I designed bunkers across the country to maximize capacity. My designs will save millions of lives. But I am not going to live in squalor. I am not going to live under a miserable ration system. Call me selfish, I really don't care at this point. I want my space. Living underground will be hard enough as it is."

"Do you honestly not care that you are going to let thousands more people die than is necessary?"

"Really don't."

"You don't care that you will never see your dad again?"

"Nope."

"You don't care about people who helped shape you, worked for you, picked up your garbage, did the right things when nobody was watching?"

"I don't, really."

* * *

Henry left, unable to find a word that communicated how he felt. *Livid* didn't quite cover it.

Now he knew what Timothy Spencer was yelling about.

Marcus was wrong, but his mind was made up. It was as good as settled. Marcus was going to live in relative luxury, and so could Henry, so long as he could accept that the luxury was in lieu of some lost soul who would have cost only minor sacrifice.

What else could he do? He didn't want to die.

He could play the saboteur like Timothy, but that would only lead to more deaths. Marcus would be content with having the entire bunker to himself if it came to it.

They were never on the same moral wavelength, but this was out of bounds.

Henry wondered if Robby knew. He headed toward his studio.

The lights were on and it was much quieter than his last visit. Robby was lying on his dilapidated couch with a sketch pad.

"I thought you were in Atlanta," Robby said, getting up to put on a shirt.

"Supposed to be, but I ran into Timothy Spencer. You knew him, right?"

"Met him a few times. Good guy. Heard Marcus canned him."

"Yeah, I didn't ask questions, you know how Marcus gets." He took a seat on a stool. "But in St. Louis, Timothy tried to tell me something, and the security guys whisked him away like he was trying to hurt me. He yelled something along the lines of, '*Ask him! Ask him how many people!*'"

"What's that supposed to mean?"

"I didn't know, so I asked Marcus. You won't believe it, man. Do you know how many people are going down in the bunker with us?"

Robby shrugged. "Probably a hundred. Marcus wouldn't want too many down there. He hates socializing."

"He is taking twelve. That's it!"

"Sheesh. With that hole you'd think he was taking a whole city."

Henry stood and paced. "Do you realize how many lives he is choosing *not* to save just so he can feel more comfortable?"

A long pause. Then: "I agree with you, dude, I do. But let me play devil's advocate for a moment. While Marcus sent you to Europe and Asia, he worked sixteen hours a day, researching and designing bunkers for the government. Out of all the experts, architects, and engineers, they unanimously chose his designs. The man is a genius and has used his abilities to save thousands of more lives than could have been saved with anyone else's plans. Those people won't be in our bunker, but they'll be safe. It's all relative."

"I know, but he is choosing not to fill ours to a reasonable capacity. To me, that is negligence. Maybe Marcus is a savior to some, but I still don't like it."

"Marcus is going to be Marcus," Robby said. "I don't know what else to say. If we didn't meet him, I'd be in jail and you would be an Average Joe sloshing through the middle class. We'd both be dead in eight months."

Henry hadn't gained an ally like he had hoped. Perhaps he was holding onto principles that did nothing but create guilt. His naiveté was creeping back in and making him feel bad. He wished he could be amoral. Every other successful person he had met shared a quality of not-giving-a-shit.

"I don't know . . . I just don't." Henry looked at the empty space in the studio. "So where is George? You put the finishing touches on him?"

"Sure did. It's already out by the lake. There is an unveiling ceremony next week."

"That is great, congratulations. I will be there," Henry said. "And not to be Debbie Downer, but I have to ask, with all that is about to happen, why go through with it? No offense."

"None taken. I did it to make people happy, even if for just a few minutes. People are going to enjoy visiting, and I enjoy creating things people haven't seen before, just like Marcus enjoys that engineering junk he's into."

Henry wondered what brought himself genuine happiness, like Robby's art and Marcus's engineering. What made him unique? What did he do to make the world a better place?

Chapter Eight

Marcus looked out the window on his final trip to D.C., glad to get out of Sherman for a day. He had his personal jet returned from Atlanta, realizing it might not have been a good idea for Henry to use it. He shouldn't have the help playing with the toys.

The jet touched down and he was met with a small motorcade. Car rides made him uneasy, but it was secure, and the distance short.

He didn't expect much from the meeting. His train tunnel to Sherman was nowhere near finished, which had him worried. But with Orlen Muehlbauer out of the way, and money being so utterly arbitrary, he could get it dug right on time.

The cars came to a stop and he waited until his door was open before they marched inside. The Pentagon was abuzz. He wanted to hear the sociologists' predictions on how the world would react. And to be truthful, Marcus wanted praise for how successful the construction projects were on his bunkers. He expected an afternoon of entertainment and pats on the back.

Marcus looked away when the other billionaires walked into the meeting room. They decided outer space was better than underground, and thought their direction was righteous and more important. One corporate magnate had already sent an armada of ships to Mars to set up a colony at last optimal orbit, but Marcus heard he was now having second thoughts about the Red Planet.

Marcus disliked the lot of them, and their short-sighted ideas.

Director Ciolli entered and everyone settled, getting in their last murmurs to neighbors. If this meeting was like the others, it would be quite repetitive for Marcus. A new set of people were brought into the fold each session and had to watch an introductory movie of what equated to a corporate training video for The End of The World.

It was sobering upon first viewing. It had finally been explicitly disclosed that it was in fact an asteroid. The video explained the trajectory of the asteroid and the impact in an animation created by Director Orkies, his team at NASA, and some special effects brains in Hollywood who thought they were working on a science fiction movie.

The video included the failed efforts at altering the asteroid's course. The ionic drive probe (code-named "Bertha") was designed to follow the asteroid and tug at it with its gravitational presence. But Bertha malfunctioned and fell away. Then a trail of nukes set out in front of the either detonated a fraction of a second too soon, or hit the target and still did nothing. The asteroid continued like nothing happened.

The video went on to show the preparations made on Earth and abroad. Bunker and space colony life was outlined with cheesy actors and all. Satellites with loads of hygroscopic silver iodide capsules were prepared to fire into the atmosphere. The scientists claimed that rainfall during and after the impact would exponentially lower debris clouds and permit human resurfacing hundreds of years earlier than expected. Every speck of water in the air would knock down a speck of dust. It was all conjecture.

The film wrapped up with an uplifting message and triumphant music, but Director Ciolli cut it off and called up Greg Meier.

"Good afternoon, everyone," Meier said. "You are probably wondering what the Secretary of Education has to do with anything. But I was put in charge of bunker bids and wanted to speak a moment about the system we devised to allocate them. Among adults, we set a hard cutoff at age fifty, with a few exceptions, some of whom are in the room."

A few people in the crowd chuckled about being above the age and getting to live while the rest of the world didn't.

"After that, we combed through medical records and eliminated a good many more millions with preexisting conditions. Again, with a few exceptions." Meier patted his robust belly and got more laughs.

Marcus wasn't amused.

"That still leaves us with a tremendous population to sift through. This is where education comes into play. Thanks to rigorous standardized testing, we know exactly which child to leave behind! We found that the children who tested poorly in our education system also did poorly as adults. No surprise there. Outliers were vetted further, some have secured bids.

"Regarding children, we have taken the cream off the top of the ninety-ninth percentile, and in most cases, their nuclear families. I am saddened to say, as Secretary of Education, that teachers were not made a priority. Schools in the bunker will be cultivated by intuitive computer programs developed aggressively over the past few years to cut wasteful spending. By their early teens, the students should take up an apprenticeship in a field of work or knowledge beneficial to the bunker population.

"None of us want our average or ill adults and children to perish, but we have to preserve the best of mankind. That means we collect people with the highest intelligence with the fewest health complications, and we carry on. I know this has been taboo for ninety years, but what will emerge from this catastrophe will be a better, stronger, smarter human race. Thank you."

Marcus knew political correctness was slipping, but he was disgusted by the casual disregard for human life.

Is this how Henry sees me?

Director Ciolli stood again.

"Unfortunately," Ciolli said, "shit is going to hit the fan. We want to tamp this down as much as possible. We've decided the best way to accomplish this is to plant false hope in the populace. The best way to lie is with a healthy dose of the truth. The truth will be that an asteroid will hit the earth. The lie will be some pseudo-science that downplays the impact, that it will not harm people at a reachable underground depth."

He paused.

"In other words, survival is possible with a little pluck and luck, the American way. Our engineers have drawn designs for homemade bunkers that most anyone can construct, ranging from single family units fashioned from in-ground swimming pools, to community projects. That is what we want to create, community and constructive action."

Marcus was skeptical of the idea that every American man was going to break out his shovel or backhoe to save his family, instead of his guns. But it was worth a shot. The propaganda spread was convincing.

The meeting went through a few more phases, geopolitics and predicted wars, civil motivation, and the like, before getting to the bunkers.

An expert spoke about resurfacing kits, and Marcus expressed his interest in securing one. Materials were passed out for food growth and rationing, underground governance models, and plans to raise radio towers from silos once the dust settled, and eventually connect to Starlink.

Marcus was in no hurry to re-addict his bunker denizens to the internet.

It was only when energy concerns came up that Marcus really perked up. The secretary of energy, Benjamin Kim, took the podium. Marcus had a close working relationship with him, and he liked that the man listened to him.

"Months ago, it came to our attention that a viable mini-reactor was designed," Kim said. "As you know, this was the holy grail of our energy needs underground. Our experts examined the plans closely, even built a few, and found that it worked incredibly well. We've gone forward and produced several for the bunkers that will require the most energy."

Behind Secretary Kim, on the screen, was the blueprint. It took Marcus a few seconds, but he recognized it. They were *his* plans.

He was caught off guard. How did they get ahold of them?

"It is my understanding that Mr. Trencher had no intention of sharing his nuclear reactor with us. By pure luck it fell into our hands." A pause. "Tell us, Mr. Trencher, why was this withheld? What do you gain from your secrecy?"

Marcus was flabbergasted by the ambush. "You don't understand, the designs are flawed. I would have–"

"Save it. You wanted to keep it all to yourself as one last trophy for outsmarting the rest of mankind's brightest minds. So, we've moved forward and kept you out of the loop. Ten bunkers have been outfitted and five more are in the final stages of installation."

Kim was genuinely upset.

"Have you no shame?"

"I was not withholding it out of some selfish, um, I don't..." Marcus struggled to compose himself. "The design is not stable long term. *You* will be responsible

69

when those reactors melt fifty, a hundred years from now. They'll work fine now, but you have to believe me, too much can go wrong."

Every head in the room faced him, shaking in disapproval. Marcus was well past flustered.

"It's too complicated to explain here," he said, "but I will meet with your team and lay it out, whatever it takes. You are making a terrible mistake."

"Mr. Trencher, we applaud your impressive first foray into nuclear energy. But our more experienced physicists have built on your prototype and they are confident that the reactors will provide power for centuries, safely. Your mistake was not coming forward willingly, and months ago. There is such a thing as collaboration. Think of all the laborious coal mining and the susceptible geothermal wells that could collapse from shifts in the Earth's crust. Tidal energy systems are susceptible to mechanical breakdown. This solves it all."

Marcus stood to object further. The other billionaires got a kick out of Marcus's discomfort. Director Orkies was genuinely concerned, and perhaps the only man in the room taking Marcus seriously. Still, he didn't speak up.

Marcus was escorted out of the meeting but left the building on his own accord. He was furious, beside himself.

How could they? How did they?

He told nobody except Robby in passing, who never saw the plans, wouldn't understand anyway, and wouldn't talk if he did.

What else had leaked? His bunker blueprints?

Then Marcus realized. He drew his bunker specifications the old-fashioned way, in a pad of architecture cartridge paper. He worked on a computer to design the mini-reactor. His computer had the finest of security software on it, custom-coded by a tech genius.

A tech genius named Timothy Spencer.

Chapter Nine

For the second time in his life, Marcus felt lost. The meeting did not go as planned. He couldn't stomach the thought of millions of lives relying on his reactors. He didn't want to stay in D.C., but Sherman didn't seem all that welcoming either.

There was someone else he had to see. He wasn't particularly excited about it, but it had to be done. He had to go see his father.

They had rarely spoken in years.

During the flight he scribbled a note in case he went coward. He filled the rest of the time staring out the window. They landed at Fort Lauderdale Executive Airport mid-day. The drive to the house was uneventful, but every inch he got closer, Marcus became more tense.

The mansion wasn't the largest, but it was beautiful. Marcus envied the palm trees and Bermuda grass. He sat for a moment, staring at the property. Then he was out of the car and at the front door, ringing the bell.

His father answered. For some reason, Marcus expected a servant, but there he was.

Thomas Trencher blinked in disbelief, then welcomed his son into his home.

"Come in. It's great to see you," he said as they entered the foyer. He sounded like he meant it.

His dad had aged well, and the birth mark on his head now sported a shock of grey in his calico hair. His wife, Minnie, Marcus's step-mom, came around the corner with a mixing bowl in hand. She disappeared quickly, gracefully exiting to the kitchen.

"What brings you to sunny Florida?" his father asked in that old-man kind of way as they walked toward the back of the house.

"Well, it's been awhile."

"You are a busy man. You like your space."

They went out back to a patio and looked out to the Atlantic. Marcus was glad they were skipping the small talk, but he wasn't exactly eager for the big talk.

"I'm sorry," Marcus said. "It was all me. I don't know how to do these things. I don't understand people, and I don't think I ever will. Family, close friends, strangers – it doesn't matter. I can read about human behavior, analyze statistics about people, and design places that make people happy and live in harmony. But face to face, I am clueless. It is frustrating."

"When you were five, we went to your Aunt Christy's wedding," his father said. "The church had a playroom to occupy all the toddlers before the ceremony. Apparently, an altercation broke out between you and another child over a toy truck. Instead of crying or prying it back, you went to an easel with a chalkboard. You looked around at the toys that were being played with and wrote down stations. Somehow you could already read a standard clock, and you divided up the time. You barked out directions to the other kids."

Marcus loved it. "Well," he said, "did it work? My stations?"

"No! They were a bunch of four-year-olds!"

They laughed.

"I swear you were not a blank slate," Tom Trencher said. "All it took was for you to come in contact with something and it was like you were remembering it, and not learning it for the first time. It was the most amazing thing to watch."

Marcus shrugged.

"But it isolated you. It really did. For years and years, you had nobody on your level. You had no peers. We worried ourselves sick about your socialization. When you and Henry asked if you could go over to that boy Robby's house down the road, we were so relieved. Your mother and I jumped up and down like we won the lottery . . ."

"Dad...I don't hate you. I don't hate Minnie, either. I was immature and selfish and didn't give her a chance." He teared up, the first time in as long as he could recall. "I'm happy you found happiness."

"Thank you. That means more than you'll ever know. I did my best, Marcus. I really tried."

"Dad, it's all over."

"I know, Marcus."

"No, dad, it's all over. Everything."

"Look at me, Marcus," his dad said, and Marcus did so. "I know. I sit on a few boards of some powerful corporations. Hell, did you see the neighborhood I live in? I've known for a while now."

"Just to be clear—"

"Yes, the asteroid. It's a bunker isn't? The site up in Sherman?"

Marcus nodded.

"Good, good. I bet it's something to see. Take good people down there with you. Find who or what makes you happy and take them with you."

"What about you and Minnie? Do you have a place?"

His father nodded slowly. "We had our choice. Georgia, Texas, or Oklahoma. We settled on Florida."

"Florida?" Marcus was perplexed. He knew the system inside and out. "What do you mean? Florida?" There were no bunkers in Florida.

"We've had a beautiful life. We've contributed what we could to the world. I am proud of you. But when it is time to go, it is time to go."

Marcus had no words. If he had a month, he wouldn't know what to say.

"I'll tell your mother everything, Marcus. She is going to be so proud of you. We'll watch the whole thing and be with you every step of the way, me and your mother."

Marcus fell to pieces. For years, he passively destroyed their relationship, and now he couldn't stand the thought of existing somewhere out there without him.

He wanted to see his mother again, too.

75

His father patted him on the shoulder one more time, then turned and left him alone on the patio.

When Marcus gathered himself, he walked back inside, unsure where his dad was.

Minnie was still in the kitchen.

"Minnie . . ." For a moment, the words left him. He paused, waiting for them to come back. ". . . I am sorry for how I treated you, and I will never forgive myself. You are a wonderful person and I regret not letting you into my life. You make my dad happy and I love you for that. I really do."

Her face melted into an expression both tearful and relieved. She hugged him, and he felt years of animosity dissipate.

Tom came into the kitchen entryway, stopped, and simply stood there.

* * *

Marcus returned to Sherman in the middle of the night, exhausted.

Before falling asleep, he sent Henry and Robby a message.

Bunker site 9 AM. Get ready for a tour.

Chapter Ten

Henry and Robby arrived at the bunker site looking rather ragged.

After Robby's presidential statue ceremony, the pair celebrated. It took a toll, and it showed. Henry fared worse than Robby if only because he was less used to drunken festivities -- or drunken anything for that matter.

As the pair approached, Marcus was so excited to show off the bunker, he was hopping in place like a little kid.

Marcus was on one of his manic upswings, far from the mood Henry dealt with at their last encounter.

Just as Marcus had promised, the massive hole was filled in. Henry expected it to be occupied with dirt and rock, but it was instead a new lake. It looked like Marcus had drained some of the nearby stripper pits into the crater. Off to the side, a concrete dome had been constructed.

"That is where the elevator is. It will keep the platform clear of debris."

Marcus shook Robby's hand and surprised Henry with a hug. "Glad to see you guys. How did the ceremony go? Sorry I couldn't make it."

Before Henry could answer, Robby jumped at the opportunity to self-deprecate. "George hated it. He tried fighting me on stage and I had to throw him down. The Secret Service beat me pretty good. Total disaster."

"Shut up," Henry said. "It was awesome. The President loved it and the people had that thing covered in mud within an hour. The fire department had to hose it down for the next round of people to get their shots in."

"How was your trip to D.C.?" Robby asked.

"A lot like your story, honestly," Marcus said. "A lot of mud thrown at me, but I also went down to Florida, . . . to see my dad."

Henry and Robby glanced at each other. Marcus hadn't seen his old man in years.

"How was he?" Henry asked.

"Good. Things are really good. Shall we?" Marcus motioned to the concrete dome. That was all they were going to get out of him regarding his dad, but it was enough.

They approached a heavy metal door. Marcus punched in a code and the door popped open.

Inside, a grated square platform took up most of the floor. A simple panel with a red and green button stood on a pole on a corner. Lights below illuminated the depths through the grate, which spooked Henry.

Marcus turned to them like a mad scientist. "Down we go!"

He pushed the green button and the platform started down. Anticipation rose as the platform descended. Henry didn't want to look up – definitely didn't want to glance down – so he watched the rock walls float past.

Marcus was fidgety with excitement.

After several minutes, the platform finally reached the bottom of the shaft. Marcus opened a small door within a much larger door and, again, entered a code. The lights in the room on the other side automatically clicked on. It took their eyes a moment to adjust.

"This is the decontamination chamber," Marcus said. "We will have to scrub down first. Don't want to drag anything in there."

Henry looked at Robby and shrugged. At least there were individual showers. There was potent soap and an abrasive scrubber, and after rinsing off, they had to put on new clothes.

In the next room, there was a podium and a dozen chairs.

"This antechamber is where we will sit the recruits down before going all the way in," Marcus said as they walked to the next door. "Later on, if our antenna works, we can broadcast from here." He punched in more codes.

They walked into a vast space. Henry and Robby gasped and cussed in astonishment.

The ceiling was close to eighty feet high. The floorspace was the size of a football field, and there was more beyond it. To their immediate right, a full-sized basketball court sat behind a wall of plexiglass. Next to it, the unmistakable blue of a swimming pool. To the left of the court and pool, a three-story climbing wall reached the ceiling.

"I call this the bunker proper," Marcus said.

The ground level was designed to look like storefronts – a movie theatre, a barber shop with a red-and-blue barber pole, and a gaming lounge. Above the ground level, there were two floors with uninterrupted balconies. The living quarters. In the forefront of it all were old-fashioned streetlamps lit with LED bulbs.

Four gargantuan pillars reached the ceiling.

"These are not just for show," Marcus said after slapping the side of a pillar. "In the base, there are ten-ton counterweights to compensate for any rattling that might occur. They use similar technology for skyscrapers in earthquake zones.

"The best part is the concrete everywhere around you. Bioengineers studied mussels from the ocean and created a synthetic adhesive they mixed in with concrete. This stuff is rigid, yet flexible. It will withstand considerable shaking. It also retards oxygen so as not to absorb it."

He led them closer to the recreational area.

"If you look next to the basketball court, you'll notice the tennis court. Jacuzzi and a spa are around the corner. On the second level there is a weight room and plenty of cardio machines."

They walked back, past another pillar, where there was a panel of windows and a door. A Red Cross plaque was on the wall beside the door – the bunker hospital. Marcus unlocked the door and they stepped inside.

"Our pharmacy is back there, locked up tight. We have everything within reason, and a few fancier items. Not sure our doctor will know how to work the MRI machine, but that's what the manual is for." Marcus led them across the room. "This is the crematorium. Hope we don't have to use this for a good long while."

Outside the hospital, Marcus pointed up to the tinted windows above it. "That is my apartment." It was separate from the other living quarters. He knew what his friends were thinking.

"What can I say? I built the place and I like my privacy."

They walked along the wall, passing a gigantic blast-proof door. Marcus made no mention of it.

"What's up with this?" Robb asked, pointing at the door.

"Oh, that is another thing I hope we don't use. There is a solid seam of coal back there. If power fails, we all become coal miners. This next door is the pantry."

Inside, there were rows upon rows of shelves full of food and supplies. The higher shelves required a sky jack to reach them. Henry felt like he was in a Costco.

Robby pointed up. "Hey, bourbon barrels!"

Marcus and Henry shook their heads.

Marcus explained most of the foodstuffs were sealed and packed to last decades, supplements to what was going to be grown. There were several immense plastic vats of cooking oils and flour, and a few smaller ones for salad dressings and condiments.

"We will eat better than most, but several meals will have to be filled with Soylent."

Marcus pointed out shelves full of clothing, everything from baby clothes to maternity garb was sealed in infomercial vacuum bags. There were shelves full of PlayStations and computers.

They came to another set of giant doors in a perpendicular wall.

"These will normally be open. I had them closed for dramatic effect."

He pushed a button and the two sides parted. The first thing noticeable was the green. Green everywhere. It looked like a park, and the grass looked real. The only thing that would have excited Henry more is if there were candy flowers and a chocolate river. Winding walkways crisscrossed the lawn, and there was a dry pond and what looked like a ditch.

"It will be a stream. We haven't turned the waterworks on just yet. The grass is fake, but we will pull it up and try to lay some turf when we get water going, and if it takes, it takes."

Immediately to the right was a café with "outdoor" seating. It was to be the place for people to take the main meals, but with a restaurant décor that was much more interesting. It was abundantly clear Marcus went to painstaking detail when it came to quality of life.

To the west was a second-floor balcony with five doors, similar to a motel. Above were faux roofs, creating the deception there was something beyond.

Marcus pointed at the apartments. "Those are for when we are more populated. For now, you will all live on the other side."

Above the apartments and everything else was, to Henry, even more astonishing. "Marcus, can you tell me why you built a *dome* in a bunker when an asteroid is about to hit us?"

"Relax, it is geodesic."

"Oh, in that case . . ."

"It's even safer than the other chamber. And you haven't seen the half of it."

They walked to the center of the domed area. There was a 12-foot tall obelisk in the center with a digital clock that seemed to come right out of the marble. There was a computer screen on another side. Marcus tapped it a few times, and the room went dark, other than a trail of dim landscaping lights.

More taps, and suddenly the sky lit up. It was the dome, but it was the sky. It authentically looked like the great outdoors. There were blue hues and clouds that gave the impression of being ten miles high. Henry slowly realized that a beacon atop the obelisk was projecting the image, like in a planetarium.

"Here, let me fast forward."

The clouds flew by, the sun went down, and the moon came up. The moon! And the stars! It was beautiful and looked *real*.

"Our circadian rhythm is going to be a little haywire, not seeing natural light. Hopefully, this will alleviate that. For the past couple of years, a tower camera at the site has been recording the sky, day and night, 24/7. This special lens projects the recording.

"That is not a true dome surface up there – it is semi-translucent flexi-glass, and three feet beyond it are a collection of screens that project forward. It adds depth and is more convincing. The stars technically shine."

Marcus flipped the switch back to basic lighting.

"Won't that bulb burn out pretty quickly?" Robby asked.

"It will last longer than you think, but yes, it will burn out eventually. Luckily, beyond the wall back there, I have a quarter mile tunnel full of light bulbs and light bulbs only." Marcus smiled. "Don't worry, Robby. I thought of everything."

They walked to the edge of the dry stream and looked to the back of the dome. The ground was torn up and carved out, where the farming apparatus was to be placed.

Marcus said the animals would be held behind a door on the back wall, which also led to the storage tunnels. He said if the vet cleared it, they might let some chickens and goats roam in the open.

"You probably won't get a tan in here, but we do have some strong plant-grow light bulbs for the gardens and grass. I've even ordered a lightweight robot that cuts grass and lights it. Sort of like a Roomba. A more reliable rig will be set up directly over the crops." Marcus led them to a well-built cedar wood gazebo.

"Romantic, isn't it?" Marcus said. "The stream will run underneath, which will come from a waterfall over here." He pointed to a wall with large protruding rocks. It looked like a waterfall, minus the water.

"It is all part of the bunker water cycle and treatment facility, which is our next stop."

There wasn't much to see of the water facility since there was no water. They went around a column to the northeast corner of the bunker.

"Nothing in there at the moment, but that will be our power plant room. We are running on generators at the moment. I have a few kinks to work out, but I'll get my system down here soon."

The next room was the brain of the bunker, a custom-built supercomputer. There were rows of what looked like bookshelves in a library, but instead of books there were circuit boards and wires. The room was noisy and chilly.

"We'll have plenty of gadgets and gizmos. This will be the cloud. We won't have the internet until Starlink is brought back online and we get a signal. For now, the guys at Google prepared a package containing the best of what was on there. Useful stuff. We'll also have just about every movie and TV show ever made, and a million video games. Just promise you guys don't turn into vegetables and ignore the girls."

Henry knew he and Robby would be content living out their remaining existence playing video games.

They continued with the tour, visiting the living quarters, the fitness facility, gaming lounge, theatre, and mundane things like the laundry room and salon. There was still work to be done, but most of the essentials were there.

As angry as Henry had been that only 12 people would be living there, he couldn't help but be overwhelmed. He expected quality, but Marcus still blew him away with what was built. It looked like life might not be so miserable underground.

There *was* room for more people, but the design planned for them to grow into it over time. Henry thought he might be able to rationalize with that.

"Where is the train tunnel going to be?" Henry asked.

"Fingers crossed, it will come through between the elevator and hospital. It won't be fancy. We left a chamber under the lake. The tunnel is being dug toward us as we speak. I wish we were digging both directions, but those mole machines are not easy to transport. Once they hit that tunnel and everything checks out stable, we will knock the wall down and meet them."

Henry frowned. Time was running out and there were miles and miles to dig. If they didn't finish before impact, or even after the public announcement, he wondered how dedicated people on the other side would be to complete it. If they hurried to finish and it collapsed, it would be impossible to link the bunkers. His parents were going to be on the other side, and he wanted to be able to visit them.

They rode the platform back to the surface and stepped out of the concrete dome. The sun was hiding behind the clouds and it was getting cold.

"What's next?" Henry asked.

"You and Robby need to find two more girls. One will do. If we have to, I'll take my secretary Brittney down with us," Marcus said.

"Britney? Hell," Robby said, "then we only have to get one. I've already told you Marcus, Brittney and I are meant to be together."

Marcus sighed. "Fine. One more."

Chapter Eleven

Henry rejoined the interview team in Charlotte, this time with Robby in tow.

Ashley looked terrible. It was probably torture for her to do dozens of interviews and know that it was all an act since Henry wasn't there to decide. She did choose two girls for a second interview.

The first of the two bombed. She started crying during the interview for no discernible reason. He could only imagine her reaction when the asteroid tried to take out the planet.

Robby teased Ashley, who he'd never met before. She took it personally.

"Seriously, Ashley?" Robby said.

"She did fine with me."

"I don't think I would have chosen her if she walked in naked." He paused. "No, actually, I probably would have." Robby and Henry laughed and punched each other in the arms like teenage boys.

"You guys are disgusting. You're playing with peoples' lives!" she said before storming out.

The next interviewee was sent in without introduction. Henry and Robby stared at her blankly for a moment.

"Hello, I am Henry Plyman and this is, um, Robert Reed."

"I am Mercedes. Nice to meet you."

"Like the car?" Robby blurted out.

She forced a friendly smile.

"Yes, spelled just like the car."

"My assistant failed to hand me your resume," Henry said. "What is it you do for a living?"

"I am a sanitation engineer," she said. "I work in a water treatment plant. I oversee day-to-day operations and keep clean water flowing. I have a hand in everything from testing pH levels to checking mechanical systems."

Henry made a note. She had clear value. Marcus would never admit it, but he did seem to have overlooked the need for a water systems expert.

"Any of the guys give you trouble in the plant?" Henry asked.

She smiled. "Some, yes, but all in fun. My father had worked there for 30 years and everybody knew not to mess with me. He showed me the ropes and I learned quickly."

Henry liked her, but he was hesitant.

Before Henry figure out an angle, Robby jumped back in.

"You are just what we were looking for. Do you have any kids or a husband?"

Henry jumped in: "The job would require you to move."

"Nope, married to my work," Mercedes said.

"Done," Robby said, completely out of place but not incorrect. "You got the job. Ashley out in the hall will take it from here. She is the one with the personality of a brick. We'll call you." Robby escorted her to the door, quite proud of himself.

Henry was speechless, staring straight ahead, shaking his head in disbelief. His interview process was not perfect, but he was a smidge more thorough than Robby. He debated with himself in his head. She had the credentials, she was pretty, but . . .

"Dude," Robby said, "Marcus is going to flip out when he sees we picked a black chick!"

Henry closed his eyes and brought his hand up to his forehead.

He should have left Robby at the airport.

* * *

Henry and Robby found Marcus in his kitchen, which was filled with the aroma of green bean casserole.

"Happy Thanksgiving!" Marcus turned, a spatula in hand, pointing it at them. "Ashley told me you guys were pricks, but you chose the right gal. Sanitation engineer. Great choice. Can't wait to meet her." He removed the casserole from the oven.

Henry looked around the kitchen. "Are you only making the casserole?"

"You think I can cook a turkey? I'd poison everyone, and I don't want to do that. Your parents are taking care of the rest."

"Oh, that's right. Man, I haven't had a proper Thanksgiving meal in years."

"Robby and I have enjoyed your mother's cooking for the past three years and I'm not about to miss this one. Let's go."

* * *

His mom yelled from the kitchen, "Just in time!" She hugged and kissed Henry. Years ago he would have been embarrassed, but this night, he soaked it in. She then hugged Marcus and Robby.

"Green bean casserole, Mrs. Plyman. I baked it just for you," Robby said with a mischievous grin.

"Hey!"

"Okay, Marcus helped a little."

Mr. Plyman led the prayer, eloquent as always. They dug in, trading bowls, plates, and playful barbs. They discussed the latest Sherman happenings and especially the success of Robby's George W. Bush mud monument.

Marcus stood up and excused himself. "I need to make a call," he said.

The others chatted quietly while Marcus was in the other room. Henry tried to listen without being obvious about it. He distinctly heard, "Bye, dad. I love you."

Marcus returned and sat back down.

"I guess I'll start?" He paused for a few moments. "I am thankful for my family, for the first time in a long time. I am also thankful for my family right here at this table. I would be nothing without each and every one of you."

Marcus looked at Robby, and Robby nodded.

"Marcus kind of stole what I was going to say, but I also wouldn't be anything without you guys. I haven't had the most luck with family, so what you've done for me could never be repaid in a thousand years. So, thank you."

Mrs. Plyman was already choked up. "I love you boys so much. You are all family. I'm . . . I'm going to miss you so much," she said, before breaking into tears.

Henry put an arm around his mom and comforted her. "Mom, we aren't going anywhere. You don't have to miss us."

Mr. Plyman looked at Henry.

"Son, we know," Mr. Plyman said.

Henry laughed for a moment. "What do you mean?"

"I had to tell them, Henry," Marcus said. "I needed their blessing."

"Why didn't you tell me?"

"Don't be upset, son," Mr. Plyman said. "You don't need us around. Your mother and I will be fine in Bloomington. Marcus is going to get that train through and we will visit, first thing. Don't you worry. We raised you right and we couldn't be prouder of you."

Henry took a moment to think. His parents, or at least his dad, knew and approved of it. He was glad Marcus had confided in them but was dismayed once again from the lack of disclosure. A negative reaction would ruin the whole holiday.

Always the last to know.

"Okay . . . okay, that's good. You're right," Henry said forcing a smile. "That tunnel is coming through and I'll be on the first train back."

Marcus smiled. "Now can we break out the pumpkin pie?"

Chapter Twelve

The rest of Fall was spent making final preparations.

Marcus went into obsessive-work mode, disappearing for days at a time to perfect the power source for the bunker. Henry didn't know what it was going to be, but he avoided asking for answers he wouldn't understand anyway.

He was more than willing to take a more active role after the recruiting was finished, but Marcus insisted that he enjoy the Last Days.

Henry had worked nonstop for nearly seven years. He was antsy having nothing to do.

After trying to spark a few new hobbies, and then downloading and deleting an addictive cellphone game, and after giving up on a book that started well before turning boring, he became a TV watcher.

When not dissecting the news, Henry enjoyed flipping back and forth between *Lunar City* and *The First Martians*, a pair of competing reality TV programs covering the colonization of the moon and Mars.

The shows were so successful that *Lunar City* had enough applicants to triple in size and the Red Planet colony would double, so long as infrastructure and supplies could keep up.

Henry preferred *The First Martians*. It wasn't because it looked like a utopia, or that he wanted to be there. It was because their struggles were so great it made for entertaining television.

The Martians' existence was abysmal. They had to sleep in special chambers to combat health problems stemming from low gravity and radiation, and they rarely came up to the surface from their tunnels. There were psychological issues, too.

While Henry was catching up on a *Lunar City* episode, Marcus came out of hiding and walked right in.

"Wow, you look like shit," Marcus said.

Henry rubbed his cheek. He hadn't shaved in a week.

"Thanks. How is your magical energy system panning out? I don't feel like becoming a coal miner."

"Finished and already running in the bunker. I worked out all the kinks and had it installed two days ago. It is stable and will give us hundreds of years' worth of low maintenance energy."

"What is it anyway?"

"Get up and let's go check it out. There is something else we need to do today."

"I thought I was on vacation."

"You were. Welcome back."

Henry got dressed appropriately for the December weather. It was an abnormally warm start to winter for Indiana, but abnormally warm starts to winter were becoming normal. Still, it was too chilly for his comfort.

They drove out to the site and Marcus told Henry to wait in the car for a moment. He disappeared into a trailer for the construction crew, and then came back out with a radio.

"It should just be a few minutes," he said. "Robby is running late. Big surprise."

Robby finally arrived in his muddy Jeep.

Marcus was already leading the charge up to the crater lake. The waters were choppy and the wind gusts were enough to knock a man over if he wasn't paying attention.

"Robby and I are hoping for a few good snow showers. It will be good for the soil. Once things thaw, we will move a few tons of rich soil into the bunker, then in goes Robby's next cycle of crops."

Henry knew the crops were important, but the cold made him ambivalent. He just wanted Marcus to get to the point.

"Are we good to go?" Marcus said into the radio.

A voice confirmed they were.

"Okay guys, just watch the lake. This is going to be awesome."

There was a faint rumble. It was either far underground or miles away from a nearby coal mine. A few seconds later, some bubbles interrupted the lake surface out in the middle, barely visible. Then they got bigger – much bigger. They felt a final explosion and water shot fifteen feet into the air.

It was hardly perceptible at first, but it became clear that the lake was draining. Millions of gallons of water were heading somewhere, and that somewhere was the bunker.

After a few more minutes, the lake was ten feet lower and still dropping.

"Explosions make for great theatrics, but isn't this jeopardizing the bunker?" Henry asked.

Marcus looked dismissive. "Plenty of safeguards, no chance of flooding. Let's go inside, there is some hot chocolate in there. Also, you guys need to meet someone."

They went into the trailer. Robby and Henry went straight for the coffeemaker and began fighting over the hot chocolate K-cups.

"Guys, I'd like you to meet Kent Grieves. He is our computer engineer. He will be joining us in the bunker."

He was of average height, wore glasses with thick black rims, and had a healthy beard. The kid was the spitting image of Timothy Spencer, only younger. The similarity was too much for Henry and Robby not to share a glance and laugh.

"Hello, nice to meet you," Kent said, standing up from a bank of computers to shake their hands.

"How are we looking?" Marcus asked, looking at the computers.

"The reservoirs are filling, and the water is cycling through steadily. It looks like it worked. In a few hours it will begin filtering and the bunker will have clean, running water," Kent said.

Marcus slapped Kent on the back a little too hard and charged out of the trailer. They gave Kent one last nod and followed Marcus.

They hustled toward the concrete dome. They were heading down to the bunker.

After the elevator ride and decontamination scrub, they entered the cavernous first chamber. It was every bit as impressive as the initial visit. Marcus was halfway across the chamber before realizing Henry and Robby were not following. He called them over.

They stood over a huge circular manhole cover, the size of the home plate area on a baseball field.

"This is one of the reservoirs. It is two-hundred feet deep and there are three more. Water is not going to be an issue. Let's go check out the power source."

Robby pointed across the chamber. "Is this what I think it is?"

Marcus turned. "Ah, yes! My art collection arrived last week! These over here are Chagall, Dali, Matisse, and Degas. Munch's 'The Scream' is hanging somewhere down here."

"How the hell did you get ahold of these?" Henry asked. Robby stared into the paint from inches away.

"Remember when I met you in Paris when you were working Europe? The art community held an auction that week to secure places for the world's most precious artwork. I won some good ones that happened to already be in America. I wanted some sculptures, but they refused to transfer them overseas. They are going to put those in some World War II Nazi bunkers. Kind of ironic."

After snapping Robby out of his trance, Marcus took them through the gardens. The waterfall was now functioning, and the stream was bubbling through. There was a pond that Marcus hoped to use as part of a fish hatchery. The sound of water was soothing. Henry imagined under the dome sky when the projection beacon was on, the chamber would be a wonderful place.

They stepped into the water treatment facility for Marcus to check a few gauges. He gave a satisfactory nod and moved next door to where his mysterious energy source was tucked away in the corner of the bunker.

"This, my friends, will free us from slavery," he said, gesturing toward the next door of the chamber.

"Instead of shoveling coal or relying on geothermal wells susceptible to collapse, we will have hands off, no-maintenance power that will last for centuries. It will allow us to live comfortably. It will also give us the ability to put effort into reclaiming the surface far sooner than anyone else."

He placed his palm on a scanner and the thick door slid open. They stepped into a circular room with metallic surfaces everywhere and flashing LED lights on tall panels flush with buttons and switches. In the center of the chamber, there was a pool of moving water. It all looked very futuristic to Henry, but he had no clue as to what it was.

"Really cool, Marcus. What is it?" Henry asked.

"It is a miniaturized nuclear reactor. Each fuel rod down there will get us a solid 50 to 100 years of power. The supercomputer in the other room is programmed to run it. It is fully automated."

Henry didn't like the idea of being in the same room as nuclear anything.

Marcus laughed at their fear. "Relax guys, I could swim in that water down there and be fine, except I guess the temperature. You are getting no more radiation than waiting for a Hot Pocket while standing in front of a microwave."

"And what if there is like, a meltdown?" Robby asked.

"It won't happen, but there are safeguards. Look around the room, what do you notice of its shape?"

They looked around. It was round.

"This reactor is inside a cylindrical container similar to an intercontinental ballistic missile silo. If anything goes wrong – which it won't – the safety measures will kick in. Ordinance will blow away any debris on the blast door above and this sucker will be launched far, far away from here."

"Underneath this nuclear reactor, there are hundreds of gallons of rocket fuel? Great," Henry said.

Robby was leaning over the rail looking into the radioactivity beneath the water.

"Relax, it is safe." He expected a little more praise from his friends, but he loved them anyway.

He led them out of the reactor room.

On the way out, they passed the paintings and the giant door that Marcus said opened into a coal seam.

"Hey Marcus, can you open this door?" Robby asked.

"It's just coal, dude, and a little power station. Maybe later."

100

They stood quiet for the elevator ride. Henry was a little frightened by something he didn't understand. Anything nuclear had a negative connotation, especially after 2023. But if anyone could pull it off, it was Marcus.

They got back to the surface to find the lake almost a third empty. Henry didn't know much about nuclear energy, but he did know it required a lot of water.

They walked around the shore, back to the vehicles.

"We have a little over a month until the public announcement," Marcus said, "I think it is time to meet all of Henry's recruits."

Henry started to say he'd start making calls right away, but Marcus cut him off.

"We will enjoy Christmas and buy up whatever the latest gadgets and games you want to bring down into the bunker. After that, we bring in the recruits. I've thought of a nice icebreaker exercise we can use to get to know them a little before going underground."

"Icebreaker? What, Trencher's band camp?" Robby said.

Marcus grinned.

"We are going to throw the biggest New Year's Eve party the Midwest has ever seen."

* * *

The party was in full swing. Robby was impossible to miss in the chaos below, always the center of attention.

"It seems my friend has lost lease of his senses," Marcus said to the man beside him.

They were perched on the east wing of the second-floor balcony, overlooking the party through a hole in the synthetic fog. Senator Greg Granger, a representative from Minnesota, was on the Intelligence Subcommittee, and one of the first investors in *Trencher Industries*. So, he *knew*.

"He is just a few weeks ahead of the game," the Senator said of Robby. Granger took a drink of his bourbon.

Marcus sipped his cocktail. A vodka drink in a martini glass. He figured he could indulge in just one.

"At least he hasn't lost his head like our poor friend, Senator Muehlbauer," Senator Granger said.

Marcus wasn't so sure the Senator knew *everything*. "Oh, yes, a shame. We had our differences, but I couldn't wish something like that on even my worst enemy."

The senator laughed. "Cut the bullshit, Marcus. I know damn well what happened. The bastard had it coming. I couldn't believe it didn't happen sooner and it is an outrage that you even had to ask." He took another sip of whiskey. "There were only five senators internally deemed unfit to be informed of our impending doom, and he was at the top of the list. You need to get those trains through, and he was standing on the tracks. Had to happen."

Marcus was uncomfortable with Granger knowing, more so for agreeing.

"Yeah, well, I am not so sure the tunnels are going to be complete. We still have over a hundred miles to dig, and the tunnel I care most about has only just begun. Orlen might have the last laugh."

"It is getting dicey out there," Granger said. "It's going to boil down to how the general public takes the news. Everyone is either going to go batshit crazy, or they'll buy into the propaganda and work in harmony. Probably a combination."

"I don't plan on taking any risks. I'll be watching the broadcast from deep underground."

"Tell you what, Marcus. I'll see what I can do to assist with your trains. The boys in D.C. aren't exactly keen on you after the mini-reactor issue, but I am sure I can pull some strings."

Marcus wanted to just say thanks and shake his hand, but he knew that wasn't all there was to it.

"That would be greatly appreciated. And what do you need from me in return?"

Granger smiled. "Well, I have a bit of a bunker population issue up in Minnesota. Not a big one, but enough to be a thorn in my side. There is a woman that is...not my wife, and a kid . . ."

Before Granger could finish, a buzz erupted from the party crowd below.

Marcus checked his watch. It was a minute before midnight.

Granger gave Marcus a hapless look, as if he was embarrassed having left the conversation in the middle of his dilemma.

"We'll pick this discussion up in a few, Senator. Let's ring in the final New Year."

A 20-foot tall screen projected live footage of Times Square. Marcus descended the staircase, not knowing where to go. He didn't know half the people he invited. He felt out of place at his own party.

He spotted Robby, as it was impossible not to. He was shirtless and wearing a tiara, jumping up and down. To his right, he saw Henry, who hardly looked better than Robby, except he still had a shirt on. Beside Henry was Mariya, one of the recruits.

With ten seconds remaining, Marcus accepted that he would watch the ball drop alone, in a sea of strangers.

"...*four*...*three*...*two*...*ONE! Happy New Year!*"

The tarpaulin on the ceiling high above released a thousand balloons. Staffers stationed on the balconies fired off black-and-white confetti and streamers in unison. People laughed, cheered, raised glasses, and kissed.

The party went into a raucous frenzy. Marcus for watched for a moment before reconvening with the Senator to finish their dealings.

The crowd started to thin out within a half hour after the ball drop. Those left standing, barely, migrated to the back of the house.

Marcus went to bed.

* * *

Henry slowly opened his eyes.

Marcus was standing over him in his morning robe holding a mug. He said nothing, only offering a grin and thumbs-up with his free hand. Then, he left.

Confused, Henry tried to sit up, but wasn't successful. At first, he thought he was covered by the world's heaviest blanket. It was no blanket.

It was Mariya.

He twitched in surprise, which, in turn, startled her awake.

He wasn't sure what to do, being trapped between the sofa and her body. He pretended to be asleep.

Mariya got up. Henry surreptitiously watched through his pretend-asleep eyes.

She gathered her dress off the floor and put it on over her head. Three times she pushed the left strap back on her shoulder as she worked the intricate lacing of her shoes.

"I know you're awake."

Damnit.

"Hey. Good morning."

"I had fun last night. Call me?"

"Sure, yeah. I'll call you."

Marcus swooped back into the room on cue. "I'll walk you to the door. Henry, get some rest."

Mariya was woozy and walking on heels. Henry kept his eyes open long enough to see them disappear around the corner, and then tried to get his dehydrated brain to recall some memory.

* * *

At the door, Mariya was clearly embarrassed.

"Mr. Trencher, I'm sorry I –"

"Don't be. Don't think for a second you are in trouble. Henry is my best friend. You aren't being

105

held to any corporate rulebook. And call me Marcus. We're nearly the same age."

Marcus opened the door to a waiting car.

"Thank you, Marcus. It was a party for the ages."

He leaned down to the open window.

"Your next trip here will be a move-in, and that will be no more than two-and-a-half weeks from now. Bring anything you feel you might want with you. Family photos, stuffed animals, whatever. We'll see you in a few weeks."

Chapter Thirteen

Timothy Spencer decided to take Marcus up on his offer, if it was still standing.

He had gleaned enough from his sources to know that the meeting in D.C. took place, and that Marcus was likely confronted in some fashion about withholding the mini-reactor designs.

In the months since his conversation with Marcus, he had run up a tab of bad luck. He was in a minor wreck with an uninsured driver. It led him to the gates of hell to face his arch nemesis, the Iowa Department of Motor Vehicles. He yet again showed up without a required document. Another paper ticket, another long wait, and another elderly woman a few seats down who hadn't talked to a soul in weeks.

His oldest daughter, Liza, was being bullied by a boy at school. It sparked a heated argument with Shelley, who told Liza it was all because the boy liked her.

Timothy became more upset with Shelley than the bully because he was sure Liza was now imbued with the belief that boys who are mean are the ones she will see as potential mates. He envisioned, deep underground a decade from then, Liza showing up to their bunker apartment with a spikey-haired teen with homemade bunker tattoos on his forearms.

He lobbied for a psychologist to unwind the damage and prevent its manifestations years down the road. He couldn't believe he had to mansplain this feminism to his wife.

Then, on his Sunday bike ride, a passing truck revved its engine, startling him so badly he nearly rode off into a ravine.

In general, people were pissing him off.

It was as if Marcus cursed him into losing faith in humanity and cursed him with a superhuman attribute he didn't want. Everyone he met, he saw their future. He couldn't help but judge every passerby's fate.

He'll die, she'll die, she has a chance, he's a goner.

Every interaction with a lower-class citizen took place in a gloomy subtext. They were third class passengers on a sinking ship, no lifeboats. He could only creep them out with heartfelt thanks for his food and packages and tip well.

Then there were the in-betweeners.

Ameya Patel was young and intelligent but was a chiropractor at a small practice in a strip mall. Would he get a bunker bid?

What about Liza's second grade teacher, Mrs. Lane, who won a prestigious award in only her fourth year of teaching? She didn't even teach at one of the poor schools, practically a prerequisite for the award. Surely, they'd want some semblance of an education system down in the bunkers.

His neighbor Rhett Nevin was a hell of an insurance salesman. Nah, *goner*.

The public announcement date, January 23, was two weeks away. Tim quietly packed away extra food and water and read end-of-the-world survivalist blogs while Shelley was at work. He bought a handgun and ammunition. He had become a level-one prepper.

Survival in the bunkers wasn't his concern. If his bunker failed, he'd be dead in an instant. That is, unless there was some protracted struggle after a vital systems failure, food or power, or something. He looked up how long a human can survive in total darkness and cursed himself for fomenting phobias.

What kept him awake at night were the moments immediately following the announcement and the months thereafter. What would society do? Collapse? Fall into martial law? Break into survivalist tribes who bond and attack as needed?

He prayed for martial law. He would gladly give up freedom for order. If there is one thing he could do, it was obeying the law. It was the other guy he worried about. Mass hysteria was a legitimate concern. He wasn't going to be a lone ranger. He had a wife and two young daughters to look after.

He loathed telling his wife, but she had to know before the announcement. It was the End Times, and he needed an ally to prepare for the shit hitting the fan.

When she got home, it didn't take long for her to suspect something was not right. He sat at the table without a thing in front of him.

He knew how it looked, but that's why he did it.

She peeled off her purse and tossed her keys in the bowl.

"Something the matter?"

"Well, yeah," he said. "But it sort of has a good ending. So, hear me out before you think I am nuts."

She crossed her arms. It was her *Go on, but I already hate what you haven't said yet* pose.

"Know how I've been spoiling the girls lately, no matter how much you get on me about it?"

"We've been over this. I don't want to raise a bunch of entitled brats who think –"

"Okay, okay. But, sorry, that is not what I wanted to talk about. Shell, please, sit down."

"Then what is it?"

"What I am about to tell you sounds crazy, but it's no joke."

She sat slowly, not breaking eye contact.

"I've been spoiling Liz and Maddie because we are not going to have much of anything soon. And I am not talking financially."

He scrunched his face as he thought of how he could say what he needed to say – without saying it.

"Shelley, I don't know how to put this, but . . . the world is about to end."

Her eyes nearly rolled out of her head. "Oh give me a –"

"Seriously, Shell. It's an asteroid. They are going to announce it in two weeks."

She gave him a cold, hard stare. It was meant as an opportunity for him to admit the joke, or that he was crazy and needed help.

He didn't take the bait.

She leaned in.

"Okay Timothy, I know things have been rough since that prick Marcus fired you, I get that. But you have a family here. Pull your shit together. I can't raise them alone."

"*Look*," he said a little more intensely than he intended.

The spike in his voice startled her.

"I am *not* joking about this. Marcus is the very reason I know about it. It's why I got fired. Our planet is about to get smoked and one-percent of us are going to survive it in deep underground bunkers. I have reservations for all of us. You, me, and the girls."

She shook her head. It was disbelief, but he was scaring her.

"I need you to stay home on the twenty-third. That is when they are making the public announcement about the asteroid. Request time off now or call in sick. I don't care. Just stay home."

He pinched the bridge of his nose and squinted his eyes closed for a moment. "If I am wrong, which I'm not, you can take the girls to your mother's and file for divorce, or whatever. I'm that sure. I'm that serious about this."

She sat back in the chair. "Fine. I'll give you the twenty-third. If your doomsday prophesy doesn't come true, we will be having another very serious talk. Maybe with an attorney, definitely a psychologist."

111

He sat up, relieved. He clasped his hands and breathed an exaggerated sigh of relief.

"We just need to ride a few months out," he said, "and then we will get to our bunker. One more thing, we need to call someone to get new doors and some security cameras. Oh, and we need to buy more water and canned goods."

It was too much for her to take in a span of minutes, but he thought it best to get it all out.

"Oh, and honey . . . I bought a gun."

Chapter Fourteen

The world was ending in six months, and at 8 PM, everyone was going to know about it.

All the recruits were in town, save for Mariya, who didn't have a clue how hard a date January 23rd – today – really was. A flight delay could leave her on the other side of the country when the announcement was made.

Henry wanted to tell her, to give her a sense of urgency, but he was under strict orders not to. What the consequences would be if he did, he couldn't guess.

He kept in touch with Mariya after their wild romp at the New Year's Eve party.

He wasn't totally sure, but he thought he could call her his girlfriend.

When he opened his messages that morning, he saw a text saying she had boarded the private *Trencher Industries* jet and she'd see him in six hours, noon. At least she took an early flight.

Sherman Airport was empty. The only traffic it ever saw was Trencher-related or when farmers dusted their crops, and that wasn't happening in January.

He paced the terminal.

The plane landed and taxied. The staircase popped out of the plane, and he took off outside to the tarmac. He ignored the biting cold. When she emerged, he thought she looked like royalty visiting a foreign country.

"Welcome back," he said, giving her a hug.

"Thank you. Wow, it is chilly here!"

They went straight to Henry's SUV and he cranked on the heat. He stole glances at her, convinced she was prettier than the last time he saw her. They drove toward town.

"Are you hungry or anything?"

"Yes, but I would like to drop my things off first, if you don't mind."

He dropped her off in front of the condo. He parked the SUV on the street, assured that the half block walk to the diner would be sufferable. When she came back down, now sporting earmuffs, he offered his arm.

"It's a short walk."

They crossed the street and walked along Trencher headquarters until they reached Milburn's Pharmacy. The diner tucked in the back of the store was a favorite of his growing up. They took a booth and awaited the waitress who was simultaneously chatting with the cooks and texting on her phone.

"Small town gem?" She looked around the diner.

"Charming, right? You won't find a healthy option on the menu even though it's in a pharmacy."

The waitress came to the booth and stood in front of them, offered a one-second smile and bluntly asked what they wanted to drink. They requested waters and Henry tacked on a vanilla shake.

Mariya ordered a breakfast platter. Henry went for a grilled cheese with pickles and fries. The food came out in no time.

"So, what's the big deal?" Mariya said. "You guys hired me months ago, and it's time to finally start work, but why is today so important? You've tried being subtle, asking whether I'd be here on time. Marcus even called to reminded me."

He dipped some fries in his vanilla shake, not ready to tell it all. "Well, I'll start by saying that it *is* a big deal. The biggest deal in the history of big deals. We are meeting everyone around six-thirty this evening, where all will be revealed."

"Exciting," she said, somewhat sarcastically.

He could only bite his tongue and take in someone else's last moments of innocence.

They finished their meal with not much else said. She looked annoyed that he wouldn't tell her anything more. He understood why she would feel that way. She had moved across the country and not been told any specifics.

"I'm sorry I can't tell you just yet, but it is a big enough deal for me to do something like this." He took a wad of cash from his wallet, all of it, and placed it on the table. "A tip, for our lovely waitress."

Mariya threw up her hands as if to say *okay, whatever*. She smiled. The act of kindness to a shitty waitress was intriguing.

They walked the frigid half-block back to the condos.

"A car will be sent to pick all of you up at six on the dot. Don't be late."

He stood awkwardly for a moment, having said all he could for the time being.

Do I kiss her?

She gave him a peck on the lips.

"See you then," she said.

Henry visited his parents. It was hard to imagine that it might be for the last time until the train tunnel is completed. If it is completed.

"We'll weather the storm," his father assured him. "There are enough level-headed people around here to outweigh the whack-jobs. We'll have six months to get to Bloomington, which is a plentiful window of opportunity."

Henry wasn't so sure. Nobody knew how people were going to react.

"I wish I could take you down with us tonight to watch the big announcement safely . . . "

His father shook his head. "Don't you worry, we'll be fine."

They said their goodbyes. His mother burst into tears.

After a long embrace, he left.

* * *

Henry checked the time. 6:30. "Where is Robby?"

"In town. Probably Dan-O's. He said he wanted to see how the people take it firsthand," Marcus said.

"What? Someone has to go get him!"

"I tried, but he refused."

"And that's it? He doesn't always have the best judgment you know."

Marcus shrugged. "I do know, and sometimes you can't change his mind. Besides, he made a good point. He can be our eyes and ears out there."

Everyone was there, minus Robby. Marcus walked away from him toward the rest of them. He wondered how Marcus was going to break the news.

"This way," Marcus said, walking to the concrete dome. He punched the code into the keypad and held the door for them, nodding at each as they passed. There were eleven of them, and they fit comfortably on the platform.

He pressed the elevator button and they began the descent. The recruits let out a collective *Ahh!*

Henry stood beside Mariya and took her hand.

She looked around. "Where is Robby?"

"Drinking," he said.

The platform screeched to a halt and Marcus moved through the cluster of recruits to the door. He directed everyone into the decontamination chamber.

"We need to scrub down before going any further. There are four showers behind the curtains. Ladies first."

When the last of the men came out dressed in their scrubs, including Marcus, he opened the next set of doors.

When they all entered, everyone naturally looked up. There were gasps and murmurs. They passed through the hospital, then the pantry and storage chamber.

"This next room is pretty neat," Marcus said. He pressed a button and the doors parted.

There were more *oohs* and *ahs*, but an uneasy mood was settling on the group. They were impressed, but nobody yet knew what they were looking at.

While they walked between the waterfall and the cafe, Henry could feel Mariya's eyes shooting daggers at him. He ignored her as best he could.

"This is a water treatment facility," Marcus said.

They skipped the reactor room, and Marcus opened the supercomputer room for the group to get a glimpse. They passed through the living quarters before going back down to the spa and pool area. Marcus let the group explore the theatre, café, barber shop, and gaming lounge.

Kent Grieve marched off to the broadcast room while Marcus got everyone's attention.

"In fifteen minutes, we will call you back to where we entered. Do not be late." With that, he was off to follow Kent.

Without Marcus around, the group spoke more freely. Henry had to deal with Mariya.

"Henry, *what* is this place?" she asked, sounding spooked.

"Please don't ask . . . please. We will all find out in fifteen minutes. All I can say is ignorance is bliss. Okay?"

"Fine, whatever. I guess I'll go explore." She took off without him and joined some of the other girls.

"Never took Marcus Trencher for a conspiracy nut," Brad Farris said.

Jenna Dothmayer overheard him. "What do you think this place is?" she asked.

"I think it is some sort of bunker. End-of-the-world type of stuff," Brad said. "There are tons of food, supplies, water, living quarters . . . everything. Honestly, I can't think of what else it could be."

Jenna was frightened, as were the others who gathered around. "I always heard he was eccentric, but I never took him for someone who has lost his mind."

"I hope he *has* lost his mind," Mercedes said. "Think of the alternative. He might know something we don't."

A few minutes later, an intercom came on. *"Test . . . testing. Okay, it's good,"* a voice said.

Henry figured it was Kent.

Marcus's voice came next.

"Everybody please return to the broadcast room, quickly. Thank you."

The recruits wandered back. Kent had a flat screen TV set up. He was still toying with some wires. A single row of ten chairs were lined up in front of the screen.

Everyone found a seat. Marcus opted to stand in the dimness behind them, pre-occupied with checking his watch over and over.

Kent adjusted a speaker, turned on the TV and took a seat.

The Presidential Seal and a blue background filled the screen.

Please stand by for an important announcement from the President of the United States were the words at the bottom.

The graphic faded to the Oval Office feed. The camera did a slow zoom while the President sat silent for an uncomfortable ten seconds.

"Fellow Americans and citizens of the world, I come to you tonight bearing grave news. One month ago, our scientists at NASA detected an asteroid of considerable size emerging from behind the sun, in what amounts to a galactic blind spot. This asteroid is heading for our planet."

He paused for several seconds. In the bunker, everyone remained quiet.

"The impact will be major, and it will render parts of our planet unlivable for years to come. But it will not destroy us. The top experts in the world are classifying it as a sub-apocalyptic event. It is projected to impact the Yellow Sea coastline of China six months from now, on July twenty-third.

"I stress to you all – it will be survivable outside of East Asia. In the coming hours, we will release guidelines on how to construct residential and community bunkers. Construction crews and contractors will undergo training across the country. Our industrial facilities will be repurposed to provide materials and food necessary for survival. All cable and television networks and internet bandwidth from this moment forward will be dedicated to informing the public on how they can be of assistance.

"It is no secret that many nations have extensive underground bunkers. We have already begun re-commissioning and stocking our own.

"Our hardworking men and women of the United Postal Service will be delivering bids won through a lottery process to citizens across our country in the coming months. A bid secures a place in one of our large-scale bunkers. Some of these bunkers are being constructed as we speak.

"Congress has declared Martial Law, effective immediately. Those who break our laws will be disqualified from the lottery process. Any law enforcement officials or military personnel who desert their posts and duties will be disqualified as well. If you work, show up tomorrow. If you don't work, you will be drafted into a service fitting to your qualifications. Not doing so will eliminate your chance at a bid. Strict adherence to the rules will assure a maximum survival rate. Looting and chaos will doom us all. Lethal force has been authorized.

"In this darkest hour, let humanity shine. Pick up shovels, not guns. Embrace your neighbors and community. Hug your children tonight. Tomorrow, get to work. This is not the end of the world. Remain calm and be proactive. After the initial blast, and no more than a few weeks' time, our experts unanimously agree that it will be safe to resurface, re-organize, and rebuild. I urge all of you to work together to ensure our survival.

"Goodnight, God bless these United States of America, and God bless our beautiful world."

The screen went dark.

Melonie went hysterical. Brad turned white as a ghost. Mariya looked infinitely sad. Henry hugged her to his chest.

Marcus walked around the row of chairs and turned the TV off. Everyone looked to him.

"Everything you just heard is a lie. Except most of the bad stuff."

Marcus never was one for sugar coating.

"An asteroid *is* heading toward Earth, but it is bigger than they are letting on. They've also known about it for nine years, not one month. The impact is being downplayed to elicit calm in the populace. The amateur bunker-building bit is a fabrication to keep people occupied with false hope. It is only bunkers such as the one you are in now that will withstand impact and sustain life long-term. The fallout will not blow over in a matter of weeks. It is more likely to linger for lifetimes."

He looked at each of them before continuing.

"I've also lied to you. All of you have been recruited not to work for Trencher Industries, but to live in this bunker, thanks to your valuable skills and traits.

"I was brought into the fold early on due to my own skillset. I designed many of the bunkers the government has constructed secretly over the past eight years, and in return, I was able to construct my own bunker with little oversight and regulation. There is not another as accommodating as this.

"We will not resurface for the next few days. We must wait and see how the nearby population reacts. When the time comes, we will retrieve your goods and bring them down. If all is calm, and I am confident it will be soon, we will travel into town. As for visiting your families . . . I doubt it will be possible. We have secured bids for them elsewhere. Kent will set up video conferencing and telecommunication, and I'll work on clearance with the military. I am afraid there is no other way about it."

Brad raised his hand. "With all due respect, I think there is. I see enough room down here for families. And this is tough news to digest, but we are adults. We could have been informed before leading us down here . . . not that we aren't thankful."

"Mr. Farris – Brad – do you know what it takes to keep such a thing quiet for over eight years? Assassinations. Hundreds of them. As for bringing more people down into this bunker, I will not negotiate. I cannot know or judge your family, but I refuse to live out my days cramped, living in squalor, and rationing food more than we already will be. Keep in mind this subterranean lifestyle will be generational. Again, I have arranged for all immediate family to receive bunker bids elsewhere. It is the best I will do, and have done, and I will speak no more of it."

* * *

Shelley Spencer burst into tears. "I'm sorry I didn't believe you!"

Timothy consoled her. He, of course, knew, but it was still surreal. After calming her, he wanted to start discussing the next step. She wasn't ready. She was still absorbing it all.

He was in survival mode, glancing out the window for any reaction from the neighbors.

"Look," he said as soothingly as possible, "we just have to lay low until our bids get delivered. We will have travel privilege and we can drive to Indiana. I'll call Marcus tomorrow. Don't worry Shell, we are fortunate."

* * *

It didn't take long for panicked Americans on the West Coast to pack up and hurry into a colossal traffic jam heading east. An asteroid splashing down across the Pacific would bring devastation from tsunamis, if nothing else. The scientists the government put on TV did little to quell the chaos. Refugee camps were setup along the mountains.

Most major U.S. cities suffered rioting and mass exodus. What were people to do? Dig through concrete?

The military did their best to turn people around and contain them, but they couldn't cover every city. Small townsfolk locked their doors and stayed in, glued to their TVs.

The message to the Chinese citizens was very different, but thanks to pirated satellite television and social media, a revolution was spurred. The full might of the Chinese military mercilessly attempted to crush it. It moved underground.

An admiral in the People's Liberation Army Navy threatened to send an armada to Peru to seek shelter in Andes bunkers. The U.S. assured them that it wasn't an option. The Chinese executed the admiral.

They also relinquished their claim on Taiwan, but Tibet was all theirs. Their next focus was to enslave more of their population to finish construction on the largest bunker complex chain in the world, beneath the Himalayas.

India, on the other side of the mountains, wasn't far behind. Nepal and others in the region had little say in the matter.

Predictably, the Middle East fought. With almost all the Jews having moved out of Israel and now in Brazil or Germany, the Lebanese, Syrian, Egyptians, Jordanian, Arabs and Palestinians turned on each other.

It was only going to be a matter of time before nukes were dropped somewhere, most likely in the Middle East or the Koreas.

The beat-down Europeans were almost glad they finally had something to unite over, or something to put them out of their misery. They did their best to inform their populations that they had a head start on bunkers, and that with cooperation, they could construct more in time.

* * *

Robby only drank a few. He wasn't so dumb as to get wasted with news of the End Times nigh.

It was a Monday, so the bar crowd was sparse. He felt safe. The TVs were on sports channels, but the announcement interrupted even those.

"Angie! Turn it up, this looks important."

The seven people in the bar gave their undivided attention. When the announcement ended, a local girl-who-never-left-town burst into tears and hugged Angie.

The crusty old men didn't say much, except, "Well, *shit*."

One walked around the bar and helped himself to a bottle of whiskey. He offered to share.

Robby waved him off politely, finished his beer, and headed for the door.

Chapter Fifteen

On the 3rd day, post-announcement, Marcus sat where he had for most of the previous two days – in his private suite. He watched through the tinted glass, taking notes on the recruits.

At one point, he snuck up to the surface. He had a corridor from his study to the decontamination chamber the others didn't need to know about.

Up on top, he met one of his men who had a military-grade fuel truck. The man plugged into a valve near the concrete dome and topped off the bunker's fuel reserves.

Despite what Marcus had told Henry and Robby, the reactor wasn't yet online.

"How are things out there?" Marcus asked.

"Chaos in the cities, I hear. But you won't see it on the news. Around here it is...peaceful. Kind of eerie, actually."

"Got the other stuff I requested?"

"In the truck." They made the exchange, and Marcus saw the man off. Next, he gathered the courage to call Robby.

"How are things in town?"

"Not bad, man. A few rednecks burnt a house down. But for the most part, people bought the story hook-line-and-sinker. I've passed a dozen residential bunker projects already."

"That's a relief. Things are only going to get better. Come on down if things get hairy out there."

"Sure thing. Wait, what makes you think things are going to get better?"

"Don't tell Henry, it's a surprise, but within the next week, bids will be delivered to each and every home in Sherman. Nobody in Sherman will have to dig."

Robby didn't speak long enough for Marcus to wonder if the call had dropped.

"How is that possible?"

"I allocated considerable bunker space up in Minnesota. Nothing special, but it beats staying on the surface. A few months from now, we will ship the whole town out."

"Damn, dude! You did a deal with that Senator, right? Henry is going to flip! Wish you would tell him already. He is still lowkey pissed at you about not bringing down enough people and all."

"It's . . . a tricky situation. All that matters is Sherman will be secure. I better go mingle and deliver the good news. Stay safe out there."

* * *

Marcus took the platform back down and returned to his study to remove his jacket. He grabbed a microphone by the tinted windows and pushed the intercom button.

"Everyone, please meet in front of the movie theatre in five. I have an announcement."

They gathered and Marcus made his appearance. He flashed a smile.

"Everyone, I have good news. The townsfolk are peaceful, according to my sources. It would be safer to keep underground from this point forward, but it is important we take advantage of the days we have left with the surface. I would like for us all to head up this evening. Before we do so, is there anyone opting out? I'll arrange transportation."

Nobody spoke up.

"Excellent! Make note of what you need to take down next time and we will make arrangements. When you call your family, tell them to expect bunker bids if they haven't already received them. Do not give away our location, and do not invite them to visit. Oh, and apologize on my behalf for your recent untimely disappearances. Thank you."

Marcus walked off. They were all on the platform and ascending within two hours.

* * *

An armed escort was arranged for the vehicles carrying the recruits. Marcus rode on his own. He wanted to check on his mansion.

People were out and about in Sherman, and as Robby reported, it appeared peaceful. Trencher Headquarters had a few windows busted out, but who cares. It was unanimously decided that it was safe for them to stay on the surface, but not in city limits.

Marcus, back at his mansion, was glad to see his security team still in place. "Any action?" he asked.

"Had to pop some shots off to scare some teenagers away," a former SEAL-turned-mercenary answered. "Quiet ever since."

* * *

Springtime flew by. It was all too fast.

In early June, Marcus received a call he had been expecting. Timothy Spencer wanted to bring his family down to beautiful Sherman, Indiana.

"No need to drive. That is still rather dangerous. I'll send a jet. I insist."

He set the date for July 15th, a little over a week before impact.

The calendar flip to July was a real punch to the gut.

The weather was warming, and Robby had his all-important garden plot on the bunker grounds. Most of the food would be grown without soil, but a last surface harvest would help the transition. Mariya kept busy with the chickens, goats, and hogs.

Preparations were nearly complete. To celebrate, Marcus invited everyone to his mansion, giving strict orders for everyone to spend the night and the entire next day as his guest.

But Marcus wasn't there.

While his recruits – and most importantly, Henry – were secluded and sleeping in his mansion, he had the entire town of Sherman sent to the airport with the help of a National Guard unit. It was time for relocation.

Parked in a slanted row was every corporate jet of *Trencher Industries*. The county road in front of the airport entrance was lined with buses.

The townsfolk hadn't seen Marcus since the announcement. Most hadn't seen him in the flesh for months, some even years. They were happy to see him. With each small group, he performed the same speech and procedure.

"I am proud to say that I was able to pull some strings and secure bids for each and every one of us. Unfortunately, I couldn't get a city-sized bunker approved here in the county, so we all must be relocated."

He stressed the inclusive words *us* and *we*.

"For security reasons, I cannot say specifically where, and I apologize, but the government demanded that a minor sedative be administered during the transportation process. I know, I know, I tried to fight it, but even I have to take orders."

Group after group complied, taking their sedatives before boarding their buses or planes. A few individuals resisted and were made examples of by being dragged away. But even that was for show. The resistors were non-uniformed National Guard actors.

In the last group, Marcus saw Timothy and his family.

"You've made the right decision."

"I sure hope so," Tim said. "We are grateful."

"Sorry about the sedative, I really did try to fight it," Marcus said.

He glanced over his shoulder.

"Between you and me, you are heading to Minnesota. Should have been a shorter trip for you, but I didn't want you driving, and I needed the plane back."

"Marcus, thank you, really. Girls, can you thank the nice man?"

The girls did so sleepily. Shelley gave Marcus a hug.

"Thank you, Marcus. You are saving our lives," she said.

"I don't know about all that. It took this man to get me thinking straight. Saving all these people wasn't in my original plans, I'm ashamed to admit. Timothy changed my mind."

An announcement interrupted. They gathered their things and lined up to board.

* * *

As the plane began to roll, Timothy fought to stay conscious for as long as possible. He felt the plane turn. His head fell in the opposite direction, and he was down for the count.

* * *

The chemical sleep yielded no dream, and no concept of time passing. He was awakened by yelling. Soldiers helped the drowsy passengers, most still unconscious, to the inflated emergency escape slide, where other soldiers carried people to a waiting bus. Timothy's daughters went down before him.

He blacked out again. The jolt of landing awoke him, briefly. He looked straight up, right into the high sun. His head rolled to face the sky elsewhere. It was the bluest he had ever seen.

A fleeting thought: It might be the last he would ever see daylight.

He couldn't be sure where he was next, but maybe it was a bus.

"This is beyond fucked up," he heard a soldier say.

Timothy tried opening his eyes. He swore he did, but he saw nothing. He reached a heavy hand up to his head and discovered it was covered with a black hood.

After another indiscernible length of time, he awoke on a moving platform.

In his next wave of consciousness, he was rolling. At some point, he was laid down, somewhere.

When he finally came to, he was underground, in a chamber rough-cut out of stone. Other dazed individuals were walking around, exploring their new habitat.

* * *

Marcus was exhausted but satisfied. He thanked the remaining National Guardsmen before they moved along to the next town. His driver took him to his mansion, where the recruits awaited his arrival. In the backseat with him were eight boxes of pizza.

As soon as Marcus entered, he put down the pizza and punched a few keys on the intercom, summoning everyone to the main hall.

"Pizza!" Melonie squealed, taking a box.

"I wanted to thank everyone for their hard work the past few months," Marcus said as everyone chowed down. "The date fast approaches, but we are ready. We will move the livestock and crops down in a week and pray for the best. Let us enjoy these last days to the fullest. Cheers!"

They toasted their pizza slices. "*Cheers!*"

Marcus sat down with everyone like a frightened kid who just moved to a new school. He kept out of their conversation, which had turned to the topic of what they would all soon miss most.

"Seeing the fog roll into the bay," Mariya said, "overtaking the Golden Gate Bridge, is something I am going to miss. I know it sounds cheesy and like I was a tourist when I lived there, but it was something I never got tired of seeing."

"I'll miss the weather – the good, bad, and ugly," Jenna said. "I grew up in Washington State and it rained all the time. Then I went to school in Texas where it was blazing hot. I think I'm just going to miss being out in the elements."

"I am going to miss the variety of humans," Robby said. "Y'all are a vibrant lot, but you're all on the high end of the spectrum. I'll miss the different sizes, shapes, and personalities of billions of people out there."

Robby turned toward Henry. "What about you, big guy?"

"My family. I think I can deal with losing the rest of the world in time," he said.

"What about you, Mr. Trencher?" Brittney asked.

"Please, Brittney. It's Marcus now."

Despite the conversation clearly going down the line, he was caught off guard. He gave a nervous laugh, then gathered his focus.

"I am going to miss progress and the freedom to pursue it. I think it is going to be arduous existing cognizant that we've passed peak as a civilization and will never reach where we are now. Not in this lifetime, at least, and probably not ever. I'm going to miss being at the top and seeing it built higher and taking part in the process. I'm afraid I'll feel as if I've made it out of Plato's Cave, experienced the bliss of truth, only to be forced back in the dark for the rest of my days."

The women nodded sympathetically. Robby and Henry tried not to laugh. The silence was discomforting, to Marcus most of all.

"Oh! I almost forgot!" Melonie said. "I am *so* going to miss trees!"

Chapter Sixteen

Timothy shook off enough of the sedative to take a walk and clear his head.

Shelley was groggy but coherent enough to keep an eye on the girls. Nobody around appeared to be any kind of threat, and it was clear they were all underground. *Nowhere to run, nowhere to hide.*

A group of men stood nearby in the makeshift triage center.

"That sumbitch," one of the men said. "He shoved us underground with no warning two weeks before impact. I didn't even have enough time to collect our family photo albums."

"It ain't right what he did," another said, "but I'd rather be here than up there. They say we could be on the surface again in a few months, anyway. It's all precaution. Our homes will still be standing."

"I wouldn't be so sure of that. Since when was the government a reliable source? I'll bet you the three bucks I have in my pocket that we won't see the sun again."

Timothy thought it was as good a time as any to introduce himself. "Hey fellas, I'm Tim." He shook hands with the men. "Can anyone fill me in on what is going on?"

"Sure, Tim. I'm Rick, this here's Stanley. That lady over there with the clipboard is signing people up for housing. Once everyone wakes up and is moving, they are going to call a meeting."

"Who is *they*?"

"Hell if I know. We don't even know what state we're under."

Tim knew they were under Minnesota – or at least he thought they were – but he didn't want to disclose anything that would link him to Marcus Trencher.

"Nice to meet you gentlemen. I better go get whatever real estate is left."

He waited patiently for his turn with the clipboard lady.

"Name please," the woman said. She looked vaguely familiar.

"Timothy Spencer."

The woman looked up, startled, then back to her clipboard. "Yes, Mr. Spencer. We have a place set aside for you and your family." She turned to a board of hooks where a few dozen keys still hung and grabbed a set. "14B is yours. It should be very accommodating." He took the keys.

"And where is that?"

"Just head that way, there are signs. My name is Ashley, and I'll be more helpful after things settle down."

The name didn't ring a bell with him, but he still thought it was possible they had met.

He returned to his family. Shelley looked woozy but was sitting up. Liza was well enough to stand. Madeleine was awake, but still lying down.

"What is going on?" Shelley asked.

"I am sure we'll find out soon enough. Want to check out our new home?"

Timothy picked up Madeleine, and Shelley led Liza. The people who were awake were peaceful but tense. The chamber was minimally lit – the bunker had all the feel of a prison.

They made it through a dim corridor, keeping close. When they reached the other side, they saw the bunker was designed like a hollowed-out hotel, with rings of balconies for a dozen or more levels.

"Where are we going?" Shelley asked.

He found a sign and stairwell nearby. "Looks like we are heading up a few flights, unless you see an elevator around here."

They didn't, so they took the stairs. He felt like they were at a ball game looking for their seats.

When they reached the 14th level, they looked for their letter. Each floor had a series of hallways radiating from the center. After walking halfway around the ring, they found their apartment.

With Maddie in one arm, he unlocked the door with his other, and they walked in. "Girls, welcome to our new home."

"I don't like it. It is too small," Liza said, and then burst into tears. "I want to go home!"

The apartment consisted of a single room with two double beds. There was a countertop with a single electric burner on one end, and a sink on the other. There was no bathroom. There were a few shelves notched into the rock wall.

"Well, it's better than nothing," Timothy said. He couldn't even fake an ounce of optimism.

"What is this? I thought Marcus said this would be the best bunker we could get?" Shelley whispered.

"I...I don't know, maybe it is. I've not seen other bunkers."

"Whatever. Can you go find the bathroom?" She picked up Maddie. "I can't believe we have to live with communal showers and toilets."

He nodded and walked out to the ring, spotting the restrooms a quarter way around. People were moving things in on all levels. He realized his family had nothing.

Two men approached.

"Welcome to the silo," a man said. It was Rick, the disgruntled man in the antechamber. "At least, that is what I am calling it."

"I'm calling it the goddamn centrifuge," the other man said. "At least until my head stops spinning."

"Hey – would you happen to know where we are supposed to get supplies? We don't even have a change of clothes."

"Look down, all the way," Rick said, pointing.

Timothy looked, but he couldn't see across the hollowed center. Strands of lights obscured the view.

"They have vacuumed bags full of clothes. Nothing fancy from what I see."

"Not much of anything fancy here," Timothy said.

Rick nodded and walked on with Stanley.

Timothy returned to his apartment.

"Alright girls, who wants to go shopping?"

As it turned out, there were elevators. The family made the descent together since neither Timothy nor Shelley felt comfortable leaving the girls.

When they reached the bottom, he took a moment to look up. A lower rung of lights strung across from the third level made it impossible to see the top. Dust hung in the air, and against the harsh light, it reminded him of getting his teeth grinded at the dentist. So far, the whole experience had been about as pleasant.

There was little clothing left when they got to the tables, but they found sizes close enough to get them by. There was no variation in style. This didn't bother him, but his wife was not pleased.

"My kind of shopping trip," Timothy said, trying to lift the mood.

Shelley glared. Before she could share her disappointment verbally, a loudspeaker squealed.

"Good evening everyone," a woman's voice sounded from the speakers. "A meeting for all residents will take place in one hour in the seventh floor chamber. Please arrive early, space is limited."

"We're heading that way anyway. C'mon."

They yielded into the stream of people in the stairwell and worked their way upward. When they arrived, they found it already half filled. They plopped down along a wall. Their vacuum bags of clothes acted as padded seating for the girls.

It didn't take long for the chamber to be packed and sweltering with body heat. The crowd spilled out to the silo, as Rick had called it. People wanted to know what was going on.

Ashley, now with a microphone rather than a clipboard, stood on a ramp before a drab green door. She was elevated enough for most of the crowd to see her, and they quieted.

"Good evening," Ashley said, "and yes, it is the evening. First off, let me introduce myself. My name is Ashley Cameron. I was a former employee of Marcus Trencher, the man responsible for you all being here. I received a bid, and for whatever reason, Mr. Trencher deemed me fit to facilitate the moving-in process.

"The government built this bunker, but I'll have you notice that they do not run it. I do not run it. *You* will run it. I am merely an organizer. After we get situated, I will take little role in governance. Mr. Trencher assured me you were a peaceful, independent people, and he fought hard to make sure this bunker was your own–"

"Where is he?" a man yelled from the crowd. "I want to thank him for all the amenities!" There were groans from the crowd, and a few laughs.

"He has been placed in a government-controlled bunker due to his valuable skillset. He'll have less freedom than you all."

"I bet he'll have his own bathroom!"

The younger folks and yokels laughed. Ashley motioned for silence.

"Maybe he will, I don't know. I do know that there are over 8 billion people who would much rather be in your position two weeks from now. Let us keep perspective."

She paused.

"Now, we are currently running on generators. That cannot last, so this brings us to the one absolute in this bunker: we must mine coal. Some of you have made a living doing this. Your skills and knowledge will be invaluable. Positions of occupation are being posted on every other level. Work will begin as soon as humanly possible. I look forward to getting to know each and every one of you. Thank you."

A distraught woman cried out: "My sister . . . she isn't here. Where is she? She was my neighbor. I know she was home."

Ashley nodded, woodenly. "Every resident in Sherman got a bid, I assure you. I'm sorry, but some had to be placed elsewhere." She turned to the door.

From next to him, Maddie yelled out: "Will we get to play outside again?"

Ashley hesitated before turning back to the crowd. "Not for now, no. Sorry."

She disappeared through the drab green door.

Everyone moved to look at the postings. As much as Timothy wanted to rush to see what occupation he was assigned, he had to watch the little ones.

Shelley was upset. Maybe it was the lingering effects of the sedatives. Maybe it was the living conditions, or the world ending. He wasn't sure. Whatever it was, he wanted to avoid finding out for as long as possible.

Chapter Seventeen

July 20, 2030. Three days left.

The bunker was stocked, livestock moved in, plants transplanted, and all systems go. There was little left to do but say goodbye to the surface. They only had a few more hours of daylight left.

Marcus set the move-in date since nobody was confident in the government's ability to track a speeding bullet through the galaxy with 100% accuracy. It was understood that getting underground a few days early was a good idea. No one wanted to be caught off-guard by an asteroid.

Nobody was cheerful, but Henry was emotionally collapsed.

"What's bothering you, man? Besides the obvious," Robby asked.

"I want to go home," Henry said. "We've spent our last days cooped up at Marcus's or out working. I want to see my home one last time. But . . . too much of a risk."

Marcus overheard and approached. "Not *that* much of a risk. Why didn't you say anything?" he said. "If you want to see Sherman again, let's do it. All of us."

Henry was skeptical and confused and found himself taking the opposite position of what he wanted. "No, it's too dangerous. We'll get taken hostage or something. Not worth it."

"I insist," Marcus said, before turning to everyone else. "Drop everything, everyone, we are heading into town."

"Knock it off, Marcus," Henry said. "I'm not in the mood."

He'd been through this several times already and thought Marcus facetious.

"I don't want another one of your safety lectures. Just leave me alone."

"I'm not kidding. I want to see it too, and we can. It isn't too dangerous. You'll see."

"Seriously?"

"Seriously." Marcus broke into a smile.

"Let's go!" Robby said, leading the charge to the vehicles.

Before getting in, Marcus popped open the back of one of the SUV's. There was an assault rifle.

"Just in case. There is another in the other vehicle. But I don't foresee any problems."

Henry didn't find the gun comforting. Marcus took a deep breath and hopped in the passenger seat, leaving Henry to drive.

The closer they got to town, and at every rural home they passed along the way, nerves heightened. The only one that appeared relaxed was Marcus.

Marcus was never relaxed in vehicles.

"I don't like this, Marcus. I've changed my mind. I'm sure it's lawless in town."

"It's fine. You'll see. Just keep up with Robby."

The south end of town was eerie. Sherman was never bustling, but they hadn't come across a single person.

"People must be scared," Mariya said.

"Or staying inside with their families," Jenna said.

They hit Trencher Street and took a right. There wasn't a soul at Dan-O's.

Rednecks had already drunk the place dry, Henry thought.

When they climbed over the railroad tracks, again, they found nobody.

"What is going on? This is creepy," Henry said. "What did you do?"

"Well, Henry. I moved the entire population of Sherman to a bunker," Marcus said. "A bunker in Minnesota, to be exact."

Henry was stunned, kind of babbled, starting and stopping but never saying anything in full. When he calmed, Marcus explained what he pulled off while they were all sequestered at his mansion.

Henry grabbed the radio from the cup holder.

"Robby! Marcus got the entire town bids! They have all been moved to a bunker in Minnesota!"

"We have the whole town to ourselves?" Robby played dumb.

Ahead, Henry watched Robby swerve and take out a fire hydrant.

"What about my parents?" asked Henry.

"They hitched a ride with the Guard to Bloomington," Marcus said. "They made it, man. They are safe."

* * *

Their first stop was Jester's Market. The first step out of the car was so spooky, it gave the group pause. They all stopped and listened.

"It's always been a quiet town . . . but never this quiet," Henry said.

They were frozen in place, breathing in the warm summer air, drawn to looking up at the waning sunlit sky.

They heard a window shatter.

The girls shrieked.

Their eyes darted from the shattered window and away to the only possible point of origin.

Robby was standing next to a parking lot light pole with a crumbled concrete base he had toppled.

"What? I thought we were here to break shit?" Robby said.

"Let's see what's left inside," Henry said, leading the way.

There wasn't much. Locals had stocked up and food distribution hit a snag after the announcement. Despite Martial Law and demands to keep working, many people didn't, and that included many truck drivers and warehouse workers. Modern food

146

traveled great distances, and the supply lines had been severed.

The store was not looted or disheveled. Floors were clean and the shelves were upright. They were just empty. After roaming every aisle, and Robby shattering a precious salsa jar, they collected cheap cola and overlooked candy and moved on.

They took a swing into the residential streets. Henry stopped for a photo of his parent's house.

"Go ahead, maybe they left something worth keeping," Marcus said.

Henry and Mariya went in. All the furniture and décor were the same, minus family photos, which was what Henry hoped to find. He had digital copies, but he wanted something tangible. His only hope was his room which served as storage for all his pre-college memorabilia.

In a Tupperware container under the bed, he found a treasure trove of old schoolwork, drawings, and high school awards. In the scattered mess, he found a small photo album.

"A-ha," he said. "This will have to do."

As Henry stood, they heard loud voices outside – *distressed* voices. Henry and Mariya ran down the stairs.

When they emerged onto the porch, they found everyone out of the vehicles standing opposite an older, distraught woman.

"You must help me! I received a travel pass to visit my sister in Missouri. There was no announcement when we'd depart for the bunker. I thought I had time. The National Guard wouldn't let me leave. When I came back, the town was empty!"

"Ma'am, the people were moved to a bunker in Minnesota. I am afraid there is nothing we can do to help you," Marcus said.

"Don't all of you have someplace? It must be nearby, or you wouldn't be here. Please, take me in! I'm useful, I can help you!" the woman said, crying.

"I'm sorry, but we are in the same boat. We are just trying to enjoy our last moments of life. We didn't receive a bid."

The woman, who was groveling and hysterical, stopped. She focused on Marcus with piercing eyes.

"You think I'm stupid? One of your peasants? I know who you are. I worked for you, like everyone else in this town. You have a bunker, out in the Stripper Pits, right? Can't cover up eight years of digging. I bet it has a spa, and gold-plated toilets. And these girls, are they your entertainment?" The woman started to laugh. "You'll burn in hell, Marcus Trencher! *Burn in hell!*"

"I'm sorry, we can't help you," Marcus said.

They got back into the vehicles and sped away, leaving the hopeless woman in the middle of the street.

Marcus broke the silence.

"It wouldn't have worked. We couldn't take her," he said, as if she were already dead.

"I know," Henry said. "You did the right thing." He really believed that, which made him uncomfortable. He didn't want that lady to live with them, even if she were completely sane. The woman's crime? Being old.

Marcus glanced over. "I think it is time we head back. It's getting dark. Can you radio Robby and Brad?"

Henry did so, and Brad complied. Robby was a different story. Robby's SUV broke away from the convoy.

"Sorry, Henry. We're going rogue."

"You can't, it's not safe. The next person you run into might have a gun."

"No problem, we found a big ass gun in the back. We'll be fine. It'll just take an hour or so. I'm going to show them where I grew up. I got the idea from you."

"You hate where you grew up. Why would you want to go there?"

"We are going to burn it down."

* * *

Near the town of Graysville, they approached Robby's first home, which was now a dilapidated mess.

Robby did as promised, and unceremoniously so. Within 15 minutes, the blaze collapsed the house.

"That is the last place I saw my father," he said.

"Sorry to hear," Kent responded.

"The guy was an asshole. He beat the hell out of me, drank too much, and told me I'd amount to nothing on his way out the door. I was seven. Fucking *seven*. Best thing that ever happened to me, him leaving. My mother and I moved in town a block from Henry and two streets from Marcus."

He abruptly got back into the SUV and started it up. He rolled down the window and yelled at the others.

"Who wants to go to the airport and spray paint a penis on Marcus's personal jet?"

149

* * *

If Marcus's jet was in the hangar, they didn't check. Robby had a change of heart.

Strewn across the tarmac were bags of luggage, children's toys, and other personal possessions.

It looked like an Auschwitz train platform.

"It's getting dark. Let's head back."

What they didn't see, beyond the runway and running the length of it, was a trench full of bodies.

Chapter Eighteen

July 23rd, 2030. Doomsday.

There were news broadcasts dedicated to the end, but they were not going to be tuned in since they had already been severed from the world a few hours ahead of schedule. The bunker antenna had been retracted.

Henry had a ball of ice in his stomach and felt nauseous. Mariya sat by his side, using his grief as a distraction from her own.

Robby pulled a recliner out to the foot of one of the pillars and occupied himself by bouncing a tennis ball off it.

Brad and Becky tried to be productive with a project in the pantry but soon retired to their chambers.

Marcus walked around, apparently unaffected.

Everyone else kept to themselves, alone and crying.

There were still last moment hopes. Results of NASA's final million-mile measures in space were likely to never be known, but they had the potential to take the edge off, even if just a little. But there was no hope for a total miss. The rock was going to hit and hit soon.

When the time came, Marcus made his rounds visiting each individual, couple, and group wherever they were.

"It is nearly time. Please gather in the common area in the living quarters," he would say.

Marcus had full confidence in his high-ceiling design elsewhere in the bunker – not a shred of doubt it would hold – but he wanted to be considerate for everyone else's fears and concerns.

The bunker residents trickled into the common room, and while there was plenty of seating, most chose to stand. A circle formed, anchored in attention at Marcus.

"We have about ten minutes," Marcus said. "Would anyone be interested in leading a prayer?"

"I'll do it."

Despite the somber circumstances, Kent's uncharacteristic forwardness was enough to make Henry and Robby exchange a confused glance.

Everyone joined hands.

"Dear Lord," Kent began. "I do not know what will happen to me today. I only know that nothing will happen that was not foreseen by You and directed to my greater good from all eternity. I adore Your holy and unfathomable plans and submit to them with all my heart for love of You, the Pope, and the Immaculate Heart of Mary. Amen."

The last bit caught some off guard.

"It's a Catholic prayer . . . " Kent said.

"It was perfect," Marcus said.

After a brief *This is it* moment of silence, Marcus spoke up again.

"We should expect some noise, some rumbling, but not much else. Just think of it as a bad thunderstorm. This hasn't happened on such a scale with humans present before, during or after, so perhaps we should all take a seat."

Marcus nodded and turned away from the circle. They dispersed into a morose game of musical chairs.

Seconds ticked, maybe minutes.

Then it hit.

It was rather unremarkable in that initial split second, only a distant ruckus.

It would be easy to believe it was only imagined.

Then, a crashing cacophony of the harshest baritone reverberated.

Rumbling followed, and it was violent. This was no thunderstorm.

Since there was no visual, there was only mental images. Countless trillions of tons of earth and stone reorganizing the globe over, tectonic plates clanking, the planet itself knocked askew of orbit.

Melonie released a childish wail.

Henry fought full panic.

Marcus peered straight ahead, possessed.

Others did variations while the earth groaned and shuddered.

When the rumbling regulated – it didn't quite reside – Marcus was the first to stand.

"That should be the worst of it. I'm going to tour the facility to look for any structural damage. I expect to find none."

The others looked at each other, partly baffled by Marcus's lack of sentiment moments after a literally earth-shaking event, and partly shaken from their own paralysis.

"So far, so good," Robby said. Another round of tremors made him reach back for the arm of his chair. He gave a meek smile. "Guess we should get used to it."

If the computer models were accurate, spherules of liquefied rock were solidifying in the atmosphere before surrendering to gravity and crashing back into the planet.

Robby was right. The blasts and tremors were not going away anytime soon.

* * *

Marcus watched the pillars as he walked the bunker. His first stop was to the coal door, and he nodded approval when he found the massive steel square was still shut.

He continued his tour, walking along the walls, running his fingers along the smooth concrete while looking high above. Closer examination would require binoculars or scaling the cables, but at first glance all appeared perfect. The highly specialized concrete held up.

After a sufficient first pass, he made his way toward the storage tunnels, walking the middle path through the gardens under the dome. The natural grass was taking nicely.

He made a stop at the obelisk to dial up the sky. He thought it would be a comforting sight when the others ventured out of the living quarters. When the dome lit up, he scanned for damaged panels. There were none.

At the gazebo, he took a moment to look back. Nobody else had yet emerged.

He crossed the arched stream bridge. After punching a four-digit code, he entered the livestock area. Beyond the next electronically locked door, the tunnels.

No damage.

He marched on, more excited and elated with each step. Quietly euphoric.

* * *

Timothy Spencer clutched Liza, his oldest daughter, with a grip more frightening than comforting. He realized this a minute into the rattling and began kissing her forehead and rubbing her back while she cried.

They sat on the edges of the flimsy double beds, facing each other. Shelley had Madeleine, who was mirroring her sister.

Shelley and Timothy couldn't comfort each other. Their hands were full.

The shaking was violent and the sound wrenching, but it became less so, and regular. After what seemed like hours, Liza and Madeleine had cried themselves out and adjusted to the tremors. Amazing, how quickly children adapt. Liza crawled from Timothy's arms, grabbed her sister's hand, and went to the other bed. They were asleep in minutes.

Timothy truly looked at his wife for the first time since the impact. After a brief pause, they embraced, and Shelley broke into sobs muffled into Timothy's shoulder.

Even at the end of times, sleeping children were worth restraint and quiet.

* * *

Timothy made his way to the outer ring of his level. He wanted to see how the bunker held up, as well as its population.

He reached the rail and looked up. The giant fan was moving. It had been shut down before the impact, so he knew it was starting rather than stopping. A good sign. The top floor was already getting stuffy.

He looked down, and saw people peeking out. At the mid-level, the congregation was dispersing. Women wailed and a distraught man with his head on the railing cried out incoherently two floors below, surrounded by others trying to comfort him.

The earth was still rumbling.

Rick approached.

"Looks like we made it through our first trial," Rick said. "Unless I'm dreaming."

"Yep, I'm sure it'll all be smooth sailing from here."

Rick gave a token nod. "Coal mining is no joke, and we'll be starting that operation as soon as possible. That was my gig before all this went down. I was a mine supervisor, underground. With all these tremors, I don't imagine it will be all that smooth."

Timothy nodded, unsure what to say.

Rick gave him a friendly pat on the shoulder. "You'll be working long hours, but I'll keep an eye out for you. Once we get all the facilities running, this place won't be so bad. We'll make the best of it."

Another tremor hit, and Timothy turned to walk back to his own quarters, swerving drunkenly in the corridor as the floor moved.

He would do whatever it took to make his family happy and comfortable. What else mattered? If he had to sling coal into a cart, he was going to sling coal into a cart. The past was the past and it did no good to dwell on it, not this deep in the earth.

Rick was right, he thought. *We'll make the best of it.*

The girls were still asleep, and Shelley was where he left her. It was clear she had been crying.

He took her back into his embrace.

"We're alive, honey, and that's something. We'll make the best of it."

Book II

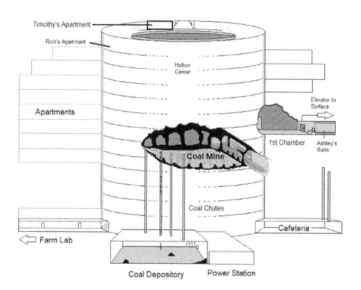

Timothy's Apartment

Rick's Apartment

Hollow
Center

Elevator to
Surface

Apartments

1st Chamber   Ashley's
Suite

Coal Mine

Coal Chutes

Cafeteria

Farm Lab

Coal Depository   Power Station

Timothy's Bunker

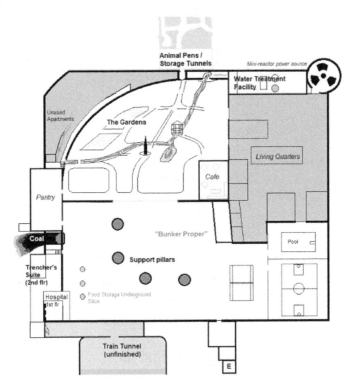

Trencher's Bunker (top down)

Chapter Nineteen

Three months later

Robby, sopping wet, stood at the edge of the pool, watching a golf cart drift toward the middle of the deep end. It listed to one side.

Melonie sat on the edge, also drenched.

Robby had only discovered the golf carts hours prior while rummaging through the storage tunnels to see what Marcus had hidden back there. They laid out a track and decided to pair up and get a cart race going.

After months of grieving, and adjusting to the strangeness of life underground, it was their first real shot at having fun again.

Henry and Mariya pulled up first. They looked into the water. Henry pointed.

"Dude don't even . . ." Robby said.

Robby didn't make the corner and skidded into the swimming pool. It was very cinematic, with water pluming into the air like a Hollywood stunt. By some minor miracle, neither Robby nor Melonie were injured.

Brittney watched from an elliptical in the fitness room above. Audrey and Jenna, Mercedes and Kent the Computer Guy, and Brad and Becky drove up just as the bubble beneath the cart rooftop, which was keeping it afloat, finally blew out. It sank to the bottom.

"I hope Marcus has insurance," Henry said.

Robby turned to glare at him, then smiled. "I was still faster than you."

"That's like saying you would have lived longer if you hadn't died first."

The ten stood around the pool, watching the remaining bubbles escape to the surface.

Jenna was the one to ask: "How are we going to get it out?"

Robby sighed. "Guess we'll have to drain the bastard."

* * *

Marcus looked on from his apartment, quite entertained. The footage would be priceless, but it came from cameras the others were not privy to. He thought it best to keep the surveillance hush. Someone might get offended.

A percolating coffeemaker drew his attention away from the monitor. 100% Columbian bean, and he had a literal half ton vacuum stored in one of the under-bunker silos. Existence without coffee? Unfathomable.

There were another couple coffeemakers in the storage tunnels. In the three months they had been down there, he hadn't gotten around to getting one out for everyone else.

Now, he thought, was the perfect time.

The sudden spark of purpose and the jolt of caffeine made him giddy. It was silly, but he let it make him happy.

After a jaunt into the tunnels, he emerged in the gardens and wheeled his loot toward the café. The others had begun congregating, well aware it was an off-Soylent day for lunch. They watched his approach with double interest – first, the coffee machine and grinder, and secondly, the fact that they hadn't seen him in over 24 hours.

"I come bearing gifts," he said.

Brad was the first to recognize. "Coffee!" Everyone was a declared coffee drinker except Robby, but he cheered along with everyone else. "Tell me we didn't forget the actual coffee?"

Marcus pulled a small bag from his back pocket and tossed it to Brad. The others lugged the machines to the counter and hooked them up. "Three months surely curbed our tolerance enough to make this that much more enjoyable."

"You're telling me," Brad said. "I thought my headache after impact was from the world ending, but pretty sure it was more the caffeine withdrawal."

"This isn't a one-off is it? I want to know just how much I should enjoy this cup," Mariya said.

"No, I think we have a few decades worth. You know that locked manhole covering the silo next to the animal feed? That one is filled with coffee beans."

"I figured that was more Soylent!" Brad said as he opened the box of graphene coffee filters.

"We should still moderate," Marcus said. "I don't want to enforce a rationing system. That'd devolve into some sort of prison economy. I'll deliver the beans every other day."

In all the excitement, Brad nearly forgot the food in the oven. They were still burning through some of the perishables, so the food was still good. He called for Becky to take the trays out.

"Everyone, we have another surprise – pizza bagels!" she announced.

Brad started the pot of coffee while everyone else rushed Becky for their portion of bagel bites. They also got an apple and tomato slices, if they so desired. Brad pulled a dozen mugs and served the coffee.

"Coffee and pizza bagels . . . this is the life," Audrey said.

"Savor those bagels, darling," Becky said. "Those *are* a one-off."

* * *

After lunch, they dispersed their separate ways. The midafternoon had unofficially become individual time, when people napped, read, exercised, or completed chores left over from the morning. Everyone would reconvene at dinner.

164

After, a majority would take part in some group event, sometimes a movie, a video game tournament, or a pickup basketball game if they were feeling energetic. It was routine that worked well so far.

Marcus rarely took part. It wasn't that he didn't want to, he did. He just didn't know how.

The old social block.

It was plainly difficult to leave his apartment if he didn't have a meaningful task to execute with a clear outcome. Otherwise, what was he going to do, hang out? Make small talk? He didn't know how.

But today he made progress. He had a purpose, an excuse, to be out-and-about: he was the coffee delivery man.

It was a far cry from billionaire magnate, but down here, for him, it was a step in the right direction.

* * *

Henry tagged alongside Mercedes in the water treatment facility, pen and pad in hand, trying to learn what he could. She had pulled the plug on the swimming pool a few hours before and was watching the digital meters as it refilled.

"What's this one?"

"Water pressure. Down slightly, but I expected that. Shouldn't last long," she said.

Most of the others had already found ways to make themselves useful – Jenna the geneticist helped Mariya with the animals, Audrey the close-enough-to-graduating doctor chipped in at Robby's farm since nobody was hurt or sick. Melonie was proving

165

most useful as a maid, hair stylist, and taking on laundry. She was a true essential worker.

Kent was constantly doing something techie, and always politely. Brittney worked out twice a day and ran a yoga class. Marcus . . . he wasn't sure what Marcus was up to. Henry hadn't found his place in the workforce.

He looked away from the screen of meters to a rectangular pool. "What's that for?"

"Sedimentation pool. Doesn't see much action in such a closed system, but it's necessary. Let's gravity do some work."

"Which part makes sure my next glass of water doesn't taste like chlorine?"

"Those tanks over there," she said pointing over his shoulder. "You won't taste any chlorine. Although, we do add some, in that tank there."

Henry nodded and pretended to write something down. He wasn't catching on.

"I'm still learning too. It's different than anything I've worked with. It was custom made for a few people in a bunker. I'm used to a facility built for a whole city."

She tapped a few icons on the screen and turned back to him.

"Honestly, the computer doesn't even tell me exactly how much water we have, at least counting the massive reservoirs beneath the bunker. And according to Marcus, it runs in a long geothermal loop, but he didn't know or tell me just how long, which is sort of important." She sighed. "At least we have plenty of water. Marcus said he drained a lake."

"That he did."

* * *

Timothy Spencer found himself lost in thought. His mind was wandering a lot these days.

Mostly, it wandered toward Marcus Trencher.

Should he be thankful that Marcus secured he and his family bunker bids, thus saving their lives?

Or, should he hate the man?

Because, after three months down there, there was no debate about one thing...

The bunker was a real *shithole*.

Timothy was manning the roof bolter well into a 12-hour shift. There was a lull in progress at the coal face, so he relaxed in the machine's surprisingly comfortable low reclining seat.

There were real coal miners down there, doing the more technical and dangerous work. The plan was to room-and-pillar six blocks deep before booting up the shearer for long wall mining – at least according to Rick, his neighbor and the mine operator. A crew was already piecing together the conveyor system, but it was months out from operational. In the interim, his shifts were split between putting bolts in the ceiling, spraying down dust, and hauling the coal out to the chutes.

He wasn't cut out for this shit.

Sonic Youth blasted in his earbuds, which were beneath a set of noise-cancelling headphones. He had been so happy to have rediscovered his phone down in the bunker, he cried.

When he turned it on, out of habit, he checked the weather app. It still showed *Sherman, IN* before timing out. No service . . . It was worth a shot.

When he remembered he had stuffed the charger in Madeleine's pink polka dot fanny pack, he danced with her around the bunker apartment. He clung to the phone like an uncashed winning Powerball ticket.

"Diamond Sea," he loved the song. It brought back memories. He had introduced it to Marcus when he was a nerdy kid showing up to college six years too early.

At the time, Timothy's apathy had put him on the brink of dropping out, and Marcus was the weird genius kid nobody wanted to deal with. Naturally, the asshole professor paired them together for a project.

Marcus was annoying, but he truly was a genius. When he showed Timothy what he was working on, Timothy knew right then this kid was going to change the world.

They *both* dropped out a few months later.

Before he could dig the phone from his pocket, a hand on his shoulder startled him. His replacement was pointing at his ears, so Timothy removed his headwear in time to hear the second whistle. His shift had ended. He checked in his equipment – belt, headlamp, and pick. He shared it with the next guy, but everyone kept their own helmet. He nodded at the crew filing in. They had clean but sullen faces. Next time he would see them, they'd have the same blackface he was wearing.

In the crowded elevator, Timothy stared at the steel-toed boots he was issued and wondered how long they would last. After three months, he doubted they would make it three more. He heard there was an amateur cobbler on the fourth floor. Perhaps he'd seek out the old man on his day off.

The elevator stopped and started, stopped and started. By the 11th floor, he was usually alone. For a fleeting moment, it was just him and the hum of the elevator. Technically, they lived on the 13th floor, but with superstition and all, they left it off the panel. 14 was the last one lit.

There was a ding, the doors opened, and he walked around the bend toward his apartment. He was covered in coal dust. It floated off him – and not only him. There was a constant sulfuric haze in the open air. The air filtration system wasn't designed to be connected to a coal mine. The coal dust suspended in the atrium didn't want to come down.

When he opened the apartment door, he was mobbed by the girls, who were unbothered by his filth.

"Daddy! Phone!" Madeleine squealed.

"Oh, darling – is that all you want me for?"

"She got it first yesterday," Liza whined, "it's not fair! It's my turn!"

Timothy supposed it was true. "Your sister is right, Maddie. It's her turn today. When her time is up, you'll get it."

There was the pause when things could go either way. Maddie's five-year-old brain processed the

169

information and didn't like it. It took a few seconds, but like a revving siren, she burst into a wail.

Liza daintily whisked the phone from daddy's hand.

"Got to be by the charger, honey. Battery is deep in the red."

He went to kiss Shelley, but she leaned away.

"Ugh, no. You smell bad and look worse."

He chuckled, she didn't.

"Hit the showers."

He put Maddie down and obeyed, pretending to be oblivious to Shelley's tone, but he always felt it. He kept the dumb smile on until he left.

At least he was going to another place of solitude. Floor 14 only had two apartments with tenants, his and Rick's, so he always had the shower to himself. Thanks to the integrated steam system in the power station at the bottom of the bunker, hot water was abundant . . . for the lower floors. By the time it got to where he was, it had cooled considerably. Still, consistently lukewarm was better than cold, and it got him clean.

This time, when he turned the knob, there was a spurt, then a ten-second trickle.

What the hell?

The water pressure had gone to shit.

He rubbed in what little water there was and scrubbed hard. It made a nice paste of coal sludge.

Great.

He turned the knob and walked back to his pile of work clothes.

He forgot a towel.

170

Chapter Twenty

Timothy returned wet in his underwear, which elicited another nasty look from Shelley.

"Water pressure is out. I'll go back in an hour."

She quarantined him in the middle of the apartment and instructed him not to touch anything.

He was exhausted and needed to lie down, which he did, on the concrete floor. He used his jeans as a pillow and his work shirt as a buffer between the cold floor and his damp skin.

Shelley came over and looked down at him, smiling. He hadn't seen much smiling since they got there. Then she wandered off.

They hadn't slept together since . . . he couldn't remember, but it was before they came underground. Well before. His current work schedule gave him one day off a week, and he slept through most of it. The couple times his off day aligned with a school day for the girls, Shelley was suddenly inspired to run errands and do chores that didn't exist.

Her bouts of depression were semi-frequent through their marriage, but the only difference between then and now was that they were once mitigated by medication. There was no pharmacy to rely on anymore.

The bunker was populated completely by Shermanites. He had only met one or two others who were not from the town of Sherman. He wondered if their assimilation was going any better.

Timothy had a few acquaintances from the mine, and there was Rick, his only neighbor on the floor. But even without them he would be fine. He was used to being alone. He was a computer programmer.

Shelley needed a job. She was a corporate workaholic before doomsday. Tim would ask around to see what she could do. For whatever reason, she wasn't assigned anything. It could have been a friendly gesture from Marcus, as a kind of favor. A real favor would have been something to get her out of the apartment, away from the girls. Make friends. Surely there was a daycare somewhere down below. He made a mental note to ask about that, too.

He drifted off.

"It's been an hour. Are you ready to check the shower?"

He sat up, blinking. "Sure, sure. Anything for you. Love you."

* * *

He got his shower, lukewarm but wet. And he remembered his towel. He got dressed in his drab, casual clothing he was issued.

He wanted to go back to the apartment and go straight to sleep, but he decided he should investigate some of his ideas to help Shelley before he forgot what they were. He returned to the apartment anyway to hang up his towel and dump his dirty clothes.

"I'll be back," he said.

"Where are you going? I've been with them all day," Shelley said.

"I was going to take one, or both if you insist."

He wasn't planning on any kids, but it was a nice recovery. At least she didn't get more upset.

"I'll take Maddie. Wouldn't want to interrupt Liza's phone time."

"Where are you going?"

"Going to pick up our ration of Soylent." He would have added *". . . that you forgot to pick up during my 12-hour shift,"* but her mood was unstable.

She acquiesced but wasn't happy about it.

Father and daughter rode the elevator down, an event Maddie always enjoyed.

"We ride this to school!" she said.

"Oh, do you? Does Mommy ever let you hit the button? Can you reach it?"

"No. Mommy doesn't come with us. Liza does it."

"What do you mean, 'Mommy doesn't come with us'?"

Maddie shrugged. "Mommy stays home, and we go to school."

He hadn't heard of any crime in the bunker, but he was still infuriated at Shelley for sending the girls off to school by themselves. There could be creeps – maybe even pedophiles. He was sure no background checks had been done. He didn't think it'd be too much to ask Shelley to shuttle them to school.

The elevator reached ground level and the doors opened. It was by far the most expansive floor, and there were quite a few people making their way around.

They went to the cafeteria first. It was not mealtime, so the joint was mostly empty, other than a few teens goofing off at a table in the corner. Timothy went to the service area, where a lone, plump woman reading a now-worthless gossip magazine pretended to ignore him.

"Excuse me, miss? Can we get our ration of Soylent?"

She looked up, annoyed. "Container?"

Timothy winced. "Oh *shoot*, I left it up at the apartment. Top floor."

The lady rolled her eyes and tossed the magazine on the counter. She might have been an actual lunch lady back in the day.

Still seated, she pulled a container from a lower cupboard, then wrestled her weight out of the chair to go to the filling station, making a great show of it.

C'mon lady, we haven't got all day.

"How many?" she asked.

"Four of us. Two toddlers."

She pulled a lever and a chalky powder filled the container in mechanized spurts. She screwed a lid on and waddled back to hand it over.

"Thanks! Hope we don't run out any time soon," he said. "I love this stuff."

Truth was he couldn't get the stuff down without pinching his nostrils.

Next stop was the gymnasium which was filled with equipment from a long-gone fitness center. Timothy noticed a partially peeled off sticker that read SHERMAN FITNESS on the elliptical near the door. He smirked at how ridiculous it was to load up fitness equipment right before the apocalypse and ship it from Sherman, Indiana, to Minnesota. Very thoughtful of Marcus Trencher.

Inside, Timothy saw a few folks going at it, running on treadmills or lifting weights. One of them was Dale, a 20-something good ol' boy who also worked in the mines.

"Sumbitch, Timmy! How are ya? Come in for a workout?"

"No, too tired. I don't see how you have the energy. I'm dead after our shifts."

"Shit, that's just it. Gotta workout until you get over that hump. It's science."

Knowing Dale cussed like a sailor, Timothy covered Maddie's ears in advance. Dale took no notice.

"Maybe I'll get there someday," Timothy said. "Say, who runs this place? I'm looking for something my wife can do to stay busy."

Dale looked confused. "Shit, she can do just about anything she wants. She don't need no permission. Nobody asked Leann over there to watch the gym, but she does." Dale turned toward the girl and winked. "Because she likes to watch me show off my guns."

Leann giggled.

Dale was right. There was no real application process. People fit in where they fit in. The person Timothy really had to talk to was Shelley.

"Okay, thanks. See you in a few hours, Dale."

They left the gym and continued down the long corridor.

"That's school!" Maddie said, pointing at a door. Timothy peeked in out of curiosity. It had all the charm of an inner-city public school.

Further down they came to a sprawling space filled with rows of grow lights and countless healthy plants flourishing beneath them. There was wheat grass, carrots, tomatoes, cucumbers, lettuce heads, lemon trees, and watermelon, among other things Timothy couldn't identify. A wall, nearly fifty yards long, was lined with chickens.

Despite all this, due to the population, he was limited to a couple real meals of fresh food per week. The rest, Soylent.

Timothy stopped a woman and asked if there was work available.

She said they were more than covered.

Shelley wouldn't have gone for it anyway. She was too urbanized. Getting her hands dirty was not really in her character.

He thanked the woman and turned back.

He looked in all the spaces they passed for ideas.

One room was full of men playing cards. They were gambling with packets of powdered alcohol.

Next door, the laundry room was chalk full of women. Nothing for Shelley there.

The next was labeled Recreation Room. It had a couple TV's and video game systems, along with some old couches. There were twenty rowdy kids and no adult in sight. No way Shelley would volunteer to supervise that.

The library on the second floor was fully staffed.

Tim and Maddie returned to the elevator, lifting her to press the button for 7.

"One more stop, honey."

The lady that administered the move in, Ashley, was his last hope. He wasn't sure what role she had in the grand scheme of things, but it was worth a shot. Her prior line of work was more or less what Shelley did before the shit hit the fan.

They stepped into the cavernous room where he first awoke three months earlier. A makeshift basketball goal was rigged up. Some boys were playing three-on-three with a worn-out ball. They'd probably play with a human head if that was all they had. They were Hoosiers, after all.

He kept Maddie close and worked his way around. He knocked on the green door and Ashley answered, only opening the door partially.

"Hello, I'm Timothy Spencer. I was hoping I could talk to you for a moment?"

She hesitated. "Yes. What can I help you with?"

"I'm sorry, could we come in? It's hard to hear out here."

She paused again, turned and looked around. "Okay, yes, sure. Come on in."

It turned out to be an office, but with a bed and kitchenette. There were rows of filing cabinets and a five-by-five table covered in blueprints.

"How can I help you?"

"My wife has been itching to get out of the apartment and make herself useful. Do you know of any work? She is highly intelligent, M.B.A. and all."

Ashley looked surprised. "She wasn't assigned anything?"

Silly question, he thought. Would he be asking for an assignment if she had one? But he only shook his head.

"I watch over the vital areas," she said. "Mostly the mine, farm lab, and power station. Otherwise, people are running themselves and doing okay at it, as far as I can tell. I'm not really HR, but I'll keep an eye out and let you know if I hear of anything."

"Thanks," he said, feeling dismayed.

* * *

When they returned to the apartment, Shelley was staring blankly in the middle of the room. She didn't react to their entry.

Liza was still tapping away at the phone in her own world.

"Liza," he said, "take your sister out and walk the ring for a bit. Get your exercise."

"But dad, I don't want–"

"*Now,* honey," he said. "And remember the rule."

"Stay away from the rail! Stay away from the rail!" Maddie chanted cheerfully.

"That's right, babe."

Liza rolled her eyes and took her sister's hand. Such attitude for an eight-year-old, Timothy thought.

He turned his focus to Shelley, who was still standing like a zombie in the middle of the room. *When was the last time she showered? Changed from that gown? Ate a meal?* He realized she was damn near emaciated.

"Shell, I looked for some work, something to keep you busy. Get you out of the apartment some." He placed the container of Soylent on the counter, afraid too loud a noise would set her off.

She moved a trembling hand to her ear, struggling to push her matted strands of hair behind it. Her eyes were socketed and soaked. She had deteriorated visibly in only an hour's time.

He approached as if she were a scared animal.

She flinched at his touch on her bony shoulders.

Suddenly, she turned, and he saw fire in her eyes.

"We should've *died. Died! I* want to *die!"*

She crumbled in his arms, beating his chest weakly.

"Oh Shell, don't say that, please. Please, we'll get through this. You'll get better. I won't let you be unhappy. I'll do anything."

He held her convulsing body and absorbed her guttural cries in a sway, kissing her over and over. For the life of him, he didn't know how he could bring her back, but he knew it was no longer a side job.

It was now the focal point of his life. Nothing else mattered.

Chapter Twenty-One

Marcus adjusted the zoom on the camera, turned up the microphone sensitivity, and thought, *this could get interesting.*

". . . Like, what were they thinking? Six single girls, well now four–" Jenna said. "...and five guys, one married. I mean, are they *that* desperate?"

The girls filled the room with laughter. Jenna, laying on her belly and in her panties, lined up all too well to Marcus's voyeuristic view.

Marcus adjusted the microphone again. *They are in a frenzy.* He noticed they all had cups. They had found a way to procure alcohol.

"I feel like I'm in a polygamist cult or something. It's like every boy's little fantasy," Audrey said, followed by more laughter. "Be careful, Becky, you might have to start sharing your husband! But at least they are all cute."

"Wait – you mean even Kent the computer guy?" Mariya said.

"Um, yes, like . . . especially."

"I'll second that," Brittney said. "Saw him working out. Pretty buff."

"Only wish he'd cut off that stupid beard. Mercedes, what about you? Eyes on any of the guys?"

"Don't get me wrong, I love me some white boys. But these motherfuckers are *white*." They laughed and clapped. "I'll sit it all out for a while, pray those trains breakthrough like Marcus promised. I'll let you all have at it. For now, I'll keep myself *entertained*."

Again, more laughter. *What's that supposed to mean?* Marcus wondered.

"And Jenna, you?"

Jenna thought for a moment. "I think I'm going big game hunting."

"Good luck," Audrey said. "I haven't even seen him in a week, other than dinner and his coffee deliveries."

Oh, Marcus thought. *They are talking about me.*

"He's always up in his room. He's probably watching us on some creepy hidden camera."

His heart leapt.

"Nope," Brittney said. "No cameras down here. I've, like, triple-checked."

That's my girl.

"Brittney, what do you think of him? You've known him longer than any of us. Has he always been such a monk?" Jenna asked.

"Not always. When I first started working for him, he had all sorts of girls around. Like, supermodels. It was kind of funny, since they were all taller than him."

"Cut to the chase – you two ever hook up?" Jenna asked.

"No, no, no. There were rumors about him and women around the office, but they were never even close to true. He was so obsessive about the actual work."

Marcus was touched by what he considered a compliment.

"But a few years ago," Brittney continued, "he stopped having all the women around. He came back from a meeting in D.C. a changed man. It was the bunker that stole all his attention. He stepped down from CEO and disappeared from the public eye. There's a good person somewhere in there, if you can crack him."

"I'll give it a shot," Jenna said, "if I can get him out of that stupid apartment."

The conversational torch was passed to the youngest – Melonie. "I'm not stupid, I know this thing with Robby is a fling. We've talked about it. We're just having fun. He said we are in an '*open relationship*,' and I understand that. It's just how things are going to be here."

Marcus thought she might be the least delusional of all of them.

"What about our other couple?" Jenna asked, looking at Mariya. "How is lover boy? He is *so* adorable!"

Mariya paused expressionless, then became animated. "Omigod, he is, isn't he?" She clutched a pillow to her chest. "He is so sweet. His complete focus is on me, and I don't even mind it. He openly adores me, which I used to always find annoying. Is it a Midwest thing, or something? I couldn't stand those so-called 'nice guys' in the Bay area, all working for startups, immature and loaded with cash. Nice, only to explode when they don't get what they think they're entitled to. Henry is different."

"It ain't a Midwest thing, or a Bay Area thing – it's a Stockholm thing," Becky said.

"Huh?" Melonie frowned.

Mercedes picked up Becky's point. "Stockholm Syndrome. Right now, these are the last dudes on earth. They ain't bad, but don't throw yourself at them. I'm telling you, they say that train tunnel could come through any day, and suddenly we will be in a network with Louisville, Indianapolis, whatever town Indiana University is in. Then what? The dating market opens up."

"Well, I can still compare them to my illustrious past, and Henry is a keeper," Mariya said. "When we were in that room to watch the President's address about the asteroid, we sat in those chairs with armrests. Henry cupped my elbow with his palm so it wouldn't touch the hard plastic, so I'd be more comfortable. I mean, who does that? It probably killed his hand. I have really bony elbows!"

The girls offered a soft *aaawww*. Becky and Mercedes shared a glance and shrug. They tried.

"But I don't even know how to show him my appreciation."

"That's an easy one," Audrey. "*You sleep with him.*"

The girls screamed laughter again.

"No shame in making him work for it," Mariya said. "I'm just waiting for him to, I don't know, take

183

me out to dinner. Or, at least, whatever the equivalent of that would be down here."

The girls let out another collective *aaawww* and Audrey put her arm around Mariya.

"Also, my bunker-brand birth control is only now kicking in."

More screams of laughter. Marcus's eardrums, nestled in headphones, were nearly blown in.

They were about to coax some dirty sex stories out of Melonie when a little red light above his door lit up and caught his eye.

He hit the power button on the computer and tucked the headphones in a drawer. He plucked a random book from the shelf and put it face-down on a chair before opening the door.

Robby came bounding in, followed by Henry, Brad, and Kent.

"The whole crew. Welcome."

The apartment was impeccably clean, and a near carbon-copy of Marcus's personal study from the estate. There was plenty of oak paneling and the same three paintings from the house hanging on the walls, along with the out-of-place print of *Maslow's Hierarchy of Needs*.

Henry grabbed the book off the chair. "Ah, Ambrose Bierce. *Tales of Soldiers and Civilians*. Have you read 'An Occurrence at Owl Creek Bridge' yet?"

Marcus shrugged. "No, just getting started."

"I won't ruin it for you, but it's a good one. Glad you are reading fiction for once, instead of technical manuals." Henry sat on an ottoman.

"Broadening my horizons," Marcus said, hoping his nervousness didn't show. "What brings you up this way?"

Robby had taken a seat at Marcus's desk, feet up and his hands behind his head. "We need to draw up plans to help Henry with his island beauty."

"Hey, watch the racial slurs," Henry said.

"What? I called her a beauty?" Robby took his feet off the desk and looked at Marcus. "We were hoping you had a few tricks up your sleeve. We want to create a special night for the lovebirds."

"Like what?" Marcus asked.

"Like, I don't know," Robby said. "There's not a hell of a lot to do here if you're over twelve."

Marcus turned to Henry. "You want to woo her."

"He wants to get *laid*," Robby said.

"No –" Henry said. "I mean yes, but . . ."

Marcus nodded. "I get it. I get it," he said, turning away and pretending to think.

Then he turned back with a slight smile.

"I know. You are going to take her out to dinner."

Chapter Twenty-Two

Timothy's request for time off from work was denied.

Dale pulled a back muscle and was expected to be laid up for a couple days. Rick said it happened on the job, but Timothy suspected it occurred in the weight room, probably showing off for Leann. Either way it made no difference. Timothy was stuck in the mine for the next half day, with a smartass teen trainee named Cory.

"How much you want for that phone?" Cory asked.

Timothy removed his earbuds and the pimply teen repeated his question.

"How much of *what?*" Tim said. "No money down here, remember? Not for sale, never going to be. Put your helmet on."

The teen stood dumbfounded while Timothy put his earbuds back in and continued spraying limestone on the newer tunnel walls.

He waved Cory out of his stupidity funk and pointed to begin spraying as well.

That was when a massive explosive picked Timothy and Cory up into the air and shot them down the tunnel like bullets.

The roar was deafening, or maybe Timothy had completely lost his hearing. Dust and debris engulfed them. They tumbled into a pile of miners as if they were pins in an underground bowling alley.

Timothy lay on the ground for a few moments, his head resting on . . . someone. He reached for his waistband and tugged on the dirty towel he kept on him and used it to cover his mouth.

He opened his eyes, but his goggles were caked with dust. He pulled them down and saw the yellowish haze was blackening by the second. His hand, he saw, was caked in blood and coal dust.

He was disoriented but rolled on his side and discovered his head was resting on someone's ass. What he could hear had a beat to it. He realized his music was still playing. He plucked the earbuds out and fumbled with his headlamp until it turned on, its weak light piercing no more than a foot into the cloud.

People were running by him, and he knew he had to get out of the way to not get trampled. Other men – or maybe the same ones, it was impossible to tell – were sprinting toward the source of the explosion to save who they could.

As Timothy sat up to get on his feet, someone stopped in front of him and gave a once-over.

"You're fine, get out," the man said before checking the guy Timothy had been laying on.

Timothy got onto his hands and knees to crawl. His outer ankle began to give in to an awakening pain. The blood on his knuckles was from abrasion. The source of the red streaks running down his right arm came from a skinned elbow. There could've been more masked by the bad lighting and adrenaline, but he felt capable enough to get the hell out.

On his crawl, he became increasingly aware of how difficult it was to breathe. With his right hand, he found the wall and stood. Running bodies were sprinting the other way. They bore no outline, just headlamps bouncing in the haze.

He was in the main tunnel, a straight shot to escape. He took on a limping gallop, keeping his right hand to the wall and his left holding the towel to his face.

When he pushed through the plastic sheeting and into the open bunker space, he collapsed at the feet of a crowd of spectators. Two men grabbed each of his arms and dragged him a quarter of the way around the circular floor to the first room – the same one in which he awoke months earlier. He was struggling to stay conscious.

The bunker doctor checked him over in seconds. "Breathe, my boy," he said, before moving on to a more serious case dragged in a moment later.

A woman grabbed some towels and dunked them in a bucket of water, then she washed his wounds while offering a few words of comfort. Then, she abandoned him as well. For a moment, it triggered panic, but he realized it was likely a good thing.

The triage filled quickly. Bodies were being placed in a row. He recognized the face of Cory, pimples concealed now by a solid layer of dust. A bolt of blood branched across his forehead. His eyes, glazed and unblinking, gazed straight ahead.

"Cory, you okay?" Timothy said, before convulsing into a coughing fit.

Cory didn't have a chance to answer and couldn't have. His body was placed on a stretcher and he was whisked off to the critical care corner of the cavern. Cory received a flood of attention for a minute, and then the doctor and nurses moved on. There was nothing they could do.

Cory wasn't the only one.

Timothy heard bits and pieces of information that trickled into the triage along with the casualties. There had been a partial collapse and there could be survivors within the rubble, though unlikely. He couldn't imagine anyone closer than him to the blast having survived it.

He sat up, and although badly shaken, his senses were getting back on track. A woman came up and asked him what hurt. He pointed at his leg and she produced a knife, slicing the side of his pants open. His leg was badly bruised and swollen, but there was no blood, no break. The cuts on his arm stung, but he was otherwise okay.

"Can you walk?" she asked.

He nodded.

"Then go," she said.

He stood up and walked out unnoticed amidst the chaos.

Outside, horrified faces stared and people shuffled out of his way. Someone asked him a question, but he ignored it.

He stumbled around the bend to an elevator.

When the doors opened to the 14th floor, he was greeted by Rick, dressed in his gear with his helmet already on his head.

"My God. What happened?"

"There was an explosion at the coal face, main tunnel."

"Goddammit! Gas pocket. This amateur bullshit wouldn't happen if we were provided with the proper machines for this kind of mining." Rick reached past him to stop the elevator door from closing. "I better get down there. We'll talk later."

Rick disappeared in the elevator. The commotion below echoed up the atrium. The balconies were lined with people looking down. Everyone in the bunker was out to see what was going on.

Everyone except my wife, Timothy thought.

He opened the door and limped inside.

Shelley was washing the Soylent cups at the sink.

Liza and Maddie were in bed together reading a book.

"Daddy!" Maddie said, first with a smile, then a frown. "What happened?"

"There was an accident at the mine. I'm okay."

She jumped up and came to him, hugging his hurt leg, but he accepted it with a grimace. Liza jumped from the bed and hugged him from the other side.

He realized his ribs were sore as well.

Shelley approached slowly. She wrapped her arms around his neck and kissed him, put her head on his shoulder, then kissed him again, and again. The dirt covering him didn't bother her this time.

Is this what it takes? Timothy thought. *Near death?*

It was the first true display of appreciation, of love, that Shelley had shown since they got down there.

"I won't be going back down there for a while." He looked into Shelley's sunken eyes. "I'll spend my time with you. I love you so much."

* * *

After the girls fell asleep, Timothy sat with Shelley and spoke about the mine explosion.

She nodded, she asked questions, she smiled. There was still an occasional tinge of mania in her eyes, Timothy noticed, but he was relieved that she was near the preferred pole of the spectrum.

The intercom buzzed – a system that functioned much like old telephone landlines. Rick asked if Timothy could come over.

He didn't want to, but he also didn't want to be rude.

"Shell, do you mind? It doesn't matter. I can stay here."

She gave a sly smile and nodded toward the door. It was the exact look that made him melt all those years ago on their first date. It was the look that made him vow *I'm going to marry this girl* before the waitress even took their order.

He kissed her, got up, and limped to the door.

"Timothy?"

191

He stopped and turned around. "Yeah?"

"I love you."

He smiled. "I love you, too."

He floated out of the apartment, despite the injuries.

Outside, flood lights illuminated the mine entrance, but elsewhere all had calmed.

He knocked at Rick's door.

Rick's apartment was the same layout as his own, except there was only one bed, and a reclining chair. His wife, a retired nurse, was still downstairs helping with the injured.

"Seven dead, a dozen or so injured," Rick said, walking back and forth. "Good men. Hell, some were just boys."

Timothy nodded, thinking of Cory.

Rick stopped pacing. "You were just far enough back for the side tunnels to take out some of the gust." He paused. "Sorry. I don't want you to think I'm trying to give you survivor's guilt. Not my intention at all. Shoot . . . we should all have a little of that being down here in the first place."

Timothy's mind was still on Shelley. He was incapable of feeling guilt at this point.

"We should've never been mining in that direction, anyhow. There's plenty of coal to the south, down the room and pillars. But that woman, Ashley, insists we dig east. Swears there is a larger pocket there. Has maps showing it and all." Rick stood, shaking his head for a moment. "But I'm not seeing it, and I've been doing this for a while. We are hitting bedrock. It's bad for the machines and bad for the people."

"I don't know much about any of that," Timothy said, "but I do know where we are. We are under Minnesota. Not sure if that helps."

"Minnesota, aye? Didn't know Minnesota even had coal."

"I haven't shared that with anyone because I found out from Marcus Trencher. We have a past. Wasn't sure how popular he was amongst the folks of Sherman, so I didn't want to be associated with him if I could help it."

Rick laughed. "Don't worry. The detectives of Sherman figured that out long ago. And I don't think you are the only associate of his down here. There's Ashley and the big colored feller, obviously, but there are more. Rough looking men. Ex-military if I were to guess."

Timothy recalled the men playing cards for powdered alcohol packets.

"I think I've seen them around."

"Able-bodied, that's for sure. Yet, they do nothing but steal the younger women and piss the guys off. With the loss of men today, I imagine they might have to start pulling their weight. I plan on mentioning it to Ashley. Quietly, though. They don't seem the type I want to cross."

"Do you think they are here in case things break down? A security force of sorts?"

"Could be." Rick sat at the edge of the bed. "I tell you, there are things down here that just don't line up, and other things that line up too well. I can't put the puzzle together, but I'll bet Ashley is a piece of it, and those military boys are another."

Timothy nodded. "I know what you mean. At first, I bought in to the self-governance bullshit. But more and more I've sensed Marcus's grip on this place. What I can't figure out is why? He is a thousand miles away in a luxury bunker."

Rick sighed. "Tim, I know you've wanted out of that mine for a while now, and I've tried. There is quite the good ol' boy network to get through, and with the loss of men, I'm afraid it's going to be even more difficult. I'll keep trying, and if I can get you downstairs to the power station, we will have eyes and ears in another crucial area of the bunker. Maybe we'll pick something up."

"How long will operations be down? In the mine?"

"I'll have a skeleton crew down there of the best men I have left to put things back together. It could be a week or less. The quotas are real and work must go on. Some digging will continue to the south, but I think I can keep you out of it. Just play up that limp."

* * *

He left Rick's apartment, exhausted from the day, disturbed yet energized by the discussion. He was a sucker for conspiracy.

He thought of Shelley and her miraculous return to sound mental health.

He looked across the hollow center to his front door, surprised to see his wife, Shelley, there, coming through it.

He stopped and smiled, taking her in. She was ghostly in her willowy white nightgown.

"Shell, what are you still doing awake?" He smiled and cocked his head to the side.

She walked to the railing with grace and serenity. She wasn't smiling. Her hands touched the metal bar.

"Timothy, I loved you. I really did."

"Shell, what do you–" And then he realized. *"Shelley -- no!"*

In one fluid movement, she climbed the railing and stepped into the open air.

He watched her sink through the illuminated dust, her right arm raised like a ballerina.

He hoped she would just look up, because if she would, he could see her face one more time. Maybe figure out a way suspend her, to save her, to rescue her. She didn't look.

He watched until he couldn't, collapsing a moment before she found the ground floor.

He wailed and wrenched.

His heart moved to his throat.

His stomach dropped.

A void in his center opened.

Rick flew out of his apartment, instinctively looking over the edge.

"My God..."

Liza and Madeleine stood sleepily before him, holding hands.

"Daddy, where did mommy go?" Maddie asked.

Liza appeared more aware that something was desperately wrong.

Timothy folded and shuddered in agony.

Rick stepped between them and the railing, escorting them away. "Let's go girls. Daddy needs to be alone right now."

Chapter Twenty-Three

Romance was in the air!

Henry and Mariya's big date excited everyone in the bunker.

Brad and Becky were in the café kitchen preparing the meal, while Jenna, Mercedes, and Brittney were opening bags of vacuum-packed designer clothes in search of the perfect outfit for Mariya.

Robby was running from camp to camp, always leaving before someone asked him to help with something. He visited the salon to see Melonie, who was doing Mariya's hair.

"Hey, that looks pretty good!"

"Thanks. I'm a beauty school dropout," Melonie said.

"Go back to high school," Robby half-sung.

He went upstairs to Marcus's and found that his creative juices were flowing as well. He was working with Kent to test the bunker-wide sound system. If it went well, there would be music for the night.

Like a dog spotting a squirrel, Robby saw Audrey crossing from the cafe toward the garden, and he was off again.

"Whatcha doin'?" he asked once he got beside her in the garden. She was in short shorts with something written across her bottom.

"Just grabbing whatever Brad asks for from the garden."

"I could've done that. I am the farmer around here."

"You could've, if you were around," she said with a smirk.

"You got me! Here, let me get that." Robby grabbed the basket from her. It had a head of lettuce and a couple potatoes in it.

They got to the café and showed the basket for admission. Brad pointed to a table with a chopping knife. Robby set the basket down. "What's on the menu? Ramen noodles? That's what I feed my dates."

"Melonie must be a lucky girl," Audrey said.

Something on the counter caught his eye. Two red circles. "Are those what I think they are?"

"You bet," Brad said. "Filet mignon, thawed and ready to cook. Everybody down here will get their own. Can't have them in the freezer much longer."

"What else is cooking?" Robby asked while opening the oven.

"Just some veggies. Go ahead and take them out. They should be ready."

Robby put on an oven mitt and grabbed an end of the glassware. He had it halfway out before realizing there was more weight than he could handle. He curled the pan back, resting it on his forearm just long enough to leave a shiny burn mark.

"Ow, fuck!"

He threw it on the counter.

The others gathered to take a look.

"That's a good one," Becky said. "Should probably put something on that." She returned to the steaks.

"Yikes, yeah," Audrey added. "That's not going to be pretty. C'mon, we'll see what the hospital has."

Audrey led him across the bunker proper and into the hospital. He paced around and finally took a seat.

"I know there is some ointment in here somewhere," Audrey said, rifling through a drawer, then another.

"Ah! Here it is," she said, turning with a tube in hand. She paused and scrunched her nose. "Do you smell that?"

Audrey followed the scent toward the crematorium door Robby opened moments earlier. She was sure it was coming from there; despite the fact they hadn't burned any bodies that she could recall. "I think it's stronger over here."

"My arm is killing me. Can we get this taken care of?"

She shook her head, apologized, and walked to the examination table. She squeezed the ointment on his arm and gently rubbed it in. She unrolled a bandage and dressed it around his forearm.

"All done. Feel better yet?" she asked.

"You are sexy."

Robby took her hand.

She blushed. "Robby . . . "

"Nobody here but us." He moved his hand to her hip.

"But what about –"

"Don't worry about that."

He pulled her in close and kissed her. Soon, she was pushing him down onto the exam table paper. She climbed up.

"All better," Robby said.

They left the hospital smelling like ointment, sex and steak.

* * *

Henry was having trouble with his formal wear. He removed his shirt when he realized he couldn't get his cuff links on, but not before a great struggle in trying.

"*Damnit, Robby,*" he said to himself.

"I'm here!" Robby said, bursting in.

"Could've used you a second ago."

"Sorry, I burnt my arm. The food is almost ready."

Henry managed to put the cuff links in and his shirt back on.

"Why are you nervous?" Robby asked. "You two have been dating for a while and you've basically moved in together. You'll never have to meet her parents."

"It's not the date. It's . . . you know . . . *after* the date."

"Ahh, don't worry. Just have fun and go with it. Just be assertive for once in your life."

Henry didn't appear to listen but said okay and grabbed his suit jacket before heading out the door.

* * *

He saw her waiting at the gazebo in a sleek black dress.

"Hey," he said.

"Hey." She took the initiative, as usual, and got on her tippy toes to kiss him. "Shall we?"

As if by magic, the lights dimmed. They looked up to see a crystal-clear night filled with stars.

They sat at a cloth-covered table for two under the gazebo. An electric candle flickered between them.

Becky brought out bread rolls and two fresh garden salads with portions of ranch dressing.

"That's not all, kiddos." Becky pulled a bottle of Screaming Eagle Cabernet Sauvignon from her apron pocket and filled their glasses.

"We get *wine!*" Mariya said.

Madonna's "Take A Bow" began playing through the gardens.

"Oh, we get music, too!" Mariya said.

Henry grinned ear to ear and shook his head.

"There's something you should know about me," he said.

"Okay . . . "

"Madonna is my musical guilty pleasure."

Mariya giggled. "Mine is *totally* Savage Garden."

"Oh my god, seriously? That's my second!"

"Wow, you like some really wimpy stuff," Mariya said.

201

This made Henry snort with laughter. Unfortunately, he had a mouthful of wine, so some shot out from his nostrils.

When he calmed down enough, he explained that freshman year in high school, he off-handedly said he liked a song playing at a store. It was Madonna.

"Robby and Marcus decided they would run with that and never let it go. They bought me albums and bring it up even to this day. I decided to own it and just accept that I actually do enjoy some of her music."

His story made for another fit of laughter between the two, which didn't stop until Becky brought the main course.

"We have something very special for you," Becky said as she sat down the plates.

They lifted the covers to reveal steak, baked potatoes, and a vegetable medley. Henry could hardly believe his eyes.

They savored every bite. They'd likely never have another meal like it.

They kept the conversation light, but as the food disappeared, so did pretenses. The only thing staving off Henry's nerves was the wine. He sprinted to a third glass and was feeling it.

"Are you nervous?" Mariya asked.

"Maybe a little."

"How experienced are you?" Mariya asked.

Henry cleared his throat. "What . . . what do you mean?"

"You know what I mean."

"Oh. Okay. Well, not . . . very."

"I am." She smiled. "Does that bother you?"

He considered this.

All those other men are dead now.

"No."

"Good."

Becky brought out dessert – cheesecake. On Henry's plate was a keycard.

"What is this?"

Becky pointed up to the unused apartments above the gardens. "Honeymoon suite."

They finished dessert while Savage Garden's "I Knew I Loved You" played.

Henry stood first, reaching for Mariya's hand, and she stood as well. They stepped out of the gazebo and danced half the song. They then crossed the stream bridge before climbing the stairs to what Becky referred to as the Honeymoon Suite.

The projected sky, which was a serene clear night before, became showered in color. Fireworks boomed and dazzled above. The dome distorted the streaks of light, as if they were dripping down the sides, making them more beautiful than the real thing.

Henry held Mariya around the waist as she looked up in awe. The song wrapped up and the fireworks were silent.

Across the dome, peeking out from a maintenance door like a trio of cartoon characters, Robby, Marcus, and Kent watched the couple. Marcus had dialed up the fireworks show before Robby wrestled the tablet back to make the next musical selection.

Robby, channeling his inner-DJ, went with "Justify My Love" by Madonna. It took a second, but Marcus started to notice the raunchy music.

"Robby, are you fucking serious?" Marcus whispered loudly.

"What? They are about to get freak-*ay* over there," Robby said with a mischievous grin.

Henry, having spotted them long ago, flipped them off. Mariya joined with both hands, laughing all the while.

Henry pulled Mariya from the balcony railing. He held her and looked into her eyes, before he led her to the door, then inside.

In the middle of the room, they kissed. And the night got more interesting from there.

Chapter Twenty-Four

Two weeks passed after the funeral until Timothy could make much of a movement beyond his bed.

Some of it was physical. His leg was much worse than he initially thought. But most of his lethargy was what he considered to be his inheritance from Shelley. He was acting just as she was the last weeks of her life.

He was grieving.

The ceremony was a blur. It was sparsely attended, which was fine. He preferred it to be private. Some non-denomination preacher who didn't know Shelley gave a generic effort with a few Bible passages. The cheap urn to hold Shelley's ashes wasn't even removed from the bubble wrap beforehand.

Timothy and the girls did not get to see her body, for obvious reasons. Their only proof of her existence was the ashes and a few photographs.

In the rare moments he could set aside his grief, he comforted his daughters. Liza's personality sunk inward. She hardly spoke. Madeleine was confused.

She understood that Mommy was in heaven, but she couldn't figure out why daddy would cry, and Liza would get upset when she played house with her paper dolls.

She spoke to the Mommy doll exactly like she spoke to Mommy when she was there, alive.

Both wanted to know why she was gone. He couldn't come up with much beyond, "Mommy was sad," which only elicited more whys.

What was he to do? Teach them about bipolar personality disorder?

Inform them that the genetics lurk within them, waiting to be triggered by traumatic events precisely like the one they just experienced?

Was he to tell them the effects would lie dormant for a decade or two before surfacing?

He could already spot it in Liza. Already gone quiet. Already gone anxious.

Rick came by often to help in any way he could. His wife offered to watch the girls. Liza and Maddie were not receptive to the idea at first, but the lady had sweets to win them over.

Timothy hoped by getting them out of the apartment, it would ease their transition back to school. Other children had lost a parent in the mine accident, but none lost a parent the way his girls had. He was afraid of what the other children might say.

On one of his visits, Rick said, "I pulled some strings finally and got you in downstairs at the power station. The only catch is that you've got to start tomorrow, or the window closes."

Timothy sat up. "Yeah?"

"I know you don't feel like doing anything, but it's time to get back on your feet. If not for you, then for –"

"For the girls. I know, I know." He rubbed his face with both hands. "I suppose you're right. I've got to start sometime."

* * *

The next morning, he arrived at the power station doors in what was left of his mining uniform. He didn't want to be there – he didn't want to be anywhere – but he couldn't let the opportunity of getting out of the mines pass him by. It was the only motivation he had. He was unshaven, unfed, and utterly apathetic. He didn't know how he'd make it through the day.

The chamber was more expansive than the farming lab down the hall. There were pillars every 40 feet. Only a quarter of the floor space was filled with coal, and the piles were not heaping. He wasn't sure what to make of the emptiness. It looked like an empty parking garage.

"Welcome," a booming voice said from behind him. "Timothy, right? I'm Steve."

Tim absent-mindedly shook Steve's hand and did a double take to confirm how gigantic the man was. "Thanks. I start work here today."

"Right, and you'll be working with me. Let me show you around."

He walked up the chamber, and Timothy followed.

Pointing toward a corner, Steve said, "Those metal tubes coming down from the ceiling are the coal chutes. I believe you were on the other end of those, correct?"

Timothy nodded.

"There is a whole row of them along this wall. Once the long wall shearer is operational in the mine upstairs, there should be a steady stream of coal raining down from them. For now, it is just a trickle."

He then walked south through the open chamber.

"There are more chutes, here, here, and here," he said, pointing to more tubes in the middle of the chamber. "These cover the room-and-pillar sections of the mine. Rule Number One is to not stand under one of these. You'll get conked on the head. Got it?"

Timothy nodded.

Steve led the way back toward the long-wall chutes, along the northern wall. There was a square window in the wall that opened to a conveyor belt.

"This is where we feed the ore. The conveyor belt acts like one in the grocery store checkout line."

He demonstrated by taking a shovel full and tossing it in. Sure enough, the belt activated and swallowed the ore.

"The belt feeds the ore into the pulverizer. It turns these chunks into a fine powder. It burns more evenly and is therefore more efficient.

"The pulverizer has its own reserves of coal powder to ensure a consistent, steady flow to keep up with base load."

He set the shovel down and pointed to a simple display screen next to the window.

"This shows us how full the reserve box is. It's in the green now, so we are good. I did some heavy lifting this morning. When it gets in the orange or red, we have work to do. Simple, right?"

Timothy nodded.

"Now, when we get peak demand and the beast is hungry, we have to use the carts and pulleys."

Steve rolled a cart to the window and lined it up. There were pulleys on each side above the window with cables and hooks hanging down. He pulled them down and fastened them to the back end of the cart. The front rolled up a short acclivity and clicked into a round groove, creating a pivot.

"Here's the part that requires teamwork. Crank the cable reel clockwise."

They did so, and Timothy's side fell behind, tilting the cart. Steve was quick to tell him it was okay, and he slowed down. The cart lifted until vertical and all the ore poured onto the conveyor belt. They lowered it in unison. Steve smiled.

"Got it," Timothy said.

"And that's about it. Coal power for dummies. You and I will manage this room. It's tough work, but we rarely have to rush and it's far safer than the mines . . . as long as you don't catch a boulder walking under a chute."

A metallic clinking noise caught Timothy's attention, and a sprinkling of coal came down a chute.

Steve said, "Most of our time will be spent pushing the coal around this room and organizing it.

Got to keep it from stacking up to the chutes or spilling in front of the conveyor window, but keep it close enough so loading isn't such a relay."

Timothy looked around and spotted two electric carts fitted with plows. There was a charging station along the western wall. "When do we use those?"

"When we get behind and the mine upstairs is raining coal on us, we push a little around using those. But for the most part, it is easier to use a shovel, barrow, and manpower. Also, the metal boxes on wheels don't use electricity, the plow carts do. Not much, but I bet if you weighed calories to kilowatts, muscle is more efficient."

"We'll have to do the math on that," Timothy said.

He smiled for the first time in weeks. He liked Steve. He was sure if anyone else was showing him the ropes, they'd portray the work as insanely difficult in order to self-validate. Steve was humble.

"Let's head to the control room. I'll introduce you to the characters in there."

They went through the doors and got a good view of where the conveyor led, which was the pulverizer. Next to it, there was a towering Plexiglas box with a riveted metal frame half-filled with coal dust.

"The excess dust from the pulverizer is diverted to that box. We've got a few days' worth stored up, but we can do better. The mine going down after the explosion dipped into the reserves."

They went through another set of doors into a corridor that hooked right and ran along the power station machinery. To avoid the noise, they kept behind the glass and didn't enter the actual room.

"After the pulverizer, you've got the furnace there. You probably know this, but it burns the coal dust, heating a coil of water. The water turns to steam, turning the spin turbine down a ways, which is ultimately connected to the generator at the end. The heated water goes through a cooling loop and is recycled." He shrugged. "And that's about it."

At the end of the corridor, they went through another set of doors into the control room. Three men sat around a myriad of panels filled with buttons, switches, and screens.

"Timothy, this is Don, Stanley, and the youngster there is Kyle."

The three stared at him, no doubt recognizing that this was the man with the wife that leapt from the top floor. Then they tried to act natural.

"Timothy, I believe we've met," Stanley said, shaking his hand.

"That's right, when we first got down here."

"Yes, that was me. Sorry I haven't seen you since. I don't get out of this room much. If you see Rick, tell that Polish prick he owes me twenty bucks from that last Colts game. He'll get a kick out of that."

"I'll do that."

Steve led them back out of the control room.

"Don't be fooled by those three. They have the easiest jobs down here. The computer does everything for them. But they're good guys."

They retraced their way back down the corridor. Steve paused at the last door and turned.

"You don't recognize me, do you?"

Timothy furrowed his brow.

"No, don't believe I do. Did you play football or something? Professional wrestling?"

He laughed. "I did play football. But, no, not from that. We've met before. St. Louis ring a bell?"

Timothy's mind worked at it.

It seemed like ages ago, but St. Louis was where he attempted to tell Henry Plyman of Marcus's bunker plans down in Sherman, Indiana. He tried to tell Henry about how few people Marcus had planned to take with him underground.

A big guy, Steve, had pulled him away before he could do much of anything. He recalled the phone call from the holding cell. It was Steve's phone.

"Yes, it does ring a bell. Sorry I called you a meathead. You were only doing your job."

Timothy's wheels started turning.

"Hey, do you know if Henry caught on to what I yelled at him?"

Steve's expression turned serious, but not unfriendly. "I wasn't close to Mr. Trencher, so I can't be sure. Henry, though, was asking a lot of questions that I couldn't answer, either because I didn't know, or because I didn't want to lose my bunker bid."

They stepped through the doors, back into the main chamber.

"I don't know if this bunker was in the plans all along, or if it really was secured through a sudden change of heart on Mr. Trencher's part," Steve continued. "As for Mr. Trencher's own bunker, I don't know if he took more down with him or not. I do know Henry started asking questions."

Timothy wasn't sure what to make of it. "Not sure it matters. Lost cause if there ever was one."

Steve cocked his head to one side. "I wouldn't be so sure about that. Those guys in that control room think I'm an idiot, or a meathead as you put it. I have an engineering degree from Purdue. I've figured out more about this power station than they'll ever learn – and something doesn't add up right with what we put in, and what we get out. Follow?"

Timothy nodded. His flame for conspiracy was rekindled.

"Interesting," Timothy said. "We might have to do the math on that."

Chapter Twenty-Five

Questions and temperatures were beginning to arise, much to Marcus's annoyance.

When are we going to raise the radio antenna? When will we connect to the Starlink internet? When will the train tunnel be complete? When are we getting the bourbon out? Why is it getting so stuffy in the bunker?

Something had gone awry with the ventilation system, sending the temperature high enough to be uncomfortable. They were nearing six relatively flawless months in. There were bound to be a few maintenance issues.

Marcus was the focal point in the impromptu gathering. He looked around at the people sitting around the table in the café.

"Look guys, the antenna is jammed. It won't raise. I have no way of knowing when the train tunnel will manifest – you'll know the exact same time I do. It could be three years from now. It could be never.

"I don't have an excuse about the bourbon – we'll break that out soon. As far as the heating and cooling, I'm working on it."

Audrey asked, "Is it because the planet is on fire and the bunker is baking like an oven?" She was fanning herself with a book.

"No, we're past that," Marcus said. "If anything, it's freezing cold. The ash in the atmosphere is blotting out the sun. That is, if NASA's models were correct."

"But we don't know for sure," Mariya said.

"Correct. We are in the dark, so to speak. That blast knocked our weather instruments offline, and likely damaged the concrete scaffolding around some of the ventilation shafts where the air is filtered. We can live off recycled air almost indefinitely, but, for whatever reason, heat is building up. I'll need to fix it sooner rather than later."

Tremors and vibrations were frequent enough to be ignored, but a blast three months earlier shook the entire bunker for the first time since the week of impact. The consensus was that gravity must have finally pulled a huge chunk of debris from space and dropped it on top of them.

"What do you have in mind?" Henry asked.

Marcus stood and stretched. "There is only one way to check our hypotheses. I'm going up."

"Up *where*? The surface?"

"Where else?"

* * *

215

The group migrated to the decontamination chamber. It was the first any of them had been there since scrubbing down for the last time.

Marcus unlocked a metal container, removed a special suit, and changed behind a curtain. He reemerged looking like an astronaut.

"Ready for liftoff?" Robby asked.

"Sure am," Marcus said.

Melonie burst into tears. Henry and Robby hugged him, and the girls followed.

Marcus wasn't terribly concerned about the trip to the surface, but they were. He told himself this was one of those moments he had to react to social cues. He milked it for all it was worth.

"Shouldn't one of us go with you?" Henry asked.

Marcus placed a gloved hand on Henry's shoulder. "It's best we minimize the risk to one person until we know what's up there. Don't worry, I'll be careful and come right back down if it is too extreme." He paused for a moment. "And if I don't return, the bunker systems are programmed to detect my watch. If it does not detect my presence for seventy-two hours, all the codes to all the doors will be wiped so that you may replace them."

He turned and opened the doors, stepping onto the elevator platform. He turned to face them, gave a solemn nod, and pressed a button.

* * *

The platform came to a smooth stop in the concrete dome that capped the elevator shaft. Automatic lights staggered on.

He double-checked the sealing of his suit. He stepped to the door.

"Here goes nothing."

He stepped out into a blighted December day. The sky was bleak, but had it been as it was during non-apocalyptic times, it would simply have been called overcast. There was a tinge of yellow to it.

Visibility wasn't great, but he could see a fair distance across the scorched and now frozen landscape – something that was a lush and lively green just months ago. Snow swirled about in a strong wind, unable to stick to the exposed dirt in hundreds of craters pockmarking the site. The half-drained lake was iced over. Black smoke billowed nearby.

He took a device from his bag and checked its readings. The temperature was in single digits, with the wind chill undoubtedly bringing it below zero.

He walked down a slope from the dome to check the vents. They were all raised and guarded by concrete barriers, as well as grated and hatted to keep rain and snow out. Steam released around them prevented icing. There was a dozen spread around the site.

The first damaged one he found had taken a direct hit.

He cursed the sky as if someone above had made a mistake.

The concrete was scattered, and the iron grate was shattered. The hat atop the pipe was smashed down, creating a complete seal.

Marcus returned to the dome for a crowbar and shovel.

He cranked the conical hat upward with the crowbar and immediately saw the cold air pour in like water down a drain. He was disappointed in how flimsy the metal was.

The next vent was in working condition, but ice was accumulating on the grate. He gave the grate a good whack with the shovel, cleared the ice, and moved on. He would need to increase the steam pressure when he got back underground.

He walked back up the hill to the back side of the dome and stopped in his tracks.

A tree, roots angled to the sky, was lodged in the concrete pillbox surrounding one of the main vents. He spun to look at the landscape. There was a skeletal tree line a half-mile away at closest. It was baffling, but he could only laugh.

The tree was mostly intact. A blast would have obliterated it.

Marcus thought for a moment. It had to have been a tornado.

"With what's been done to you," Marcus said to the earth, "I guess winter tornadoes are fair enough."

He examined the damage more closely once atop the box and cracked grate. One of the limbs stabbed through the pipe and hat. Marcus become more disappointed in the vents. He was sure they would

218

require frequent manual maintenance. He returned to the dome to get an axe and saw.

It was an awkward angle and a confined space. The oak was tough and frozen and taking forever to saw through. He finally got pissed off and chopped at the hat, lopping it off. He eliminated the wood in his way and chopped the obstructing limb away, clearing the vent.

He sat on the edge of the pillbox and caught his breath for a minute before making his way back to the dome entry. He had worked up a sweat in the insulated suit.

He stopped by the silo cover housing the radio antenna. It, too, had taken a direct hit. The circular manhole cover was dented inward, and the hinges were snapped.

Marcus laughed. His lie about the antenna being jammed turned out to be truth.

He returned the tools to the dome, but he was in no rush to go back underground. He stepped out and walked twenty yards straight ahead. The cratered field, the blowing snow, the collapsed fence line in the distance, all reminded him of No Man's Land.

He took off his helmet. He took a deep, stinging breath and exhaled a cloud of steam, eyes closed, head tilted to the sky.

Then he stripped completely.

His naked body did its best to defy the biting cold. He laughed, growing maniacal, before tapering off to a harsh pant.

He fell to his knees and clutched the snow in his fists, rubbing it all over his bare skin, alternately grimacing at the pain and laughing at life.

"Not bad! Not bad at all!" he shouted to the sky.

After another minute of his mania, he gathered his suit and returned to the dome. He returned to his calm demeanor, suppressing the shivering. He dressed during the elevator descent, replacing his helmet only a moment before the doors opened to his waiting friends.

* * *

"How was it?" Henry asked.

Marcus stepped into the room and removed his helmet, not immediately answering.

"So bad," he said.

He collapsed to the floor.

Jenna was the first to put his hands on him.

"He is *freezing!*" she said. "Get some blankets!"

Others scattered about the room to look for anything to wrap him up in.

Marcus' teeth chattered and his body shook uncontrollably.

"The . . . the vents are . . . are c-c-cleared," he said.

"Don't talk, just warm up. There will time for that later," Jenna said. She put a comforting hand on his forehead.

* * *

They got him out of the suit and into a robe, and then he was escorted, bent like an elderly man, back to the café.

Brad put on some coffee.

Jenna sat beside him, rubbing his back.

They waited until Marcus was ready to talk.

"Well . . . " Marcus began. "It was cold."

Robby laughed. "No shit?"

"It was barren, unrecognizable. Everything is gone," he said. "The ground is frozen. The air is filled with ash – I could only see a few feet in front of my face. I had to be careful not to get lost. Every few feet there was a crater. I can confirm that we were bombarded. Two of the vents and the antenna silo cover took direct hits. I thought I designed them to withstand that type of impact. I'm sorry, it was my fault."

They denied his guilt.

Jenna pulled him in closer. He put his arm around her and his head on her shoulder while he feigned sadness. She smelled so good, and she was so warm.

He collected himself and continued.

"I felt the cold creeping in through the suit, but I didn't realize how much. I knew I had to get the vents cleared. The suit is designed to withstand subarctic temperatures. There must be a tear or something. I forgot to check my thermometer, but it had to have been 50 below."

He paused, licking his lips.

"I began to feel disoriented near one of the outer vents. But I *did* get every vent cleared."

Marcus stood slowly, with help from Jenna. "I'll be fine. I better go adjust the steam pressure now before the ice builds back up."

As he walked away, he heard hushed praise.

He's so brave!

He kept his slouched posture but couldn't keep from smiling. He composed himself before stopping and turning around.

"Oh, and about the bourbon. We shall have some tonight. It is Christmas Eve, after all."

They cheered.

* * *

Marcus and Robby rolled out the bourbon barrel to great fanfare. Carefully following the manufacturer's instructions, they inserted the tap with only minor spillage.

"Hold up! Nobody drink yet!" Marcus said. He high stepped it back to the pantry. Robby got two shots in before he returned.

He held two boxes in his arms, gift wrapped. "Since we will all be hungover tomorrow, we might as well open presents tonight. Merry Christmas, everyone!"

Robby snatched one of the boxes, while Becky was closest to the other, so she opened that one.

"Capri Suns?" Robby said. "*Fuck yeah!*"

He and Becky doled out the mercurial bags of sugar water while Brad retrieved some glasses.

"Okay, now we can drink."

"First, a toast to our brave leader," Henry said. "We wouldn't be here without him, and most, if not all of us would not be alive. He has always been courageous and willing to make the tough decisions.

222

And it's already feeling cooler down here. Thanks, brother! Cheers!"

They clanked glasses.

Marcus made gracious and dismissive gestures while smiling. "Okay, okay – *now* we drink!"

And drink they did.

Melonie was the first to puncture the Capri Sun and pour some in her glass for a perverse mixed drink of mixed childhood and adulthood. The girls followed suit.

Robby praised her, but declared that he was a man, and could therefore only drink the bourbon straight. He was three deep before anyone else had finished their first.

"Can we at least get some music in here?" Robby asked.

"Good idea," Marcus said.

He went to the café panel display and typed in the passcode for the music library. The code was necessary due to Robby abusing the privilege when he serenaded the bunker with Chris De Burgh's "Lady in Red" and Rupert Holmes' "Escape (The Pina Colada Song)" on repeat while he hid in the tunnels. It was unforgiveable.

After a six-month temperance policy, nobody had any alcohol tolerance. They were loosening up in record time.

Mariya was the first to dance. Her choice of partner was not Henry, but rather a few of the other girls.

Jenna stayed near Marcus. He knew from his surveillance that she was trying to get close to him. Without the spying, he would've been clueless. He was closing in on five years of celibacy. It was mostly unintentional but snowballed as he became more focused on designing the bunkers. He hadn't the time. Sex had to take a backseat. And besides, his bedside manners were becoming *aggressive.*

He couldn't pin down his feelings. Sure, she was beautiful and intelligent, but back in his early billionaire days, he'd date a supermodel, get bored, and find another. Women were an abundant resource, disposable.

In moments of self-reflection, he deflected the blame on his father. He didn't have a good model at home on how to show affection, thus the shallow serial dating. *Never get close. That's what you do, right dad? Get close, they die, and then move on, right? Why bother?*

He wasn't afraid to admit he had daddy issues – if only to himself. It was a fine excuse for never getting close to any female other than his mother. Maybe it was mommy issues. Regardless, they were all convenient excuses. Loneliness was his passive, self-defeating revenge.

Welcoming Jenna's advance would require him to open a compartment within him that had rusted shut. And it would have to be different than his serial dating days. Women were a finite resource now, and this one wouldn't go away at his behest. He'd have to open up emotionally, if he ever figured out how. The prospect scared him to no end.

He had secrets he couldn't tell a soul.

* * *

"I call this move the pterodactyl!"

Marcus was awakened from his moping by Henry doing a ridiculous dance move in which his arms were bent at the elbows, while he stepped back and forth in no particular rhythm.

Henry was very drunk.

Marcus was startled even further from his pondering when Jenna returned with a drink for him.

"You're falling behind," she said.

"Oh, thanks." Another wouldn't hurt.

"Do you dance?"

"God no," he said. "It's not my thing."

She laughed. "It's okay. I don't care for it either. It's what birds and insects do to find a mate."

"True." He had used that line before to get someone to leave him alone about dancing. There was hope for this girl.

He began realizing his curt answers were killing the conversation.

This is where you talk, Marcus, he told himself.

Knowing not what to say, he drank more.

"You don't dance but it looks like you drink," Jenna said. "I'll get you another."

One more wouldn't hurt.

She returned, holding another. "Here you go." She stared him down, and in the first time in years, he felt intimidated. "So, no dancing, some drinking. Do you like movies?"

"Sure, yeah. I like movies." He took a gulp of bourbon.

"What's your favorite?"

He couldn't recall a single movie. "I don't know. I guess I'm more into documentaries."

"That's cool. We should watch one together."

"I'll have to see if any are loaded up on the cloud," he said. He realized the deflection in his answer. "If not, we can watch whatever."

"It's a date," she said. "I bet there are a thousand documentaries loaded on that thing. It has every movie I've ever seen."

He hoped she was placated and would move on. She didn't, but she did back off. They watched the others.

He attempted a few more words with Jenna. The alcohol loosened him up, but in the back of his mind, he knew he shouldn't risk getting *too* drunk.

"I better get to bed. I'm tired after all the events today."

He stood and the alcohol nearly sat him back down. Jenna laughed and braced him so he wouldn't fall.

"Good night, Marcus. Don't forget our date!"

"Right, right. Good night."

Jenna joined the others.

Before leaving the café, Marcus snuck another refill of bourbon. He was already drunk so another drink sounded like a good idea.

He stumbled to his suite.

* * *

"Come up," Marcus said into the intercom next to his bed.

*Two or twenty minutes later -- he couldn't tell –
she came up.*

*Through his bloodshot eyes, she appeared to
materialize straight out of the floor. "Strip."*

*"Yes, daddy," she said. She stripped. She lied
down on the bed.*

"Too drunk," he said.

She got on top of him.

*It was sloppy and selfish, but he didn't have the
mind to care. He could control this one.*

*Two or twenty minutes later -- he couldn't tell –
it was over.*

"You can't stay," he said.

She left.

Chapter Twenty-Six

Christmas was cancelled, or at least, the gift-giving part. According to bunker literature, it would be "ill-advised to foment any sense of entitlement in such an environment of limited resources."

Timothy was able to secure a coloring book and pack of crayons for Madeleine and an assortment of ribbons for Liza's hair. It was a far cry from the Kiddie Smart Watch Liza was begging for before the asteroid. Maddie had her eyes on *Allie AI*, the cute doll with "Advanced AI." Neither the watch nor doll existed underground.

Instead of gift-giving, bunker literature encouraged a focus on the religious aspect of the holiday. There would be a service and meal in the dining hall, repeated three times so no one would miss out. Timothy couldn't pass up a holiday meal. The Thanksgiving "feast" was better than anything else they'd served.

But as for the religion, he was done with that.

"Okay Maddie, you know the drill. Start crying during the service so we can get a good spot in line."

"But daddy, won't God be mad?"

I've still got some Catholic guilt to wring out of you yet.

"No honey, He won't mind." He crouched down to her level. "God is going to do whatever makes Him happy, and He wants you to do the same, as long as you don't hurt anyone. Following rules is usually good, but sometimes listening to everyone else and doing what they tell you, sacrificing yourself, only makes you unhappy and hungry. God doesn't want that."

He felt guilty saying it, and she looked perplexed. He didn't want to raise little monsters pushing people down and out of the way, but he also didn't want them to be pushovers.

He turned to Liza. "And after the meal, Liza, act sick so we can get away from the old ladies."

"Dad, I am sick," Liza said, which was true. She had been running a fever for a week.

"Well, play it up so we can get out of there." He kissed her warm forehead.

* * *

He walked the girls to the back of the dining hall, told Maddie she could stop her fake crying, and he listened to the announcements.

A day of fasting was to take place each Saturday for everyone not involved in labor-intensive work. This would be offset, the preacher insisted, by an

229

extra real-food meal each week. As it turns out, the farmers were doing a heck of a job.

The workers were not off the hook. There was a new sustenance to be introduced. Some sort of protein paste. The preacher didn't even sugar coat it. He said it tasted "pretty bad" but it was the equivalent of a superfood. Timothy wasn't sure it was possible to get any worse than Soylent.

The preacher announced social gatherings and opportunities designed to boost morale. Much to Timothy's dismay, the preacher released the congregation by rows for the meal. His plan to jump the line had backfired.

Steve passed, leaning in. "Jump in. Nobody will say anything."

Timothy pulled the girls in line. While no one said anything – Steve was right about that – he could feel their leers burning the back of his head.

"You are with a big black dude. What are they going to do?" Steve said.

Timothy got his tray of food and made sure the girls got everything. Sliced carrots, green beans, a small chunk of watermelon, and a prized scoop of chicken salad, which was basically chicken and celery. Everyone received a cup of tart lemonade as well. Nobody complained. It was the best meal they'd had since Thanksgiving.

Rick sat down. "Not mother's cooking, but it'll have to do."

Timothy introduced Rick to Steve, Steve to Rick. Rick was a Purdue fan, so they talked about the football program as if it still existed and was going to rebound next season.

The crew of military-types walked into the dining hall. The four did not attended the service. They sat the next table over and made their appearance known.

"There's a sweet thing on the fifth floor, got her scouted out," one of the men said. "Probably fifteen or so. But if there's grass on the field, I'll play."

The others booed him and punched his arms.

"I'm on that chick in the gym. She's slutty but that's what I like. I'll share, don't worry."

Timothy couldn't take the crude conversation, especially with his daughters sitting right there. Idiot frat boys cussing up a storm right next to children was not cool.

He turned around. "Excuse me, fellas – can you keep it down? I've got young girls over here. Thanks."

"Oh, we've noticed the *girls*," one of the men said.

Timothy didn't turn to look, but it was more laughing and punching, he imagined.

"Shut the fuck up dude, stop talking shit," another one said. "There are fucking children around and shit!"

They were having a grand time.

Steve was clenching the table as if he'd fly off if he didn't. He looked at Timothy, watching for the slightest nod.

Timothy shook his head. "Let it go. We don't need to start some bunker blood feud that lasts through the centuries. We're done anyway. Let's go."

They filed past the table of men with their trays. Steve stopped in front of the young men and stared. Timothy nudged Steve in the back to get him moving forward, but Steve didn't budge. It took several seconds, but Steve finally moved on.

Outside the dining hall, children were playing under the open space.

"Girls, go join your friends for a bit. The adults need to chat."

Madeleine jumped right into the fray. It appeared that she had made friends at school. Liza walked shyly around the edges. It pained Timothy to know she wasn't feeling well. He wanted to be a dad and help her out, but Rick and Steve had pressing issues to speak about.

They strolled away from the children. Steve was the first to speak. "We need to map this place out."

"That's a great idea," Timothy said.

The bunker was expansive and housed over a thousand people, give or take. There were concentric rings of halls on all residential floors, and dead-end corridors that extended further, all lined with apartments as small as Timothy's, and smaller. He had done some exploring in a few of the service areas on the ground floor, but not elsewhere, and not in any organized manner.

"I have a notepad upstairs and a few pens," Rick said. "Tim, you want to give it a try?"

"Absolutely, sure."

"About those military boys back there," Rick said. "Two of them are being put to work in the mine,

232

and one of them downstairs with you. They don't know it yet."

"Oh, great," Timothy said. "But there are four. What about the other guy?"

"Ashley was vague as ever. Says they've been doing maintenance stuff. Don't believe her, but she said she needed to keep at least one free."

Rick glanced around, making sure they were alone. "She did say one of them was a bit more civilized than the rest. A quiet guy. He is the one that will be working with you two. See if you can't get on his good side and get something out of him. You know, without making it obvious."

They stopped at the end of the corridor, before the farm lab, then turned to walk back.

"How is the mine?" Timothy asked.

Rick shook his head. "The room and pillar sector is still producing, but we are butting irreplaceable machinery against nothing but solid rock on the long wall."

"Why still do it?"

"I ask myself that every day. Ashley insists, won't shut up about it. Says there are gobs of coal on the other side that will last us forever. Says the bunker was built here specifically because of the coal on the other side. I'm not seeing it. Going to give it a few more meters, and if I don't hit black, I'm turning the tunnel one way or the other. Hell, she won't know. Don't know why I listen to a word she says."

The trio made their way back to the bunker center. The children were still playing. Timothy spotted Madeleine in the middle of a ring of bouncy toddlers. She was a magnet for attention. He scanned around and found Liza sitting at the edge of the action, interacting with no one.

He turned to his two friends. "Better go let this food settle. See you tomorrow, bright and early." He called the girls over.

"Not sure how bright it'll be," Steve said, "but it'll be early."

* * *

The overnight shift in the mines left multiple heaping piles under the room-and-pillar shafts. The task for Steve and Timothy was to collect the ore and cart it closer to the conveyor window that fed the pulverizer and power station.

Steve gave pointers on how not to hurt your back and work the shoveling muscles in a more balanced manner.

Timothy was already feeling stronger from the work. He enjoyed the simple, physical exertion. It had its perks over the sedentary computer work he had done all his adult life.

Once their system for moving the coal was worked out for the shift, their conversation turned to the state of the bunker. They spoke of what Timothy should look for during his mapping expedition. Steve said he should secure a length of string marked off for distance to help with scaling.

"Excuse me," a voice said behind them. "I—I start work here today."

Timothy had no idea how long the young man had been standing there. It was one of the young soldiers. He had a buzzed head with a horseshoe scar on his scalp. His face ticked and his eyes darted downward. He was a ball of nervous energy.

"Right," Steve said. "Let's show you the ropes. This here is Timothy, I'm Steve. You?"

"I'm – my name is Jared. Jared Roberts."

"Jared, got it. First things first, never stand under one of these things." Steve pointed to the shaft above with his shovel.

"Oh, okay. Yes, sir." Jared gave a twitching smile.

"Let's head over to the conveyor window and begin there."

"Before we start," Jared said, "I . . . I just want to apologize for my friends yesterday. I'm–I am not like that . . . like them."

Timothy and Steve looked at each other for a moment, then each nodded.

"No hard feelings," Steve said. They began walking toward the conveyor window.

"Jared, were you a soldier?" Timothy asked.

"Yes, yes sir. Got this scar in Korea," Jared said. "I'm–I was a SEAL, believe it or not."

"You are elite, my friend! Thanks for your service," Timothy said.

"Oh, thanks. It–it was nothing."

Nothing? Timothy thought. *Shit, son. A SEAL? And look at your head. It was* something.

"Besides," Jared said, "not sure we what we were trying to accomplish in Korea."

Timothy had ideas. The obstinate Hermit Kingdom had ambitions in space and a record of giving the middle finger to the international community. If they caught wind of the asteroid, who knows what would have happened if a preemptive war wasn't waged to destroy or distract them.

"Yeah, it was questionable, I guess. And now the United States doesn't even exist."

"Oh, it still exists," Jared said.

Steve and Timothy stopped and looked at him.

"I mean, I don't know that. But I bet our government is still alive in some form." He shrugged. "I mean, I don't *know* that."

While Steve explained the conveyor window, Timothy noticed that Jared wasn't listening. Rather, he was staring intensely between them.

"...Just like at a grocery checkout line, the conveyor only moves when it detects..." Steve stopped, noticing Jared's lack of attention. "Are you listening?"

"Sorry. Yes, sir."

"It's not rocket science. We just push piles of coal around and occasionally toss some in this window." Steve smiled and patted Jared on the back. "Just do what we do, and you'll be an expert in no time. And enough with the 'yes, sir' stuff. We are not superior to you."

"Yes, sir. I mean, okay. I'm a hard worker."

"That's all you need to be. We are equal here. If you have any suggestions, we'll try them out. We are not your bosses or anything."

They got to work and let Jared talk.

He was a southern Georgia boy who had been to as many countries in the military as he had been to states in the U.S. before joining up. After Korea, he did some domestic work. He said he didn't want to talk about it, but Timothy knew it would come out all in due time. They just had to build trust.

"After we did . . . stuff, you know, for the government, I got sent to watch Mr. Trencher's place. You know Marcus Trencher? The billionaire guy?"

"Actually, we do," Timothy said. "I helped him found his company. In return, he blessed me and my family with bunker bids." His sarcasm was ambiguous enough to work either way.

Steve said, "I worked security detail for his friend, Henry Plyman. Good guy."

"Mr. Trencher is why I am down here, too." Jared abruptly stopped talking and scraped a shovelful of coal and tossed it into the cart.

"Was your bunker bid a reward, or are you still working for Mr. Trencher?" Timothy asked.

Jared laughed nervously. "Nah, it was a reward I guess you could say. Besides, he ain't here is he?"

"Nope. But sometimes I feel his presence. Guess because he designed the place."

Jared hesitated before the next shovelful. "I will say, that guy gave me the creeps. He wasn't much better than the government."

A whistle blew for lunch. They went to the break room. A woman from the farm lab delivered a head of lettuce and a used peanut butter jar full of the new mystery protein paste.

"Figure it out," the woman said.

They tore off folds of lettuce and put a dab of the paste onto the leaves. It looked fecal. It tasted like it looked.

Timothy gagged.

Jared refused. "I'd rather starve," he said.

Chapter Twenty-Seven

Marcus's heroic trip to the surface brought other things to the surface.

To see it again, the planet and sky, gave him a jolt of euphoria. It was also funny to have tricked everyone still down below. But it didn't take long for the past to come bubbling back up. It had been doing that more and more lately.

He had processed none of the end of the world trauma.

All the things he did, and all that was done to him, to get the bunker, was all best to bury in the back of his brain. It wouldn't stay there, though.

He delayed his date with Jenna. A two-day hangover bought him some miserable time.

He was in no mood for the whole thing. Just going along because that is what he is supposed to do. He was supposed to do things he didn't want to in order to be normal, to be like everyone else.

That introverted premonition of knowing he was about to not have a good time was strong. Alas, he went.

Jenna met him in front of the theatre in jeans and a t-shirt. He was slightly better dressed, but not enough for her to notice.

"Shall we?" Jenna said, offering her arm.

He hooked it and they walked into the cozy theatre. Marcus was hesitant to sit on the couch since he knew of and had watched Robby and Melonie's exploits on the cushions. He managed to put the graphic imagery aside.

"So, what is this documentary about?" she asked.

"We should watch a movie. Most of the documentaries I liked are no longer relevant. You know, a regular movie, with actors and stuff. I don't know the last time I saw one. Your choice."

Jenna manipulating the remote through the alphabetical list of titles. She stopped in the E's.

"This one – *Eternal Sunshine of the Spotless Mind!* Have you seen it?"

Marcus shook his head.

"It's so good. It's a smart people movie. You'll love it."

He was skeptical but soon became engrossed.

The concept of erasing memories, the basis of the film, sent him into deep thought. Would he do it? Was there value in moments of suffering? Would he erase memory of everything preceding life in the bunker, so that it may seem only normal?

He couldn't decide. Where would he be had he only carried memories of comfort? Discomfort drove him to do great things. It also drove him mad.

When things fell apart in the film, so did he.

His throat constricted and his eyes flooded. It was only then that he became aware of Jenna again. He wanted to keep himself together. But he couldn't. He sobbed, catching Jenna's attention. She lifted her head off his shoulder and looked at him.

"I'm sorry. We can stop, we don't have to –"

He put his head on her shoulder. He used to do the same with his mother when he came home from a day of bullying at school.

Jenna put her hand on his head and neck and rubbed them soothingly. She was confused and unsure of what to do or say.

"I want to forget," he said. "I want to forget."

"Shh, it's okay," she said. "You can talk to me. I understand."

Talk? The word flipped a switch within him.

He lifted his head, going from inconsolable to cold.

"You don't understand. I can't talk to you, or anyone. I did things to get this bunker... all wrong. We had better options. I should have thought of something better."

"Something better? Marcus, you can't put the weight of the world on your shoulders when the universe is throwing stones at it. I mean, really, what options did we have?"

Oh, how little she knows. He wavered a moment, as if he wanted to tell her everything.

Then he laughed dismissively.

"I can't say." He stood up. "I have to go."

And he was gone. She called after him, but he didn't turn around.

* * *

Marcus paced furiously in his study, back and forth, the length of his desk. His hands trembled at his side when they weren't running through his hair over and over.

How could she understand? She couldn't. And talk? She only wanted gossip. I don't gossip. What I know is beyond gossip. Options? There were options, but I gave up on them. I and everyone else in power gave up on humanity and its uncanny ability to solve problems at the last possible moment. Instead, I bought in to bunkers and systematic death. I was sworn to secrecy and now had to play prison warden, be a prisoner, all until our sentences are carried out.

He walked into the bathroom and stood before a long mirror, placed his hands on the frame, and leaned on it. When he took his weight off, there was a click and release. The mirror glided open on its hinges. He stepped inside.

He descended a set of metal stairs then opened another door. He flipped the lights on.

Before him were 25 miles of tunnel awaiting connection. 25 miles of his little secret. It was nothing but 25 miles to a dead end, for now.

He walked 30 yards. To his left, a ghostly train station platform.

He had hoped people would be able to board a train and travel to Bloomington, then Indianapolis, or outer Louisville. His bunker would become a vacation destination, a tourist attraction. That was the original plan, at least. He had the recreational space.

But he had no plans of staying. He wasn't going to die underground.

He had secured a tunnel-boring machine for the construction of the bunker and used it primarily to carve out the storage tunnels. He then logged the 25 miles of tunnel toward Bloomington in two years before the machine broke down and replacement parts were impossible to come by.

This left approximately 30 miles to be completed from the other end. He was told there was good progress before everyone moved underground, but now he was in the dark.

A tripod stood in the middle of the tunnel with a seismograph device on top. He turned it on and awaited a reading. Nothing. No distant rumble of a tunnel-boring machine. It was his only means of knowing whether they were getting close.

He picked it up and took it another half-mile forward, but still nothing. He lifted it up and slammed it against the tunnel wall.

He turned and walked back, locking up before returning to his suite. Immediately upon stepping into the bathroom, there was a buzz and the light above his door was flashing.

He had a visitor.

He checked the panel display. It was Henry.

He pushed the button to the intercom. "Go away."

"Come on Marcus. You need to talk."

He very much disagreed but pushed the button to let him in anyhow.

Marcus laid down on his leather couch, put his hands behind his head, and waited for the psychiatric session.

Henry took the chair beside him.

"Just tell me what's on your mind," Henry said.

"I don't look forward to the upkeep and attention required to keep a relationship running."

"Okay," Henry said, "you don't have to spend every day with her. Keep it casual. Just be who you are. It's not do or die."

"I've never been capable with people, never will be. An impossible deficit to overcome. I once masked it through accomplishments, but none of that matters now. I'm obsolete."

"I get that you think forming relationships purely for pleasure and not for some epic industrial purpose is not your thing. But maybe you can make it your thing. Your next project."

Marcus shook his head. "I'm rundown, Henry. I outran it all for a while, but now my feet are planted ankle-deep and the concrete is dry. I'm stuck."

"You are not stuck. If anyone can change and adapt, it's you."

"Not this time, and not in this place. Remember that liberal studies psychology stuff you got into – egocentrism, heliocentrism?"

"I think it was sociocentrism. Heliocentrism is the sun being the center of the universe, I think."

"Whatever. My universe expanded to include a company of a million employees, and eventually, whole societies. It brought me a lot of pleasure. But the planets, or people, were all a great distance away from me, and I liked it. But then it all collapsed, and now I'm in a black hole."

Henry pinched the bridge of his nose. "You were stuck in concrete, now you're in a black hole."

Marcus continued: "Other than you and Robby, and Timothy, I never had a small group. I'm claustrophobic down here, socially. It strikes me as childish, what you guys do. I don't know how to 'hang out' or dance or joke around. Or talk to people on a personal level."

"The vast majority of people never reach a level where they have to focus on whole societies in their sociocentrism, or whatever, so they focus on their own smaller groups. It's a natural way of finding meaning and relevancy. Having fun and dancing *is* childish. But I've got to say, I was much happier as a child, and I think you were, too. It's okay to return to that once in a while."

"You ever hear that quote, *'Great minds discuss ideas; average minds discuss events; simple minds discuss people'*?

"I've lived by that." Marcus sat up. "Down here there *are* only people. No ideas, no events – just eleven other people. Maybe my head was always in the clouds, but at least it was above the masses of narcissists wallowing in social media. Now there are no idealistic clouds for me to hide in. I have no history of breaking into small groups. I'm obsolete."

"You are not. You are my best friend. Robby's, too. Everybody down here likes you whether you think so or not."

Marcus returned to lying down. "Whatever." He closed his eyes, then added in a more friendly tone, "Thanks."

Henry stood, hesitated. "This is usually none of my business, but have you been taking your medication?"

"Yeah, yeah. I had a lifetime supply brought down. I keep it up here. I'm all good on that front."

Marcus had no such stash. He saw the end of the world as opportunity to sever dependence on a medication of which he was always skeptical of the efficacy.

"You aren't going to stay up here for a week, are you?"

"You'll see me when you see me."

Henry moved to the door.

"Henry?"

"Yes?"

"If you could have the most painful experiences in your life erased, would you?"

Henry thought for a moment. "No. I believe there is some intangible value in suffering. Even the worst of the worst." He waited for a response, and when none came, he opened the door.

"Henry?"

"Yeah?"

"I miss poor people. Fat, fucking poor, stupid people."

Henry laughed, uneasily. "Me too, Marcus."

Chapter Twenty-Eight

Timothy had been snooping around in his free time, mapping out every corner of the bunker where he could gain access. There were anomalies.

He pulled Rick aside. "We should have a meeting."

"We who?"

"You, me and Steve."

"What about Jared?"

Timothy considered this for a moment. "Can we trust him?"

"I haven't seen a reason why not."

"Okay. When and where?"

"Tonight? We can meet at my place, and my wife can watch your girls."

Timothy nodded. "I'll bring the Soylent."

* * *

Rick unfolded a card table in the center of the room and Timothy scattered his drawings on it, each piece of paper labeled in the top right corner with the floor number. He flipped to the 14th floor.

"We'll start at the top of the bunker. It's a smaller floor, with six apartments on the center ring. We are here," Timothy said, pointing his pen to Rick's apartment. "This one is mine. These four are empty. There is a half ring down this hall past my place to the west with six more apartments, but nobody lives in them. The girls play back there. Kind of creeps me out."

Steve crossed his arms and cocked his head. "You're telling me there are eight vacant apartments up here? We are packed like sardines downstairs. Plus, these apartments look larger than the ones downstairs."

"I've tried the doors. They are all locked. But pretty sure they are apartments."

"Does the council know anything about this?" Steve asked. "Maybe we could spread some people out. Make things more comfortable for the folks down in third class."

Rick said, "We could bring it up to them."

Timothy's initial thought was to object out of pure selfishness: He liked his space and the fact there were fewer people upstairs. But he kept it to himself.

"Anyway, that was fourteen. Twelve is the same in the middle, but I think it is full occupancy." Timothy flipped the next page. "Eleven is where it gets interesting."

Steve un-crossed his arms and leaned in.

"The outer ring is a half-ring," Timothy said, pointing. "It doesn't extend north beyond the east-west hall. It gets even smaller on eight because of the mine below it." He flipped through the next four pages. "It stays this way until the seventh floor – but even there, nothing extends past Ashley's suite to the north. Nobody knows how far north the elevator is. But presumably, it's got to be further out than the outer ring on twelve."

"That's a lot of dead space," Steve said.

Rick borrowed Timothy's pen and redrew the long mining tunnel, slightly angled north. He also added to the room-and-pillar section to the south.

"I changed course northward a few degrees on the tunnel, without Ashley's permission. I've put more men to the south in the rooms to keep up on production."

Timothy nodded. "The full outer rings pick back up on four, three and two, with long dead-end halls in each direction. I can't be totally sure, but I counted 245 apartments of varying sizes. But check this out." He pulled the paper from the bottom of the pile. "I drew a vertical representation of the bunker, viewed from east to west. What do you notice?"

"A void, there." Rick pointed to the blank spot.

"Exactly." Timothy circled the area of emptiness. "Nothing. Except I think there is something there."

"What are these lines?" Steve asked, pointing.

"Y'all are being confusing about this. Look – the bunker is shaped like a tall circle," Jared said.

"You mean a cylinder?" Timothy said.

"Yeah, whatever. Like a giant Coke can. There's a big dent in the side of the Coke can, to the north, and we want to know what's in that dented area."

The others looked at each other, confounded by the simple brilliance: The bunker was, more or less, shaped like a dented Coke can.

"Oh, I almost forgot." Timothy threw pages on the floor until he found the two he was looking for. "You know those Soylent dispensers in the cafeteria? They are encased in pillars up to the sixth floor, and don't reappear on eleven. I even knocked on a few doors to go into apartments to check."

"Six stories of Soylent?" Steve said. "Makes starvation sound appealing."

"I know. But the pillars all stop somewhere after six. Not sure what's in them. Could just be infrastructure stuff. Or more Soylent. But worth noting."

"What else did you find? Any secret rooms?" Rick asked.

"There is this one room on ground level." He flipped to the page. "Here. It's tucked in the corner of the Farm Lab. None of the workers could tell me what was there, and I don't think it's a closet."

"That?" Jared said. "I know what that is, and I can get you in. It's pretty neat."

"Well, what is it?" Timothy asked.

"It's a surprise. I'll show you tomorrow. You'll get a kick out of it."

Timothy preferred he just say it, but apparently it was not important enough to tell them now, but interesting enough for him to show it off later.

Steve picked up the ground level page. "There's something missing. Did you ever come across any sort of water treatment facility?"

Timothy shook his head. They all looked baffled.

249

"Is that what's back there?" Timothy asked Jared.

"No, it's not that." He smiled like the Cheshire cat.

"It's got to be somewhere. Could be like a water tower," Rick said.

Timothy collected the papers. "Okay then, checklist time. Jared shows me the mystery room tomorrow, we figure out what is in this void, and find out where the hell our water comes from."

* * *

In the coal depository, Timothy waited anxiously for Jared to arrive, and he showed up chipper and grinning.

"Let's head on over," Timothy said.

"Sorry, can't just yet," Jared said. "Gotta wait 'til after lunch. The workers clear out of the Farm Lab. And, uh . . . my Navy pals. They work in that room before lunch. After, they go play cards and video games."

Timothy's intrigue was renewed: A secret room inhabited by Navy SEALs. He had to see it.

* * *

When the lunch whistle blew, they went to the break room. A woman dropped off a head of lettuce and a fresh jar of protein paste. Timothy could barely stand it, but he forced the stuff down. Between the manual labor, the cutback on calories, and his weeks of grieving where he could hardly swallow, he had dropped thirty pounds. He needed to eat whatever he could get, even if it tasted like shit.

Timothy shoveled some in and did his ritual gagging.

Jared giggled like a child.

Timothy scowled at him.

"Okay," Jared said. "We can go."

They walked down the hall. The Farm Lab was mostly empty, other than a few older ladies. It was full of lush plants. It was one bright spot in the bunker.

"Hey, Wanda!" Jared said.

"Hi Jack, how are you?"

"Just fine, nice seein' you."

They walked toward the door in the back corner.

"Jack?" Timothy asked.

"She's a bit senile, never remembers my name."

Jared dug in his pocket. "I kept a key."

The door opened and Timothy was hit by a strong, earthy smell.

There were two long, rectangular boxes on either side of the room that looked like freezers. In the middle of the room, there was a stout vat, also steel. Pipes and valves meandered between them all. Atop the vat, there was a lid with a thick glossy window.

Timothy couldn't see inside. "What's in there?"

Jared smiled. "Go on, open it."

Timothy released a latch and opened the door slowly. Whatever was in the vat was dark and had a vaguely liquid motion.

"It's our new sustainable food source! These boxes over here have rows of corrugated plastic slabs covered in 'em. Easy to take care of, really. Just need a dark, warm place. They eat about anything."

Timothy put his face closer to the opening, peering with squinted eyes, trying to see.

Then the first one flew up and hit him in his face.

"What the fuck!"

Two more came out and landed on his shirt. He swatted them away.

"Roaches! They're goddamn cockroaches!"

Jared laughed hysterically. "Close the lid! Close the lid!"

Before he could, a glut of roaches bubbled out of the opening, like an overflowing sewer on a low-lying street. He smashed the lid down and winced at the crunch. Bright, slimy innards spewed around the rim. He slid off of the vat, flailing at the swarm running on him while racing past Jared to outside the chamber. There, he stumbled to a table of carrots and vomited through them.

Jared shouted from the door. "Hold up! I better kill as many as I can real quick!" He came out minutes later in a hurry. "We better get the hell outta here!"

They returned to the coal depository, Jared cackling. Timothy was green faced.

Steve leaned on his shovel. "Well, what was in the mystery room?"

"Fucking cockroaches."

"Cockroaches? Seriously? Why the hell do we have those down here?"

Jared was doubled over from laughter. "You – You guys know that protein paste?"

"Oh no fucking way!" Timothy said, hunched over, ready to vomit again. "You've gotta be kidding me!"

"Nope – great source of protein! Know what we feed 'em? Human hair, from the salon on two!"

Timothy was down on all fours, dry heaving.

* * *

Timothy turned. "I'm about done with this pile. Jared, why don't you get a start on the new chute. If you get a cart under it now, might save you some work."

No response.

"Jared?"

"I-I-I'd rather not. I'd rather not work b-back there."

Timothy frowned. "Why not? Afraid of the dark?"

"No, it ain't that." He stomped off.

Timothy looked at Steve, who shrugged. Timothy walked to the back corner, dragging his cart behind him. He stood in front of the minor pile, which was about a foot up the wall.

Something caught his eye.

Part of the wall was different than the rest of the chamber. It was a lighter grey, even in the lack of light.

He stepped up to it, careful not to get under the chute where chunks of coal could land on his head. He ran his hand along the wall, and flakes broke off. He found the clear division between the carved bedrock and the artificial stone.

253

It was concrete.

"Steve, check this out," he yelled across the chamber. "There's a wall here."

"No shit," Steve said as he approached.

"No, I mean – look. It's cheap concrete. See?" He jabbed at it with his shovel.

A slat crumbled off into the coal below. Within the crater left on the wall, there was a half-dollar sized hole. Timothy and Steve exchanged a silent glance before Timothy struck again, opening a slightly larger gap.

He stepped up and put his face to the hole.

"It's hollow, but pitch black."

He backed away and put his shirt to his nose.

"And it smells *awful*."

Jared sprinted back into the chamber, yelling.

"Tim! We-We didn't close the lid all the way and, and, and . . . "

They ran to him.

"Whoa, slow down. What happened?"

"The-the door. The r-roaches are out." He ran his hand over his head like he wanted to tear his scalp off. "The bugs are all over the c-crops." He began sobbing. "I-I fucked up. I fucked up big time. I didn't close, I didn't close . . . they are going to kill me!"

"It's okay, nobody is going to kill you."

Before Timothy could put a hand of comfort on his shoulder, Jared stood straight up and stared past them at the wall and the hole they had just made.

He backed away.

"He-he made us do it. We h-had to kill them so-so we could be here."

"Calm down, Jared. Who? What do you mean?" Timothy said.

Jared's eyes stayed on the back wall. He took more steps backward toward the center of the chamber.

"You shouldn't stand there," Timothy said as the sound rock and tin came from above.

As Jared finally broke his gaze and looked upward into the chute, he was buried in a hailstorm of coal.

"Jared!"

They rushed forward to grab him and pull him out.

He was knocked out cold.

Screams came from the hall, and the doors burst open. Three soldiers sprinted to them.

"You're a dead man, Roberts!" one said.

They grabbed Jared's limp body right out of Timothy and Steve's hands and dragged him away.

One of the SEALs pulled a knife. "Not another step."

They backed away, hands up.

"If either of you step out of this place in the next ten minutes, you are both dead men."

"He needs to go to the medical center," Timothy said.

The man smirked. "That's exactly where we are taking him. Don't get any big ideas, fella."

The man backed away before turning and sprinting to catch up to the other two carrying Jared. Timothy scaled the wall and gained solid footing onto the coal. He put his face in the hole and turned his light on.

"*Oh God.*"

He fell down and continued to kick away, scooting back from the wall.

"Tim? What is it?"

"Bodies."

He looked up at Steve.

"Stacks of them."

Chapter Twenty-Nine

Timothy and Steve stood away from the wall. Steve peered into the alcove and nearly got as sick as Timothy.

There were 20, perhaps 30 bodies neatly stacked in the chamber. Most wore a uniform, some still had helmets on. It was a crew of workers.

"They were the last of the bunker construction team. Skeleton crew." Timothy wiped the sweat from his brow.

"They'll be skeletons in a couple years."

"It's like they were executed shortly after so nobody would know the whereabouts."

"But why this?" Steve asked. "They have a crematorium down here."

"Too many of them? Too close to the move in date? The wall looks like it was put up in a hurry."

"Do we tell anyone about this?"

"I don't think we can. Who do we tell? It's clear who did the execution. Jared wouldn't even step within thirty yards of this corner." Tim pointed at the wall. "If we say anything, we join them. We'll have to cover it up when we get enough coal back here."

Steve nodded. "We better find where they are holding Jared. I'm starting to believe what he said."

"Believe what?"

"That they'll kill him."

* * *

Outside of the chamber, an alarm honked, and red lights whirled. There was no sign of the mercenary soldiers, but there were hundreds of others flooding the hall, heading toward the farm lab.

Timothy grabbed Dale, his old mining partner, who was running by. "What's going on?"

"A bunch of fuckin' bugs got out from somewhere. We are getting as many people in the lab as we can to kill'em quick and save the crops."

He ran off.

Timothy and Steve headed for the holding cells, going against the stream of people. The cells were vacant, save for one old man. With no serious crimes committed, it was nothing more than a drunk tank.

They headed back toward the medical center. In the atrium, bugs were already flying under the lights.

Timothy saw Ashley and stopped her.

"What are they doing to Jared?" he asked.

"He jeopardized our food source by breaking into the roach farm," she said, angry. "Jared is no longer with us."

"You can't *kill* him!"

"I'm afraid it is already done."

"He at least deserves a trial," Timothy said, frantic. "Talk to the committee!"

"I don't think you are listening. It is done. He is already dead."

They charged past her. When they made it to the medical center door, the four soldiers were exiting.

"What did you do to him?" Timothy asked.

"Jared performed an act of terrorism on the bunker and we all might starve because of it. We did what needed to be done."

"You son of a bitch! You are just as guilty!" Timothy was yelling. "If you were there instead of getting drunk or playing video games, this wouldn't have happened. You abandoned your post!"

Steve held Timothy back.

A soldier got in Timothy's face. "I don't think he was alone. I think you were with him. We might have to *investigate* this further if you want to *push* this further."

The soldiers walked away. Through the medical center window, and through the crematorium oven #2 window, flames flickered.

Timothy turned and saw Ashley. He put a finger in her face.

"*You* have some explaining to do."

"You as well." She looked around. "Not here. Let's go to my office."

* * *

Ashley filled three glasses of water, then handed them out to Timothy and Steve.

259

"You've been snooping around, Mr. Spencer," she said. "What is this map-making venture you've been on? Asking to go into people's apartments and such? It's got people uneasy."

"Amateur cartography. A hobby. I just want to know my surroundings."

She smirked. "Find any secret passageways?"

"There are anomalies." Timothy pointed. "What's to the north?"

Ashley looked confused. "Nothing. Other than the elevator that brought us down here."

"The Soylent silos only go up to floor six or seven. There are no apartments to the north. There is something other than an elevator there."

"Nothing but rock." She raised an eyebrow. "Cooking up a conspiracy theory, are we?"

"Where is the water treatment facility?" Steve asked. "There are a thousand people down here with running water. Where does it come from?"

"We are in the land of lakes. Nobody knows this, but we are under Minnesota. We siphoned off a lake." She paused, frowning. "Sorry. The treatment plant *is* to the north. It slipped my mind. It's beyond the big metal door beside my quarters, off the corridor to the elevator. Totally automated, and we haven't had an issue yet."

"My water pressure went out a few months back," Timothy said.

"And it corrected itself. Computers do amazing things these days."

"We want to see it."

"Denied. Anything else?"

"The power station. We are cranking out nearly double the power necessary for this bunker," Steve said.

"Just an issue of scaling. Smaller stations are not as efficient as megawatt plants." Ashley frowned again. "I was disappointed about this as well, honestly, but we can overcome the technical shortfall with hard work. We have the coal."

Timothy sat back, frustrated. She had an answer for everything. None satisfactory, but answers nonetheless.

He decided to come out blazing.

"What about the bodies in the walls?"

Ashley straightened her posture, as if on alert. "What *bodies*?"

"The last of the bunker construction crew, stacked up behind a flaky concrete wall in the coal depository."

She sighed, eyes closed. "Look, Mr. Trencher went through hell and high water to secure a thousand bids in another state to put these people down here – to save them. He simply couldn't let word get out. Harsh, but it had to be done."

"Why not let them stay in the house they built? After all, they earned it." He leaned forward. "Because they knew Marcus's dirty secrets about this place?"

"Oh, have a look around!" She gestured wildly. "You'll find nothing else. Just face it, you are stuck underground. Accept the things you cannot change."

"And have the courage to change the things I can." He stood. "I *am* going to find out what those workers knew."

Steve moved toward the door.

"One last question," Timothy said. "What's in the attic?"

"Computers. The bunker brain."

"Really? I'm quite good with computers. Was one of the best programmers in the world. You should let me have a look."

"If we have a crash, you'll be the first person I call. Have a nice day."

He followed Steve out.

Steve shook his head when they were alone. "Lies, lies, lies, all lies."

"Yeah, I don't believe a word she said," Timothy said.

They watched the frenzy of people, running, stomping, slapping, trying to kill or capture the roaches. More than likely, the bugs would outlive all of them.

Timothy turned to Steve. "I better go pick up some Soylent while I still can and go see my girls." He paused. "You take care of yourself. I don't think we are safe here."

* * *

Timothy entered the apartment and found Liza reading and Madeleine playing with her paper dolls. It concerned him that they were alone after his run in with the soldiers. He set the Soylent down.

"Daddy! Today at school we learned about bugs!" Madeleine said.

Liza looked up. "The only good bug is a dead bug, they told us." Then she put her head back into her book.

"Yes, we have a bug problem, which means we might have a food problem soon."

Liza dropped her book to her lap. "Dad, we already have a food problem. I can't stand this soy stuff. I think it's making me sick."

He sat beside her and hugged her close. Her forehead was still warm. "Hang in there, darling."

The book in her lap was Elie Wiesel's *Night*. It was entirely too heavy of a read for an eight-year-old. He was horrified. He handed her his phone.

"Play some games."

Later, after he tucked the girls in, he lay awake. He ran the events of the day through his mind over and over.

There was a buzz at the door.

He sat up, his heart starting to race. He approached the door cautiously. "Who is it?"

"Rick."

In Timothy's state of paranoia, he still didn't open the door. Too many movies with a gunman out of sight beside the door.

"Sorry to wake you, but there's something you need to see."

"Are you alone?"

"Of course. Found something in the mine. Get dressed."

"Okay. Just a minute."

When he opened the door, Rick was, in fact, alone.

They went down to the 7th floor and into the mine, walking the darkened long wall tunnel. They passed weary, blackened faces of the night shift. It was always night in the mine. They put on their hats and turned the miner lights on.

Rick led him to the end of the tunnel, or at least the back end of the boring machine. Rick turned to the northern wall. "Look here," he said.

There was a hole only about the size of a quarter.

"There's not dead bodies or bugs back there, is there?" Timothy asked.

"What? No." Rick looked at him as if he were crazy. "Here, use this flashlight for a better angle."

Timothy leaned in for the light to flow through the drill hole.

"You see there, at the end? The stone, the light catches a different shade, a brighter hue."

Timothy pulled his head away and looked at Rick.

"I think it's concrete. And, look again."

Timothy looked.

"Nothing but blackness at the end," Rick said. "It's hollow. There is something back there."

"Another gas pocket?"

"Nope. Checked." Rick waved a device in his hand. "I have the area cordoned off and all my men in the room-and-pillar sector, but eventually they'll wander back here. We must act soon. There is something manmade on the other side of that wall. It's no more than five feet, and I think we could blast —"

Before Rick could finish, the outline of a man appeared and lunged at him, plunging a knife in his gut.

Timothy jumped back.

Rick clawed at the attacker's shirt, bringing the man down on top of him.

The man pulled the knife from Rick's belly, and rapidly stabbed him twice more. Blood and steel glinted in Timothy's headlamp light.

Timothy glanced away and spotted a pick leaning against the machinery. He went for it.

The man lunged at him, but was tripped up in Rick's legs, falling to the ground.

Timothy planted the pick in the man's temple, pinning his body to the floor and freezing a malevolent expression of floating white eyes, white teeth, and red lips.

The attacker was in black head to toe, with his face scrubbed in coal dust. Probably one of the soldiers. Hardly any blood escaped the tightly wedged pick in the right side of his face.

Timothy let go and left the pick in, hurrying to Rick.

His friend was gurgling blood, bright red. Bubbles foamed at the corner of his lips. He coughed and lines of red splashed on his nose and cheeks. With a trembling hand, he dug into his pocket.

Timothy leaned over him and Rick reached for him, but only had the strength to brush his hand on Timothy's shoulder. With his other hand, he lifted a set of keys. He dropped them, and they landed on his chest.

"*T* . . . *N* . . . *T*."

He relaxed and was gone.

Timothy said a prayer over his friend, choking and crying between lines.

He took the soldier's knife and tucked it down his back. He took off down the mine. Near the entrance, he stopped at a door. His hands were shaking feverishly but he was finally able to get the key in, unlocked the door, and entered the storage room.

He scanned the equipment and replacement parts, until his eyes fell onto a stack of small, wooden crates.

TNT.

He picked a crate up – it was all he could carry – and stepped out of the room, locking the door behind him.

He considered doing the deed right then – moving Rick's body, rigging up the explosives, and blasting through. But he decided it was a task best saved for later, with Steve at his side.

The TNT had to be stashed.

He rode the elevator to the ground floor. He buried the box hastily under a stack of coal. Not safe, not smart, but it was the best he could do for now. He sprinted back to the elevator and hit the button for 14.

If only one of the soldiers was sent, it was probably to assassinate one person. Timothy's presence was unexpected. If the soldier was alone, that meant the others might be . . .

Timothy burst through the elevator doors. He sprinted the quarter length around the atrium, turned the corner into his corridor . . . and froze.

"Daddy!" Madeleine screamed.

Behind her and Liza, two of the soldiers. One had a knife entirely too close to Liza's cheek.

"That's far enough, Spencer."

"Let them go! They're children!"

"We are going to go for a walk. Back the way you came."

"Okay, okay. But at least take the knife away from my daughter's face." He looked at Liza. "Honey, just be calm. It'll be okay."

He looked back up at the soldiers, and then past them.

Behind the soldiers was the only hope in a hopeless situation. Timothy did his best not to give away what he saw.

It was Steve.

Timothy held up his hands. "Okay, okay. I'm moving." He took slow steps backwards.

Steve crept silently behind them, gaining inches.

Timothy backed up to the railing. It didn't escape him that he was touching the very spot Shelley leapt from.

"You are hurting her," Timothy said to the soldiers.

"Shut up. Keep moving to the elevator."

He did, and the soldiers followed his route. Steve moved closer and assumed an athletic crouch. As the soldiers came close to the railing, Steve pounced.

At the same moment, Timothy lunged for his girls.

Steve clocked one soldier before he knew what hit him.

Timothy had a grip on Madeleine's wrist.

The man flipped over the railing like a ragdoll.

The other soldier released Liza and went for Steve.

Steve clamped one hand around the knife-wielding hand of his assailant, and then he got other around the man's neck in a death grip.

The soldier chopped at Steve's arm, like chopping at a tree with a pool noodle.

"Come here girls, don't look." Timothy hugged his girls close. He didn't want them to see Steve kill the man.

The soldier dropped the knife and pulled hopelessly at Steve's arm. His face was turning purple. He was four inches off the ground.

Steve put his other hand around the man's neck and lifted him higher.

Timothy wondered if he was about to toss him over the edge as well.

He didn't. The man passed out.

They took him into the apartment. Steve had a roll of duct tape, and they wrapped him to the chair. They emptied his pockets, which only contained powdered alcohol packets and a set of keys to the holding cells.

"Thank God. Thank *you*." Timothy sat on the edge of a bed. "What are we going to do when he wakes up?"

"Ask him about the other ones. Still two more of these guys out there. If I were to guess, they are with Ashley, waiting to report on this kidnapping attempt. Or assassination attempt."

Timothy didn't want his girls out of his sight, but he didn't want them to see the interrogation. He sent them to the furthest corner, the best he could do. They were frightened, doe-eyed, and docile.

"Steve," Timothy said, half-whispering, "Rick is dead. He came up to get me and showed me something in the mine. When we were there, one of these guys killed him. I . . . I got lucky and hit the guy with a mining pick. So that means there's only one left."

"Jesus. What did Rick want to show you?"

"He had drilled through the north wall. About five feet through, there is some sort of open chamber. Before he died, he gave me keys and told me to get the TNT. I stashed a box down in the coal room."

The soldier mumbled. He was coming to.

Timothy tapped him on the cheek to help him along.

"What's your name?"

The man's eyes were half scared, but only half. "Grant."

"Okay, Grant. Where are your friends?"

"Fuck off."

Steve punched him, bloodied his nose.

They gave the man a moment.

The soldier licked his lips. "Sammy went to the mine to make quick work of that mine supervisor."

"Sammy's dead," Timothy said. "I killed him."

The soldier laughed through the blood.

Timothy pulled the knife out, removing the soldier's doubt. Grant looked shocked, then defeated.

"Congratulations, you killed an American hero."

"That hero *did* kill Rick, and he tried to kill me."
Timothy put the knife to the man's bruised throat.
"And you were going to kill my family."

"Okay... okay."

Timothy backed the blade away, stealing a glance
at his daughters.

"What about the other one?" Steve asked. "Who
was he headed out to kill?"

"Blaine stayed back. Drank too much last night,
and we didn't think we needed him."

"Where is he? Is he with Ashley?"

The soldier laughed. "We wouldn't mess with
her." He spit a blood-and-saliva mixture to the side.
"Blaine was with a woman on the third floor, Nora."

"What for?"

"What do you *think*? Room three-three-five." He
gave a sleazy smirk.

"Who is giving you these orders? Is it Ashley?"

He rolled his eyes. "My orders come from
Marcus Trencher. Know him?"

Timothy and Steve exchanged a look.

"You are in communication with Mr. Trencher?"
Steve asked.

"Not exactly. Before impact he hired us to watch
his property. Gave us bunker bids as a reward. Made
us take sedatives, put us on a helicopter. Made us
wear blindfolds on the way down and all. Told us to
maintain order by any means we see fit."

"Judge, jury, and executioners, just like that?"
Timothy said.

"Jared set off a catastrophe that might lead to starvation. You two . . . you guys were snooping around."

"Scared we might find something? Like a false wall hiding dead bodies?"

Grant released a long sigh and his head sunk for a moment. His head then rose as he inhaled deeply.

"We got down here, blindfolded, like I said. Mr. Trencher walked us to the coal depository and told us to wait outside. We listened through the door. Mr. Trencher congratulated the workers and gave a little speech. He had a table set up with cake and soda. They cheered. That niche in the chamber was the last modification made to the bunker.

"When he came out, he told us, 'Shoot them all, put the bodies in the alcove, and wall it over. The concrete mixer is in the southwest corner. Others will be down in two days. You'll find a nice care package in your assigned rooms.' He tossed us an envelope with our keys, and told us to have a nice life, and not to forget to mop up."

Grant licked his bloody lips again.

"It was surreal, and I don't know why we did it. I guess we felt we had to. We walked in, and just sprayed them. They were cornered. It really messed Jared up. Poor kid already had a brain injury. I don't think he fired. We all wished we didn't. But we unloaded the clips and broke down the guns and tossed them in the niche. A sick ceremony. We stacked the bodies on top of the guns, walled it up, and tried to forget about it."

His eyes looked woeful.

"I don't know what happened to me. I used to believe in the missions, but they became progressively fucked up those last few months. Yet, I kept following orders without question. A bunker bid, a pass to live, is a powerful bargaining chip."

The soldier slouched and stared into his lap.

"I'm sick of this shit. I loved Jared, really did, and I stood by and watched his throat . . ."

He grimaced and cocked his head to the side. He looked up at them.

"I understand you guys have to do what you have to do, but I can help you if you let me."

Timothy shook his head. "You said 'people.' You mean us? We came down two days later? So Marcus flew from Minnesota back to Sherman, Indiana, then back here for the move-in?"

The soldier looked confused.

"Minnesota?"

Chapter Thirty

Steve dragged Grant, still duct-taped to a chair, out in the hall. Timothy put the girls to bed.

"What do we do? We can't just let him go." Timothy tried to whisper quietly enough to not keep the girls awake and to not let the soldier hear from the other side of the door.

"There are the holding cells," Steve said.

"Where are the keys?"

They went into the hall and asked Grant.

"Blaine has them," he said.

"So we have to go to the third floor to get the keys from Blaine?" Timothy asked. "What if he won't give them to us?"

Grant smirked. "You'll have to convince him."

"Okay, well, you're going to help us, or you are going to rot in one of those cells downstairs."

"You'll need to untie me."

"I don't think so," Timothy said.

They cut Grant loose from the chair, then re-duct-taped his wrists for handcuffs.

It was 2 AM. The bunker was quiet, other than a few people on ground level still chasing bugs.

They got on the elevator.

"What room is this woman in?" Timothy asked.

"Three-three-five," Grant said.

"And who is she?" Steve asked.

"Nora is an outsider like you. She got here in an exchange of favors with Senator Granger from Minnesota. I guess Marcus owed him."

Grant cocked his head. "I don't know what Marcus got out of it – maybe this entire bunker – but the Senator got to stash Nora, his mistress, and his illegitimate son. Granger will never see them again, and it kept her quiet."

Maybe Marcus did get the bunker, Timothy thought as the elevator stopped at 3, but it seemed a lop-sided exchange. The Senator was a philanderer, and Marcus got a bunker in exchange for hiding a woman and a kid? The Senator was powerful, but so much prime underground real estate for a personal cover-up? Seemed unlikely. Marcus had to trade something to avert scrutiny on his selfish bunker project.

They headed down the hall and knocked on 335.

A woman's voice said: "Not now, I've already got someone."

Timothy nodded to Grant.

"Nora, it's Grant. I came to drag Blaine out of there. That's all, I promise."

The handle turned and the door opened.

"He's on the –" She stopped. Her eyes darted between Steve and Timothy, and the duct tape around Grant's hands. "What is this?"

"I've been a bad boy, Nora," Grant said with a smile.

She didn't laugh.

"We are only here for Blaine, honest."

Timothy saw she was a scared woman. Ragged and scrawny, but still attractive. There was also something hauntingly familiar about her. Timothy couldn't help but wonder what she looked like in good condition. Good enough to lure a married U.S. Senator, he figured.

She warily moved aside so they could go through the doorway.

Blaine was splayed on the bed with blood and a crust of powder caked on his nostrils. On a cafeteria tray beside the bed, there were lines of powdered alcohol.

"Idiot," Grant said. "Snorting that shit is terrible. Turns straight to glue and gives you an instant headache." He shuffled to the bed and nudged Blaine with his taped fists. "Blaine, get up."

The man mumbled something and went back to sleep. He wasn't walking out without help.

Timothy turned to Grant. "Where are the keys?"

"In his pocket, I guess."

Timothy and Steve picked Blaine up. As they got him upright, Nora dug in his pockets, pulling out a set of keys and tossing them on the bed. She stashed the alcohol packets.

Steve tossed Blaine over his shoulder and Timothy picked up the keys, feeling a pang of pity for the woman.

"Sorry, miss," Timothy said. "So sorry."

A baby began crying from the basic crib in the corner.

They made their way out of the apartment and back to the elevators.

"I feel bad for her," Grant said. "She was a doctor. A cardiologist. She didn't take the break-up with the Senator too well. We had all these alcohol packets from Mr. Trencher's care packages, a whole crate full, and we used them like money. The guys, Blaine mostly, got Nora hooked and used that to his advantage. She is an alcoholic, an addict thanks to them."

"The baby never bothered you guys?" Timothy asked.

"Don't look at me. I never partook. Neither did Jared. But, yeah, the baby bothered me. I don't think it bothered them. If we had Child Protective Services down here, I doubt she'd get to keep the little guy."

Inside the elevator, Timothy pressed the ground floor button. He was disgusted with Grant. The man had a knife on one of his daughters not long before.

They made their way to the holding cells, and Timothy opened one using the keys they confiscated. The old man was still in there, so they released him. Steve laid Blaine on the cot, as Timothy cut Grant free from the duct tape.

"We'll bring you food and water tomorrow morning," Timothy said as he began to shut the door.

"I remember the walk," Grant said before Timothy could lock it. "I am a SEAL, remember? I memorized the step counts. Ashley has some sort of map of the bunker – a layout. I've seen it. The elevator isn't on it. If you can steal that blueprint, I could show you where it goes. It's . . . odd."

"Don't need to steal a map," Timothy said. "I've made my own. Tomorrow, maybe."

Timothy shut the door with a satisfying *clink*.

Chapter Thirty-One

The prediction that no one would see Marcus for a week turned out to be false.

It was closer to three.

He fumed over the embarrassing date. It was only a simple movie date, yet he cried – and almost *talked*. It was a show of weakness he vowed would never happen again.

A few days after the date, Jenna approached his door and buzzed.

"Marcus, can we talk?" she said into the intercom.

He didn't answer.

What could possibly be the basis of their relationship? What could he possibly say? He had only entertained the company of women for showmanship and sex, in exchange for expensive jewelry or prestige, or whatever they wanted. He never asked. What would be the arrangement with Jenna? *Feelings?* Immaterial, unquantifiable. What about . . . *love?*

How pathetic, he thought. Deep down, he wanted that motherly embrace, exactly the way Jenna held him in the theatre.

He couldn't control the desire. Worse, he couldn't express it.

Prisoner in his own mind, his own apartment.

* * *

Life went on elsewhere in the bunker, but with an air of melancholy. Marcus rarely added any enjoyment when he was present yet was somehow able to detract from it with his absence. Fun and laughter felt inappropriate with someone suffering in their midst, even if it was detached, antisocial Marcus locked in his room.

The bunker *was* Marcus. Even absent, he was everywhere. It was Trencher's bunker.

"Is he collecting his piss in jars yet?" Robby asked while digging into a plate of scrambled eggs.

"No, but he isn't doing so hot," Henry said, the only one who had seen Marcus in the last 20 days.

"Has he ever done this before?" Mercedes asked.

"Oh, yeah," Robby said. "Since childhood. He's disappeared for days and come out like nothing happened, miraculously self-cured from whatever the fuck he had. That's why I'm not too worried. I've seen it before."

"Shouldn't we do something, though?" Audrey asked. "We can't just forget about him."

"Might not have to do anything," Brittney said. "He'll be starved out any day now."

279

Henry shook his head, "Marcus can survive on Soylent longer than any of us. I'm sure he has a stash up there."

"Three weeks' worth?"

Henry shrugged. "He might have snuck out at night for refills."

"Let's cook him a real meal. What's his favorite food?" Becky asked.

"Chicken fingers and fries," Robby said. "Any of that still in the freezer?"

"We'll make it from scratch," Becky said. "We can spare a chicken."

"With honey mustard," Robby added. "It's a deal breaker."

"Got it. We'll make it tonight. I'll deliver it," Brad said.

"Are you going to try to talk him down?" Mariya asked.

"Absolutely not," Brad said. "I'm going to give him his chicken fingers and fries, and honey mustard. Then I'll ask if he needs anything else, and leave. If he wants to talk, I'll listen. Otherwise, telling him what to do will only make it worse. People in his state, especially as smart as he is, can sense motive from a mile away, even if one's not there."

* * *

Brad crossed the bunker, plate in hand, and buzzed at Marcus's door. The lock was instantly released. Apparently, he was expected.

The apartment was impeccably clean. Marcus sat in an overstuffed chair in the living room just as he entered.

"What's up, Brad?" Marcus said with more cheer than Brad expected.

"We made chicken tenders and fries downstairs. Henry and Robby said you might like some."

Marcus looked surprised. "Wow. Sure, sounds good."

Brad placed the plate on the ottoman in front of Marcus.

Marcus didn't move. His fingers were tapping the armrest rapidly and his right foot on his crossed leg bounced so fast it was a blur.

Brad headed to the door but stopped and turned as he put his hand on the knob.

"Did you want anything to drink?"

Marcus already had fries stuffed in his mouth. He shook his head as he chewed and swallowed. "No, no drink."

Brad lingered for a moment. It seemed that was as much interaction as he was going to get. Not even a thank you. He turned once again for the door.

"This is amazing, Brad," Marcus said around a mouthful of food. "What do you put in it?"

Brad smiled. "Secret family recipe, my mother's. The key is to keep it simple."

Marcus grunted in agreement.

"It was my inheritance, no joke," Brad said. "My mother passed away when I was in high school."

Marcus hesitated. He took the next bite in a slower motion.

"Breast cancer. She was still young, a single mom. We didn't have much. The lawyer literally handed me a scrap of paper with that recipe. Turned out to be the most valuable item."

Marcus remained silent, avoided eye contact. He chewed a little slower.

"To make things worse," Brad continued, "my idiot sister wrecked the car, then my girlfriend broke up with me later that school year. She said I was depressed and no fun. Don't blame her now, but it only made me more depressed. I don't buy into all that Freudian bullshit. I'm a simple man, but the loss of my mother, then my high school sweetheart, really fucked me up for a while. You know, regarding women."

Marcus took another bite, but still didn't say anything.

"I skidded by, graduated barely, and was on track to becoming your run-of-the-mill food industry fuck up. Tattoos, pills, and grills, man. Long story short, I met Becky. Hot little part-time waitress finishing nursing school. She took care of me, like my mother. Didn't put up with my mopey bullshit, also like my mother. Hell, even in one dark moment I accused her of trying to replace my mother – my last-ditch effort at scaring her off and staying comfortably unhappy. It didn't work."

He paused, wondering if he was wearing out his welcome. Marcus didn't indicate one way or the other.

"Got into culinary school. Tried quitting that, but Becky wouldn't let me. Finally, I just said *Fuck it, I'm going to be happy.* Finished school, opened a restaurant that saved my life in more ways than one, and I've been happy ever since."

Marcus had stopped eating but kept his eyes on his plate.

"That's good," Marcus said. "Sorry for your loss."

"Everything happens for a reason." Brad held up his hands. "I'm rambling, sorry. Enjoy your meal." He turned to leave.

"Brad? Can you do me a favor?"

"Sure."

"Can you send Robby up?"

"Sure." Brad nodded and left.

* * *

Marcus finished the last of the chicken tenders. Brad's sob story wasn't enough to kill his appetite.

What was he trying to do? Get me to talk about my mom? Friendly gesture and talk...or passive-aggressive ploy to let me know my problems are not unique, and to get over it? Nice try.

He picked up his laptop and opened the surveillance program. He had watched the plotting and inception of the meal idea. He'd done hardly anything except watch them, all of them, for the past three weeks.

Not once did he hear anyone say a bad thing about him. Not once. Only concern. It hurt him that they cared for such a despicable person.

He watched Brad return to the café to an eager audience. *Here is where he gloats about his clever*

283

psychobabble bullshit. He tried to outsmart you, Marcus. He's a snake. Watch him bask in praise.

"Well, how was it?" Jenna asked. "What'd he look like? Did he have a beard?"

"It was fine," Brad said. "He was clean-shaven."

"C'mon, Brad," Jenna said. "What did you talk about?"

"Can't say. That's between us. But he did like the food."

They were stunned.

"You were up there for five minutes. You didn't just watch him eat. What did he say?"

"I'm sorry, but I wouldn't be a trustworthy person if I ran back down here and gave you a transcript of our conversation. Can't do it. Won't do it."

They took the hint. But you could almost see the gears turning in their head.

Brad held up a hand with one finger.

"He did ask for one thing. He asked that Robby come up."

Robby looked around at each face as if he were trying to think of an excuse. "I was going to go for a swim."

The others groaned, and Brittney threw a French fry at his head, missing.

"Fine," he said, standing up. "I'll go."

Marcus set the laptop on the arm of the chair.

* * *

Marcus met him at the door and hugged him. "Robby, my man! How are you?"

Robby smiled. "I'm good, bro. Livin' the dream."

"Oh, how is – what's her name again?"

"Melonie." Robby frowned. "She's pregnant."

Marcus's face was blank for a moment, and something seemed to connect in his eyes. Then he broke out a smile.

"Congratulations! We'll have to have a shower! Wait, that's for the women. We'll throw a party!"

Robby was skeptical of Marcus's elated response, but it was better than anything he expected. "Thanks, but we haven't told anyone yet."

"Why not?"

"I am a little worried Audrey might get upset that Melonie is pregnant. She likes me. So, I'm trying to think up a way to break the news."

"I don't know. I'm not exactly the most experienced guy to get advice from. Perhaps tell Audrey privately first, and then make the announcement to everyone else. Just don't shock her in front of everyone."

"Listen to you, love guru." Robby grinned. "You should start an advice column."

Marcus shook his head. "I don't have a clue. I'm hopeless on that front."

"Look man," Robby said, "I would love to dick around with you up here, but I have court time reserved. I'd invite you, but I have a bet with the others that you'll stay up here for another week."

"Hah! You are just scared. Still have that feeble backhand?"

"You still on that soft second serve bullshit?"

285

Marcus was laughing.

"Seriously, want to play? Everybody else down here sucks," Robby said.

Marcus paused, then nodded. "Yeah. Yeah, I do."

"Big mistake, but okay. Let's go."

As Marcus moved forward to stand, his right palm mashed down on the laptop keyboard. Mute was toggled on.

"... *needs to be refrigerated after opening ... I got the dishes, don't worry ...* "

Robby cocked his head. It was Becky's voice coming out of the computer, out of the café.

Marcus slammed the laptop shut.

Robby stared Marcus down.

"... What was that?" Robby took a step closer. "Answer very carefully."

Marcus stood, palms out, mouth agape. He only shook his head.

"Just audio, or do you have video too?"

No answer.

Robby cocked his head again, then shook it.

"I'm sorry," Marcus said. "Look – watch me, I'll delete the program. Please –"

"You're sick, Marcus. Been for a while."

"I'll delete it, right now. Robby, you can't tell the others." Marcus grabbed Robby's forearm.

Robby yanked his arm away and burned his gaze into Marcus. "Delete it. I won't tell, but only because it would ruin all sense of comfort we've managed to work up in this fucked up place."

Robby looked away for a moment, shook his head, then stared back at Marcus. "And you . . . you can go *fuck yourself.*"

* * *

Marcus stood at his door, shaking. After a minute, he went to the laptop and opened the menu to uninstall. He wiped away tears.

Then, he didn't do it.

He hit the tab key, changing the camera footage each time. He hit it again and again, looking for nothing in particular, seeing different aspects of life in the bunker as it happened live.

He stopped on Robby's room. He was thrashing about and throwing things. He picked up a chair and placed it in the corner directly beneath the hidden camera, disguised as a Wi-Fi device. Robby scowled before punching it as hard as he could.

Marcus recoiled as if Robby had hit him.

The broadcast ceased.

* * *

Robby's hand was gashed and bleeding profusely. Audrey appeared in the open doorway.

"Robby, what happened?"

He held up his trembling hand, blood streaking down his forearm.

"We have to go to the hospital now."

She grabbed him and dragged him to the elevator and across the bunker proper.

Robby watched Marcus's windows until he was under them at the hospital doors.

Audrey washed the cuts. He didn't say a word while she bandaged him up.

"Do I need stitches?"

"No. Can you tell me what happened up there?"

He ignored her question. "Remember what happened last time we were in here?"

There was no flirtation in his voice. Still, she blushed.

She looked around and bit her lip. "Are you sure you are –"

He pulled her hair down as he stood and towered over her. He kissed her forcefully. He spun her around.

She became submissive.

He was rough. Then he was done and collapsed over her.

Audrey caught her breath and managed to slide from beneath him.

He stood hunched over the table.

She adjusted her clothing.

She put her hands on his shoulders and said, *"You animal."*

She tried kissing his cheek, but he shrugged her off.

"What's wrong?"

"Melonie is pregnant."

He walked out.

Chapter Thirty-Two

Liza's fever remained persistent, even worsening over the week. She missed school, and Steve covered for Timothy in the coal depository, also making most of the food and water deliveries to their prisoners.

Timothy hadn't a clue what was making his daughter sick.

He couldn't stand the thought of asking anything from Susan, Rick's widow, since her dead husband's association with Timothy led to his death. She showed no animosity, but he felt guilty.

When she began seeing the girls less and less, she confronted Timothy, said there was no need for forgiveness because he did nothing wrong. She loved the girls and wanted to see them. It helped her through her grieving more than anything. As for the fever, she couldn't figure it out either, but said she knew how to alleviate it.

Timothy had taken Liza to the bunker doctor, but he just shrugged carelessly and spared a few aspirin. *No more than an out-of-practice small town pill pusher,* Timothy thought.

He knew of another doctor – Nora, the Senator's alcoholic mistress, and part-time prostitute. He didn't think bunker authorities were aware of her medical expertise, because she was never assigned any work. Perhaps her habit got in the way. He decided it was worth paying her a visit.

"I'm not feeling well, sorry," she said through the closed door.

"Neither is my daughter. She's had a fever for over a month now. I was hoping you could help."

There was a pause, and then much to Timothy's relief, she cracked the door and peered out. She was frightfully pale and gaunt, wearing a white gown. Timothy was struck by her similarities to Shelley. She wore the same standard-issue gown as Shelley had on the night of her death.

Nora closed her eyes and rubbed her head. "Come in, I can't stand long."

He stood awkwardly in the middle of the room. She made straight for the bed, laid down, and continued rubbing her head with her eyes closed.

The baby began to fuss.

Timothy approached the crib. "May I? Do you mind?"

She flicked her hand to indicate it was okay.

He picked up and gently rocked the baby. He pulled up a chair, wondering how long it had been since she held the boy.

"I have to use formula to feed him," she said. "I'm trying to get clean now. I'm a week in. It's not easy without proper food and medicine. I rationed what powder I had left to lessen the blow, but that ran out two days ago."

"I'd like to help." He moved the baby boy to his knee. The baby giggled and swung his arms.

"He likes you." She managed a painful smile that quickly faded. "It was only two of them."

"Pardon?"

She sat up, an agonizing process. "I only *entertained* two of those soldiers, and not as often as you might think. And both are dead."

Timothy made a nonjudgmental expression.

"I brought my disease down here with me. I had no expectations of living, no notification of a bunker bid, they called it. I hired a nanny and drank too much. I hardly remember the first six months of his life. His birthday is coming up. January twenty-third."

The day of the public announcement about the asteroid.

"These men in black took my son and me without warning, straight to the middle of nowhere in Indiana about a week before impact. I was on the same plane as you, you know, right beside your family. I was going to introduce myself, but then came the sedative and blindfolds." She paused. "Sorry for your loss."

Timothy tried to recall the plane. Madeleine was in rare form and Shelley wasn't happy. He couldn't recall much else.

"I bet you are wondering who the father is."

He already knew, but he didn't say.

"My son's name is Benjamin, Benjamin Weinstein. I'll be damned if I let him have his father's last name." She paused, taking a drink of water. "I was a career woman, worked twice as hard as any man around me. The upper classes were full of assholes, but that didn't stop me from falling for the king of them all. I began a relationship with Greg Granger, Senator from Minnesota."

Timothy kept his expression as neutral as possible. He didn't want to let on what he knew. It was best to let her talk.

"I started attending fundraising events during that Medicare fiasco. Met him at one. Boy did he ever have the dark triad – narcissism, Machiavellianism, psychopathy – had them in spades. These things have a built-in invisibility cloak upon first impression. I was swept off my feet."

She licked her lips, eyes half-shut.

"It only took a simple Google search to find out he was married, but I was too far gone. It's embarrassing, especially as a highly educated woman, but I fell for it all. He was going to leave her after the next election, et cetera, et cetera. He gave me gifts, was a great lover, and took me out toward the end when it no longer mattered. He even took me to Marcus Trencher's New Year's Eve party. After that, he cut off contact. He suddenly decided to become an ideal husband."

Nora went quiet.

"I knew Marcus very well," Timothy said. "He's why I'm down here, for better or worse." He paused. "He made some sort of deal with Senator Granger to secure the bunker bids for this place. Almost everyone down here is from Sherman, Indiana. Would you know anything about that?"

She thought for a moment. "No, sorry. I was kept in the dark regarding his political dealings. He preferred to ignore my intelligence and I didn't so much mind it. I suppose I had something to do with it."

Timothy moved Benjamin to his shoulder, who was beginning to fuss. "It just doesn't make any sense. It doesn't seem feasible for Marcus to gain a whole bunker in Senator Granger's home state just to hide a mistress. No offense."

"None taken." She looked confused. "So, you are telling me we are in Minnesota? Or, under it?"

Timothy nodded.

"I was flown to Indiana, put on a plane, drugged, and then flown right back to Minnesota?"

He nodded again.

"You are right, doesn't make sense," she said. "But these are powerful men we are talking about. Rules and logic don't necessarily apply to them. Build a bridge to nowhere, ignore science, deal a bunker for a mistress and illegitimate child – politics as usual."

Timothy placed Benjamin in the crib and went to her.

She got to her feet.

Timothy put his hand on her bony back to support her. When she nearly fell, without thinking, he placed his other hand on her upper chest. He could feel her heart thumping. She put her arm around him, looked him in the eyes, somehow unashamed and unembarrassed. They were intimately close. He removed his hand from her chest and looked away. She gained her balance.

"Let's go see your daughter."

"Are you sure you feel okay enough?"

"It'll be good for me to get out. Let me get dressed." She turned and lifted her gown over her head. She wore nothing underneath.

Timothy turned away, unashamed and unembarrassed, and unsure how he felt about it.

* * *

The girls were in the apartment with Susan. Madeleine was playing with her paper dolls on the floor. Liza was in bed with Susan sitting at her side, stroking her hair.

"Hi, Daddy," Madeleine said. "Who is that?"

"This is Benjamin. Want to play with him?"

She lit up as Timothy set the baby down and made sure he could sit upright by himself.

"And this is Nora," Timothy said. "She's a doctor."

Madeleine, already enamored by the real live baby, didn't respond.

Nora walked to Liza's bedside and Susan, the former nurse, caught her up as best she could. Then Susan got up, and hugged Timothy. "I think she's in good hands. I'll see them tomorrow." She nodded to Nora, and then left.

"You said it had gotten worse this week?" Nora asked.

Timothy nodded.

"What have you eaten this week?" Nora asked Liza.

"Nothing. Just the soy stuff. And I drink water." Nora put a hand on her burning cheek and gave a comforting smile before standing and turning to Timothy.

"I think it's a minor allergy to something in the Soylent, but when that's all she is getting, it's enough to make her fairly sick."

Timothy nodded slowly. "The more I think about it, she did improve after the Christmas meal, and she skipped the Soylent meal before and after." It seemed obvious to Timothy, and the solution seemed even more obvious, but he still asked. "What should we do?"

"She needs real food."

"Not the easiest thing to get around here these days."

Nora sighed. "I know. We have to talk to that woman in charge, or the committee, tomorrow. I'll go with you. Maybe they'll listen to a doctor."

Timothy thanked her and offered to escort her back to her apartment. She picked Benjamin up, insisted that she was feeling better, and left. He closed the door behind her, lingered a moment, and returned to Liza's side.

"Dad, she looks sicker than me."

"She is, honey, she is." He patted her head. "But we are going to help her, and she is going to help us."

"She's pretty," Liza said.

"She's a doctor. I'm glad I found her to help you."

"Daddy," Madeleine said, "I like Benjamin. He's my friend." She put her paper doll down and sighed in deep five-year-old thought. "Well, he's really more like my little brother."

295

Chapter Thirty-Three

Steve gave Timothy a hard time for stashing a box of dynamite under a pile of coal next to a wall that butted against the bunker power station. They moved it to a safer location down chamber and covered it up with equipment and unused bags of cement.

"How's Liza?" Steve asked.

"Not good, but I think we finally figured out what was wrong. Nora thinks it's an allergy to something in the Soylent. It makes sense."

"So, Liza needs real food, right? How are you going to arrange that in the middle of a famine?" He wiped sweat from his brow. "I haven't dropped this much weight this fast since the time I tried squatting 650 in college."

"I don't know, man. I'm meeting Nora at lunch and we are going to go to Ashley to see if we can get some green ration cards."

Steve looked at him, a little smirk on his face.

Timothy had caught an odd look from Susan the night before, and Maddie's comment about Benjamin being like her brother . . . Apparently, they were all thinking things about him and Nora, which was weird. Maybe it was just his imagination.

"Our boys in the clink are getting pretty cranky," Steve said. "I almost feel bad for them."

"Don't. But we do need to talk to them. We'll do that after lunch."

* * *

Timothy knew the real food was still being grown from the undamaged crops, and the chickens were still laying eggs. In fact, the chickens were the only happy and well-fed residents of the bunker after the roach infestation.

The miners had priority over everyone, while the farmers took their fair share. Monitors were implemented to make sure *"fair"* was very little. A one real meal per week for everyone else was tentatively scheduled to begin in two weeks. That would be too long for Liza to wait.

Both Steve and Timothy found it unfair that they did not fall under the same category as the miners. Their job was every bit as physical. Timothy decided it would be his backup angle if Ashley showed no sympathy for his daughter's plight.

The line at the cafeteria resembled photos from the Great Depression. People were unhappy but didn't dare to act up and jeopardize their meager ration of Soylent.

Timothy spotted Nora ahead of them in the line with Benjamin's head on her shoulder. She turned and saw him, smiling wanly. She received her serving of Soylent and some baby formula, and then waited on the side for them.

The soup pots were filled with premixed Soylent. The grumpy lunch lady ladled a bowlful for each of them and waved them along. Before the next in line pushed him along, he handed the lunch lady a note.

"I'm in charge of feeding the prisoners."

She begrudgingly spared him one bowl and they met up with Nora and Benjamin.

"Hello, Nora. This is Steve."

"We've met. Glad to know your name." She smiled.

They found a table along the edge where the line no longer stretched. Nora shook up the formula and fed Benjamin. Timothy and Steve ate the chalky sustenance. They made faces like they were taking shots of moonshine.

"You look nice," Timothy said. "I mean, better."

"Don't feel it but thank you." She wiped Benjamin's mouth.

"Nora, the whole arrangement made to get us down here isn't the only strange thing we've uncovered."

She looked up from Benjamin as if to say, *Oh really?* and returned her attention to the baby.

"We mapped the place out and a few things don't make sense. For example –"

"There's our girl," Nora said.

Ashley had walked right past them. Timothy saw her pants were noticeably tight.

"I'm sorry, but I've got to say it – she is *definitely* gaining weight," Timothy said.

"That's for damn sure," Steve said. "I think she might be causing the famine, not the roaches."

Nora looked at them like they were stupid. "You guys are not only mean, but you don't know anything, do you?"

Timothy opened his mouth to reply, but nothing came out. He didn't have a clue.

"She's pregnant," Nora said.

"No way." He took another look at Ashley.

"Watch," Nora said. "She is going to that pantry for neonatal vitamins. It's where the baby formula is stored."

Sure enough, Ashley made her way past the counter and grabbed something from the pantry. She also got a fill of Soylent (cutting line in front of twenty people) before making her way back toward them. Timothy turned back to Nora, who was grinning.

"Who the hell would..." Timothy paused. "Now, for the record, I *never* talk this poorly about women – but who would ever..."

Steve elbowed Timothy. Ashley was passing.

Nora laughed.

"Excuse me, Ashley," Timothy said, raising his hand. "Ashley!"

She stopped, sighed loudly, and turned around. She tucked the vitamins in her elastic waistband. "What is it, Mr. Spencer?"

"I know our last meeting wasn't pleasant, but I was hoping you could help me with something."

She looked at him impatiently.

"My daughter is allergic to something in the Soylent. She is getting very sick. She needs real food."

"It's true," Nora said. "I examined her, and symptoms are consistent with an allergy."

"And you are?"

"Doctor Nora Weinstein."

"Huh." She raised her chin and looked back at Timothy. "Well I'm sorry, but that is something you should take to the committee. You people think I run things around here. I don't. Have a nice day." She left the dining hall.

Timothy got up and went after her. He came up behind her in the hallway.

"Who's the father?"

She froze, and then turned slowly. "What are you talking about, Spencer?"

"Who is the father?"

"None of your business."

Timothy realized she wasn't so much *unattractive* as she was indescribably *plain*.

"I have a livelier social life down here than you give me credit for."

Of all the lies she had told, this was the most unbelievable. Still, he didn't like how personal he had gotten and didn't want to take it any further if he didn't have to.

"Look, I'm sorry about your daughter." Her guard came down, a little. "The committee overlooked you guys down in the coal depository. There are only two of you and you do some heavy lifting. Maybe I can convince them to include you with the miners. It's the best I can do, honest."

"Do it now."

"Tonight?" She smirked. "I need to go take my vitamins. Are we done here?"

Timothy nodded.

He returned to the dining hall and relayed the news.

"My ration is Liza's," Steve said. "If we get that increase, along with yours, that will cover, what, five meals a week? It's better than nothing."

"Steve, I can't possibly ask you to do that."

"You aren't. I'm doing it no matter what. I've still got a good twenty pounds to spare."

"I hardly have an appetite," Nora said. "I'll give whatever I get. I can make up for some of it in baby formula. They don't keep close inventory on it, and it tastes better than Soylent."

Timothy was speechless. He took a hand from both and squeezed. He never imagined he'd have such friends.

* * *

Grant stood as soon as the cell door opened. Blaine was lying on the floor.

Grant went right for the bowl of Soylent. But instead of slurping it down, he brought to his friend. He ignored Timothy, Steve, and Nora while he delicately elevated Blaine's head and fed him. He followed it with what remained in their water jug.

Steve took the water bottle and refilled it at a spout outside the door. The disappointment of receiving only one bowl was shown in Grant's face, but he didn't say anything out loud.

"No sympathy for the devil, right?" He patted Blaine's chest.

"How's he doing?" Timothy asked.

"For the first week he was saying crazy shit, shook like a leaf."

"Delirium tremens," Nora said. "I wasn't far from it myself."

"I thought he wasn't going to make it. Now, it's just the worse hangover of his life."

Grant took the full jug from Steve and thanked him. He took a swig and gave Blaine another sip.

"How are ya, Timmy?" Grant asked. "Haven't seen you in a while."

"It's Timothy. I've been busy." He reminded himself that Grant had a knife near his five-year-old daughter.

"Right." Grant moved to the cot and sat. "Hey Timothy, did you bring those drawings down? I've been dying to show you. Been paranoid for weeks I'd forget the steps, but I didn't."

Timothy pulled a paper from his back pocket and unfolded it. "This is a drawing of the seventh floor." He set it on Blaine's chest in front of Grant.

"Got a pen?"

"I'll do the drawing." He didn't trust the trained killer.

"Okay, we'll have to go and draw it backwards." Grant closed his eyes. "Off the elevator, it went 16 west, door, 18, door –"

"Slow down, slow down." Timothy moved the paper to the floor for a better writing surface. "Ready."

"Numbers are steps, about three feet." He closed his eyes again. "After that last door, it was 63 headed south, southwest. Then big door, 30, another big door, and . . . and that's it." He opened his eyes.

Timothy scribbled the sequence at the top of the page. He nodded at Grant to join him on the floor. Steve moved next to him.

Timothy pointed his pen on the map at the big metal door west of Ashley's office. He drew a dotted line directly north, scaled roughly to 90 feet. Grant nodded approval. He drew a dark dash to symbolize a door.

"This next part, you said south, southwest? How much south and how much west?"

"I'm not going to do anything stupid. Give me the pen and I'll get the line started. You can finish since you know the scale."

Timothy thought for a moment, then handed him the pen.

At the end of the long, slanted line, he angled directly east, drew in two dashes for doors, and put a box around the letter E for the elevator. They studied it.

Timothy shook his head. "Must be off. This doesn't clear the outer rings on 11 or 12."

"I think you are dead on," Grant said. "I wasn't the only one counting steps. We're SEALs, after all. One day we got curious and explored, kind of like you. We knocked on room 1118. It was a thud. We tried knocking the door down, but it was solid, there was no give. Nothing but concrete behind it. Same on 1218. They're fakes. Elevator runs right through there."

"I'll have to check those floor plans."

"Check away," Grant said. "Not even Steve over here could break those doors down. It's there."

Steve crouched down to get a better look. He put a finger on the corridor closest to the bunker. "Did you hear any running water in here?"

"Come to think of it . . . no. But along here, I did." He pointed to the long, diagonal line.

"Maybe Ashley was telling the truth about the water treatment facility, but it is further out than she made it sound."

"That whole stretch, we were walking on plastic. I think we were in a tube, like in that part in *E.T.*, you know? I could feel it in the air. The others could, too. Sammy coughed on purpose, and the echo seemed off."

Timothy didn't know anything about water treatment facilities, but he knew they had several components and required a lot of space. It seemed ordinary. Ashley was telling the truth.

He pointed further up the line. "Here, looks like you passed right over the Soylent feed tanks on the north end of the cafeteria. I'll have to double check the ground floor sketch, but I'm almost positive."

Grant thought. "I know I didn't step on anything abnormal, but Jared said he did. He must have veered, because we were all in a line and nobody else felt it. Said it was rounded, like a manhole cover. I thought he was full of shit, feeling that through the plastic and all, but maybe it really was the top of the Soylent tanks."

But does it matter? Timothy thought.

Timothy's eye wandered from the new lines on the page to Rick's amendments to the mining tunnel. He realized he hadn't drawn in the space on the other side of the northern wall. He drew a question mark above the tunnel and circled it. Relative to most everything else, it was in the middle of nowhere.

"What's that for?" Grant asked.

"The night your friend killed Rick, he was showing me something in the mine. He drilled about five feet into the northern wall and broke through into an open space . . . a cavity of some sort. We think it is manmade."

"How are you going to get through?"

"I was hoping you could help us with that. That mine has nearly collapsed once before, and I haven't a clue on how to work dynamite."

"*I do,*" a voice said.

They all turned.

It was Blaine, back from the dead.

"I'm Irish," he said. "I drink, fight, and blow stuff up." His eyes were still closed.

Steve and Timothy stood and walked to the cell door. Timothy knew what Grant wanted.

"Nurse him back to health," Timothy said. "We'll get you all we can."

Steve refilled the water jug.

"After we blow that wall down," Timothy said, "you'll be free to go."

They shook on it.

Chapter Thirty-Four

Robby would give little detail about his visit with Marcus. He only said Marcus insulted his intelligence, they scuffled, and it was over. He hurt his hand during the confrontation. That was it.

Henry said he found it believable that Marcus insulted Robby, but he could hardly believe it came to blows. They ragged on each other all the time, for years. They never actually fought.

Audrey also expressed doubt about the fighting, or at least Robby's injury. She claimed to have seen him immediately after leaving Marcus's apartment, and hadn't noticed his bleeding hand. But Audrey said she heard a commotion in Robby's room and went to check on him, and only then she saw his hand injured. She also noted that he had scrapes, not bruises.

Melonie made a sarcastic remark about Audrey checking his room, and then *they* were at it.

Marcus was taking no visitors, which at this point was normal.

Henry wanted to mediate. He'd done it before. But Marcus would not acknowledge him, and Robby kept shrugging him off.

* * *

Robby destroyed as many cameras as he could find. He cornered Kent and made him take him around to every supposed Wi-Fi device in the bunker, without telling him why.

When Kent picked up the shattered pieces of one and recognized the components, he said: "This is a camera."

He checked his tablet and found that access to the cloud didn't falter. He caught on. If it had been a Wi-Fi access point, he would only get spinning wheels.

"Did you know about this?" Robby asked.

"No, I didn't."

They worked as a team and avoided the others, picking off cameras only when they knew they wouldn't be seen.

Robby swore Kent to secrecy. Kent understood the ramifications. The only person that scared Kent more than Robby was Marcus.

* * *

With the cameras and speakers being taken out in the bunker, Marcus grew paranoid. Or rather, more paranoid. They were plotting against him.

He could pick up just enough conversation to glean what was going on. They were so *open* about it.

He assumed Robby told everyone about the cameras. Kent helped him remove them. Marcus only saw those two, but he was certain the others were off camera, pointing them out for them.

Henry was distancing himself. *Judas.*

And Mariya encouraged him.

Marcus was sure Brad didn't tell everyone about their conversation. At first. But he did later. He even embellished it, told everyone that Marcus had cried. He was a liar, a snake.

He had been right all along, about all of them. His paranoia told him so.

It told him that even his beloved Brittney joined in. She had befriended all the women he dated behind his back. The women made fun of him, even insulting his performance in bed. Now Brittney was telling everyone in the bunker, men and women.

His paranoia informed him that Jenna was mocking him and admitted that she only wanted his secrets. He was right about her, too.

He was positive he foiled an assassination attempt. The others convinced Mercedes to poison his water supply through the pipes leading to his apartment. She didn't want to, but she did. He had the sewage blueprints memorized, and after scrutinizing them long enough, he found the pipe she was using. The poison would be removed before it reached anywhere else. She was smart about it. But he was smarter.

Instead of water, he had to mix his Soylent with vodka. A chemical reaction removed the effects of the alcohol, so he wouldn't get drunk.

He was smarter than them all, than all of them combined.

There was one concern, and it dampened his mood considerably. People were breaking into his bedroom. He could hear them.

He locked the double doors and blocked them with the sofa.

Did Senator Muehlbauer get to the bunker construction crew? He must have. There was no other way.

But it didn't matter. He was leaving soon.

He heard the tunnel boring machine approaching, felt the vibrations. His state of mind gave him superhuman senses, his mind told him. The tunnel connection was only hours away, and that was all that mattered. He could make his escape then.

He checked the tunnel every 27 minutes. After his last check, as soon as he had returned to his bathroom, he heard a blast. The workers, 25 miles down the tunnel, decided to blast the final separation in celebration. It was reckless, but he loved it! It was hilarious! He packed a bottle of cognac in his bag so he could congratulate the workers when he saw them.

The wait proved to be too much. He knew the workers were still miles down the tunnel, but he wanted to see their lights if he could.

When he opened the door, he was stunned to see a worker the others had sent ahead. He must've had a vehicle. He got there so fast.

"You there! Welcome!" Marcus jogged to greet the man, the first contact between the bunkers.

Marcus hugged him.

The man looked every bit as surprised as he was.

309

"So glad you made it, and not a moment too soon!" He patted the man on the back. "I heard you blast through the end there . . . I love it!"

The man looked back down the tunnel but couldn't find any words.

"Here, I brought you something." Marcus took out the bottle of cognac and shoved it in the man's hands. "To celebrate! Go share it with the others, or not, I don't care. I'll bring more!"

"Thanks, mister," the man said.

"I just need to gather a few things. I'll meet everyone here in a couple hours when they catch up to you. Then I'll be ready to go."

Marcus ran back down the tunnel. In his apartment, he gathered his things. He put a bottle of champagne in his bag for the workers, thought about it, took it out, and replaced it with whiskey. He opened a cabinet and grabbed a pistol. He laughed at the thought of shooting out his windows.

Instead, he refrained and stuck it in his jacket pocket.

Before he left, he decided he needed his favorite drink. Coffee. It was, he mused, the only thing he would miss.

* * *

Melonie asked Henry and Mariya to make sure nobody skipped as they gathered in the café for dinner. Nobody else was tipped off about the surprise.

310

Audrey and Marcus were the only two missing. Robby waited outside the café in the gardens. He stood in the gazebo and watched the others trickle in. He thought about life, Melonie, Audrey, his unborn child, his mother and father. None of it made him happy.

A fish, belly up, was stuck to the rocks in the stream beneath him.

He looked up at the dome. Storm clouds were gathering.

"Come on, babe," Melonie said. "It's time." She took his hand and led him back into the café.

He grabbed a glass and tapped it with a spoon. "Everyone, Melonie and I have an announcement." He looked at her and retook her hand. "We're pregnant."

Everyone broke out in cheer. They threw their hands up and hugged each other, and then lined up to hug and kiss the expecting parents.

Mercedes said, "*I knew it!*"

It was all enough to make Robby smile, something he hadn't done in a while.

Then it grew quiet.

Marcus appeared, casually walking across the café, straight to the coffee machine. He ignored everyone and the excitement that had erupted a moment before.

Henry stepped forward.

"Marcus, did you hear? Melonie's pregnant. Robby is going to be a father."

Marcus ground his beans and filled the filter.

"Marcus?"

"Predictable," Marcus said, not bothering to turn around.

It grew even quieter.

"What did you say?" Robby asked.

"I said *pre-dict-a-ble.* I mean, it's *predictable* that the two dumbest people in the bunker would copulate and breed before any of the smart people. Just like the Old World."

"You *motherfucker!*" Robby lunged for him.

Brad and Kent held him back with the hysteric help of some of the girls.

Marcus went about with making his coffee until Henry pushed him from behind.

"What's your problem?"

"What's my problem? You, all of you, are trying to *undermine* me."

"Marcus, you're drunk. Go back upstairs and sober up. You are saying things you don't mean."

Marcus unscrewed the cap from a flask and poured liquor in his mug as the coffee trickled down. "I've always heard about this, but never tried it."

"Marcus, go up –"

"Don't tell me what to do!"

At that moment, the lights flickered. Drunken Marcus turned and rolled along the counter to keep his balance.

By the time the attention of the others returned to Marcus, he had drawn a pistol.

Chapter Thirty-Five

Sometime during the night, a card was slipped under Timothy's door. It regretfully informed him that the committee rejected his request for more green rations on behalf of his ailing daughter. Handwritten at the bottom, it said coal depository workers would receive one extra real food meal a week.

He ripped it up and threw it in the trash.

It was almost unbearable to wake his girls for another miserable day of existence, but he realized that was through his own eyes. Madeleine was blissfully unaware and adapted like a champ. Liza, on the other hand, was worse off than he was.

"Time to get up, Maddie."

She rubbed her eyes and sat up.

He gently shook Liza. She moaned and pouted.

"Liza, just give it ten minutes and let's see how you feel. Maybe you'll be up for going to school today."

"I can already tell. My head hurts and my whole body aches."

"Just sit up while we get ready and maybe you'll feel a little better."

"I don't want to go to school anyway. All we talk about is the Bible."

Timothy put on a shirt. "What about math?"

"We do some, but it's easy. Then Mrs. Haag just talks about God some more."

"Is that really why you don't want to go, or are there bullies?" He sat at her side and felt her forehead. "Yikes. That answers that. Your head is on fire. Get some rest, Susan will be over later. I'll get you some food today, I promise."

He kissed her forehead and wasn't sure if it was her fever or his half-hearted promise that burned his lips.

* * *

After dropping Madeleine off at the school room, Timothy walked down the hall to the coal depository. Steve, as usual, was already there.

Steve asked about Liza and the request to the committee.

"Rejected." Timothy sighed as he picked up his shovel. "We got our ration raise, though. As soon as I get mine today, I'm running the food straight up to her."

"Hate to tell you, but we aren't getting ours until Friday."

Timothy threw his shovel down. "It's Tuesday. What am I supposed to do?"

Beyond fed up, he stomped out of the chamber.

He passed the school room, the game lounge, and approached the farm lab. Thirty feet before he reached the doors, a guard stepped out, stretched, and yawned.

Timothy quickly turned around. He looked into the school room window to appear less suspicious but realized that probably didn't help. With nowhere to go, he returned to the coal depository.

"They have guards posted at the farm lab now." He picked his shovel up. "I was going to hold the joint up."

Steve laughed. "You know, the miners get a meal today and Thursday. If you still have any pals up there, maybe one would be willing to bargain with you."

He considered this. "Worth a shot. Don't know what else I can do."

* * *

At lunch time, Timothy hung out outside the cafeteria. Guards were posted there as well. He looked for a familiar face and spotted one.

"Dale, hey!"

"Hi, how are you? I was about to get some grub before my shift. It's real food day!"

"I heard. Actually, wanted to talk to you about that." Timothy paused, frowning. "Dale, my daughter is allergic to something in the Soylent. She has a serious fever and is really sick. She needs real food."

Dale ran his hand through his hair and shook his head. "I don't know, Tim. That's a lot to ask. I'm witherin' away myself and I work all day."

"I'm not asking for charity. I have something to trade." He pulled his phone and earphones from his pocket.

"Who the hell am I going to call down here?"

"No, Dale, it's loaded with music. I used to rock out all shift when I was in the mines. Makes the time fly by." He showed him how it was full of songs.

"My, that is fancy. Just for a meal?"

"It's a rental – let's say, two days for one meal. I can't give it away; my daughters would kill me. They need this thing almost as much as they need food."

Dale thought for a moment. "Make it three days and throw in a Soylent. I'll need something in my tummy."

Timothy put out his hand and they shook. He handed the phone over and waited outside the cafeteria. Dale returned, handing him a tray of food.

"Better be some good tunes on here."

"There are. Thanks, Dale!"

* * *

She ate what she could, and he told her to save every speck on the plate for later. She thanked him and resumed feeling miserable.

He wasn't sure what he expected. An instant cure? It was one meal in one day, with the next a couple days off. It wasn't enough.

By the time he returned to the depository, he was more beat down than that morning. A father who can't provide for his children is no father at all. Liza's life was in danger and Madeleine was undernourished. The future was bleak.

He picked up his shovel but couldn't even begin. "We're doing it tonight."

Steve turned to him. "You talking about what I think you are?"

"At dinner time, when the mine clears out. If there is something significant beyond that wall, it won't matter if we get caught. I don't think I care either way." He struck his first shovelful and dumped it in the cart. "Who knows, maybe we're next to a forgotten Cold War bunker chock-full of rations."

"Wouldn't that be nice?"

* * *

They opened the cell door a little before 6 PM. Steve filled the water jug.

"Is he going to be ready to go?" Timothy asked.

"He's a little groggy," Grant said, "but much better. Hungry more than anything."

As if on cue, Blaine sat up. "You got the ordinance, soldier?"

Timothy lifted his shirt. He had ten sticks of dynamite taped around his torso like a suicide bomber.

"Jesus jumpin' Christ, man. We won't need but a couple of those." Blaine laughed for a moment before he stood and stretched. "Let's get this show on the road."

He seemed better than Grant thought he was.

They loitered outside the mine and waited for the whistle, followed by the lunchtime exodus. When it emptied out, they stepped through the hanging plastic sheets and into the entryway.

Timothy unlocked the storage closet and they pulled out uniforms and helmets. Steve was out of luck. Nothing in his size. He opted to stay posted outside.

Timothy had to backtrack to find the drill rod he'd put in the wall. "Here."

They pulled the rod out and Blaine looked through.

"There's definitely something back there." He put his hand out. "Dynamite, please."

Timothy pulled a few sticks and handed them over. Grant gave him a match booklet.

"Might as well make your way back down the tunnel," Blaine said. "This'll just take a minute. And ditch the rest of those sticks." Blaine was plugging in the first stick as they left.

Timothy removed his suicide vest and put it in storage. When he came out, Blaine was already jogging toward them.

"Any sec –"

The explosion startled them despite expecting it. After a minute, a cloud of black-on-black tumbled toward them in the distance.

Blaine found great pleasure in his work. "Might've been a bit much, but nothing wrong with being thorough." He grinned. "Now we just need to wait for the dust to settle."

"We don't have time for that." Timothy charged ahead and disappeared into the black cloud.

He kept to the northern wall, moving by feel as much as sight. When he hit the debris, Timothy could hardly contain himself.

What was on the other side?

The blast left a hole large enough to crawl through. He waited as the others caught up. Grant went first, followed by Timothy and Blaine.

It was a tunnel – a long one. The walls were rounded and encased in large, curved sections of concrete. The ground was covered in fine gravel chewed up by whatever machine that had eaten its way through. It stretched as far as they could see in each direction.

"What is this place?" Blaine asked. He yelled *"Hello!"* at the top of his lungs. While the echo traveled far, there was no answer.

Timothy looked east. His headlamp could only reveal more of the same, a nondescript tunnel.

"Grant, are you *sure* you counted those steps right? Maybe the elevator is somewhere to the west."

"I counted them right. At least enough to be in the ballpark. We're not even on the grid here."

Their headlamps swung all around.

"Hey, be quiet. Maybe we'll hear water."

They stood completely silent. They heard nothing.

"Found something." Grant picked up a small black device. "I think it's a survey tool. Shoots a laser to measure distance and stuff. Too bad it's shattered."

Blaine looked it over. "Nothing like we had with the SEALs, but I suppose you're right."

Grant tossed it back on the ground.

In each direction, it looked the same. Timothy didn't know what the tunnel was for, but he'd seen enough for now. He turned to leave.

"Where are you going?" Grant asked.

"I'm getting Ashley. I'll drag her down here by her hair if I have to. She has some answering to do."

The two soldiers shrugged and followed him out.

"When we get back, we'll walk the tunnel west back toward the bunker. We're bound to run into something."

On the other side of the hole, they found Dale.

"Timothy, what the hell are you doin' up here? I heard the blast."

"How's the music treating you?"

"I . . . I'm not so sure about this weirdo Radiohead stuff, more of a country fan, but . . . what the hell is *that?*" He looked past them.

"That? That is a secret tunnel. Go have a look around. Crawl through and take a left. See what you can find. We'll be back in a minute."

They ran back down the mine tunnel, slowing to a head-down walk when passing the men returning from lunch. The blast was loud, but apparently didn't draw attention away from the real food being served in the dining hall.

* * *

They caught Steve up on their findings during the jog around the atrium. Timothy knocked on Ashley's door.

320

He shouted, as calmly as he could, through the door. "It's Timothy. I wanted to thank you for getting us our increase in rations."

"You're welcome." A pause. "Is that it?"

"No. I wanted to talk to you about something else, too. Will you open up?"

"I'm sick as a dog. Come back tomorrow."

Timothy was done with the nice guy tactics. He took a step back and plowed his shoulder into the door as hard as he could.

"*Ouch!*"

The door didn't budge.

Steve moved him aside. He tried the handle. It was unlocked. Steve stepped through, and Timothy followed, closing the door behind him. Blaine and Grant remained outside.

"What is this?" Ashley asked. She was sitting at the edge of her bed over a trash bin.

"We blasted through a wall in the mine, to the north. We discovered a rather substantial tunnel."

"You did *what?*" She put her face in her hands. "Shit. You guys messed up. You have no idea."

"Why? What is it? Why is it there?"

She only shook her head.

"*Answer me!*"

"It was a project to connect to another bunker, in . . . in Minneapolis. It was abandoned and will never be finished. It would just upset people if they found out. Remember how Detroit started cranking out all those tunnel boring machines instead of cars? For all those projects across the country? They were really to connect bunkers. This one didn't get finished in time."

321

"I don't believe a fucking word you are saying."

"Yeah? Prove me wrong." She had the gall to laugh at him. "Keep digging for the truth. Heck, dig the rest of the tunnel! I'd love for you to prove me right in about fifty years."

Timothy had a nearly uncontrollable desire to punch her in the face. He looked up to the ceiling and noticed the pulldown attic staircase.

"Mind if I have a look upstairs?" He didn't wait for an answer. He jumped and yanked the cord, and it came flying off.

"Allow me," Steve said. He reached the built-in handle in the panel and tugged, but it was locked tight. He used both hands and pulled harder until he was doing a pull up from the door. There was a sound of wrenching metal, and the door became ajar. He pulled twice more, then *pop!* The stairs came down.

Timothy began climbing.

Ashley jumped up and pulled at him. Steve pulled her back.

At the top, Timothy pushed through a trapdoor with some difficulty. It was covered by a carpet. He kept trying and managed to break through.

It was a bedroom. The bed was covered with fine silk sheets and half a dozen neatly arranged pillows. But it didn't look slept in. The furniture was expensive and unique. The walls were wood-paneled. A small chandelier hung in the center of the room. A set of closed doors led further north. It was luxurious.

He sifted through the drawers. Men's clothing.

Were these confiscated from the deceased miners? They couldn't have been. Nobody in the bunker wore clothes like this.

"It's nice up here, like a luxury hotel suite," Timothy yelled down.

He skimmed through the closet full of suit jackets and dress pants. The bed was nice, but there was a perfectly fine one downstairs. Seemed like too much trouble to climb up. And who replaced the carpet over the door?

"Ever going to tell us who the mystery lover is?" he shouted down.

She didn't answer.

He moved to the French doors. He didn't think it was another closet. They were locked, solid oak, and well-built, with a divider between for more support.

He moved along the western wall, tracing his hand along.

There must be something here.

He knocked on the panels. Solid. On the third, there was a hollow noise. He pushed it, and it released.

There were three switches. Two were unlabeled, while the third only said, *Power Conserve* above it on a plastic strip.

He threw the middle one. Nothing happened, at least that he could perceive. He threw the other unlabeled switch. Again, nothing. He threw the last.

The lights flickered. There was silence, then a great *whirr*.

He heard Grant shouting: "Timothy, come quick! You are going to want to see this!"

323

Timothy climbed down and joined the others outside as Ashley sat despondent on her bed.

He looked through the opening in the chamber toward the atrium. The lights were cascading on and off by floors. The chamber went dark for a full second and came back on.

"That's not it," Grant said. "Look – the door opened!"

The giant steel door he had passed through, unconsciously, with his wife and daughters months earlier, was cracked open.

He looked at the others, who looked back at him.

He moved to the door.

Chapter Thirty-Six

"I tried to protect all of you. I tried to save you."

Marcus swung his gun back and forth, freezing everyone in the café.

"I see how you are looking at me. You think I'm self-destructing – but you, *you* are the destructive ones!"

He jabbed his gun into the air for unneeded emphasis.

"Marcus," Henry said, "put the gun down. Let's just talk. We'll listen." He stood to the right of Marcus and was the closest to him. By speaking, Henry drew his aim.

"Don't speak to me, traitor!"

Marcus moved the muzzle back to the others, ending up on Robby.

"You, too," Marcus said. "I know you told everyone."

"I didn't say a thing," Robby said.

Robby's calm demeanor disturbed Henry, and angered Marcus.

"Yes, you did! I *heard* you!" He raised the pistol and tapped the barrel above his ear.

Henry turned to Robby. "What is he talking about?"

Marcus swung the gun again at Henry.

Robby didn't answer. He remained in a stare-down with Marcus.

Marcus answered for him.

"I had cameras and microphones installed throughout the bunker, but Robby and Kent destroyed them."

"You had *what?*" Mercedes said before covering her mouth.

"I have suffered from a social deficit my entire life. I used the camera to study your interactions to help me understand all of you. I only used it for your own good. But I've cured myself, and now I know how you work – and you are all saboteurs!"

There was a wild, far-off glint in Marcus's eyes. Callous and cold, diabolical, inimical. His lips were taut, and his teeth showed through a slit grin.

Henry thought he might be drunk. He had been drinking, but he was steady and calculated in his movements.

No, he decided, Marcus was simply mad.

"It's too late," Marcus said. "It's all over now."

The lights flickered. In the momentary darkness, several made a move to escape.

Dim battery-powered lights kicked on.

Marcus turned and fired into their huddled mass.

Brad was hit in the upper chest, but managed to stay on his feet, turning to run.

The others scattered.

Marcus fired again, a bullet going over the head of a scurrying Mariya.

Henry was on the other side of the tables and couldn't get to her. He turned and ran.

Becky ran with Brad, but Marcus pursued them out of the café into the gardens. Henry stopped at the gazebo and looked back.

The obelisk at the center of the gardens projected a fierce springtime storm onto the dome above.

Jenna had been knocked down in the rush to escape and was the last to vacate the café. She held her hand above her right eye.

Marcus fired at her and missed.

In her state of panic, she did not follow the others into the living quarters, staying instead in the gardens. Her only hope was the pantry door.

"Stupid, *stupid* girl!" Marcus fired again, again missed.

His third shot did not. It hit her right side.

Jenna stumbled forward. A red blotch grew on her side, and she fell into the stream.

Marcus turned his attention to Henry.

Henry only needed to see Marcus's dead eyes for a split second before he took off toward the storage tunnels.

Marcus sprinted after him.

Henry erred while entering the code. Fine motor skills were shot. *And he would be shot, too, if he didn't get this damn – got it!*

Henry raced past the animals and their noises and opened the storage tunnel door as Marcus slammed through the previous.

The tunnel lights blinked on and off in consecutive sections, creating a rolling strobe effect.

Henry didn't know where he was going, but he ran as far and fast as he could to create the greatest amount of distance.

The strobing lights moved faster than he did, making him feel as if he were moving backward.

Henry turned left, then right, another left, and soon . . . he wasn't sure.

He stopped to get his bearings. He hadn't a clue.

It was deathly quiet.

He couldn't hear any footfalls.

He flinched at a loud noise. It wasn't a gunshot. It was a bassline.

It was music.

The intercom sound system received power priority. Marcus must've dialed up the music from one of the display panels plugged in at each intersection. He was covering his noise.

Henry glanced at a display panel near him and saw *Artist Name: Ciccone Youth, Song: Into the Groovey.*

He continued to roam the tangled tunnels, wondering when it'd be better to stop and hide between some crates, or in one.

He tried to focus through the music, but it was blaring. The guitar riff was jagged and angular, almost skin-piercing. A frequent *clack-clack-clack* amplified through the tunnels. He kept moving. He looked for some pattern in the lights, but it only disoriented him further.

In the background of his mind, he recognized the song lyrics. It was a grunge-y Madonna cover song.

He was only getting more disoriented.

The Madonna imposter was telling him to *Get into the groove.*

And, *Boy you've got to prove your love to me...*

Asking, *Boy what will it be?*

Henry walked into an open intersection.

When he looked to his right, there stood Marcus, waiting.

"What will it be, Henry?"

He was smiling.

"You don't have to do this – any of this," Henry screamed over the music.

At that moment, the song ended.

"Marcus, we can work through it."

"Whew, boy. You have no idea. We had to do it, you know. People had to die, lots of them – *most* of them."

"I realize that. I accepted it. You were right. Limited space, and all that."

Marcus shook his head and then began to laugh. And then it seemed like he couldn't stop. He even had to hunch over.

Several waves of light rolled past, the silence more deafening after the blaring music had stopped.

Henry became impatient.

"I don't find this funny."

"Maybe this will get you," Marcus said, laughing again before letting out a long sigh to gather himself.

Then stared at Henry for a long moment.

"There was never any asteroid."

* * *

He's lost his mind, Henry thought.

". . . But the impact . . . we felt it. It shook the whole bunker."

"The stabilization pillars, Henry — get those counterweights at the bottom moving in conflicting motion, and it creates quite a stir. Also had some special effects to shake the room I planned for us to gather in. As for the aftershocks, most of those were the pillars, too, but some of it was ordinance above ground set to detonate on a schedule. The military placed packages around the site before taking off. Probably bombs from old Vietnam stockpiles. More were dropped later. Idiots placed them a little too close. Damaged some of the vents."

"You were freezing when you came back down from the surface," Henry said. "The sun was blotted out."

"It was December! I stripped my suit off to play it up."

Henry's head was spinning.

"There were people on the surface and flying planes and dropping bombs over bunkers?"

"Nobody flies planes anymore."

"Drones?"

"Drones would imply human control. They were *machines*."

"But . . . *why?*"

"Well, Henry . . . we gave up. Humanity – those in power, at least – *gave up*. Too many people, too many problems caused by the people, and not enough solutions for the people. We went past the tipping point. Drastic times call for drastic measures.

"The Powers That Be orchestrated an abrupt, controlled decline of the human population. They calculated it was better than World War III, or slogging through a thousand stopgap measures that wouldn't solve the inevitable, or the chaos of another pandemic."

Henry tried to process this. "So this is some kind of environmental thing?"

"Mostly, yes. But really, what was going right?"

"Your invention...it slashed emissions below protocol. It solved everything."

"I'm flattered, but it was not the technological ark that would save mankind from global warming, at least not without these drastic measures. There were other things: overpopulation, unemployment, the wealth gap, famine, drought, flooding, disease, colony collapse disorder, unsustainable fishing, species extinctions. I could go on and on. All problems too big to solve. We might knock out one or two here and there, but not all. We are killing all these birds with one massive, imaginary space stone."

"But I don't understand," Henry said. "Why?"

"When it comes to people, the primary issue was what to do with the *Useless Class* created by automation and AI. We don't need these people. But you know what really did us in? The oceans! They were turning to acid!"

"We aren't solving anything down here."

331

"Actually, we are! As we speak the planet is being induced into a coma. Stratospheric aerosol injection, it's called. Basically, sulfur and the like are being pumped into the atmosphere to block sunlight and regenerate the ice caps. It's more acid, and it won't fix the oceanic acidification issue, but we are human, kicking the can further down the road is what we do. It's going to get much colder, arctic cold. Therein lies the necessity for bunkers."

Henry hadn't felt so confused since Marcus told him about the asteroid. Now, it never existed.

"The experts' hope," Marcus continued, "is that the sulfur clouds will be offset by us no longer polluting. Mother Nature will blow through a few thousand water cycles, the forests will grow back, and a much smaller, more efficient human race shall inherit the Earth."

"How long?"

"Three, maybe four decades"

"But what about the people? The ones that didn't get bids?"

"*Everybody* got bids! Communication towers and satellites were shut down, social media messaging was blocked, so Sally in Santa Monica couldn't call Auntie Anne in Indianapolis, and Patty couldn't humble brag about her bid on Facebook.

"Imagine . . . you win the apocalypse lottery, a bunker bid, to stay alive. You ask no questions, be a good citizen, and show up with your family at your designated time and site. You are led through giant doors in the rock face for orientation and to place your things in your designated living space. Instead, you are promptly gassed to death. It's barely an alteration of a Nazi death camp."

"Impossible. Nobody could coordinate this."

"True. Why do you think there was war in the Koreas? Pakistan and India? Eastern Europe? The science was irrefutable. Our planet was on its dying breath. Those that wouldn't get in line were put there."

"On an individual level? Millions chose to die and didn't go to bunkers or those gas chambers. They're still alive, then?"

"Sure, they lived. Maybe a billion still up there. Ironic, right? Whole third world countries haven't been touched. Low priority.

"But look on the bright side! All the real and manufactured urgency brought out the best in us. We colonized the moon. Mars! The space elevator will crash back down in a few years, but what an advance! The last generation of overpopulation pulled its attention up from its gadgets and accomplished a few last great things. When we retake the surface, there will be plenty for everyone. A true resource-based economy! Peace! Longevity! In D.C., I heard rumors of a major CRISPR breakthrough in reversing aging that they've held back. Didn't want it out there when we were already overpopulated. The future will be bright, once the sun comes back out!"

"And what about us, down here? Will we see it? Are you going to kill us all?"

Marcus looked disappointed.

"Henry, I'm not going to kill you. You're my best friend! Now come on, let's go meet our neighbors."

333

* * *

Timothy Spencer led the way around the first giant door, and crept cautiously toward the next, 90 feet ahead. The levers he pulled in that strange room above Ashley's apartment must've opened these doors. Light shone through from the other side.

Three quarters of the way down, the door behind them closed.

"It's Ashley! She's shutting the doors!"

Timothy sprinted forward. Steve surpassed him, crashing against the door and pushing back with all his might. He could only slow it.

"Come on! Go, go, go!"

Timothy slid beneath Steve's arms, followed by Grant. Blaine was nearly caught but made it.

At the last possible second, Steve eked through.

They stood in awe.

* * *

Henry reemerged from the supply tunnels with Marcus behind him.

The gardens were empty.

Someone had retrieved Jenna, or her body. But there were people ahead, through the wide opening into the bunker proper. Marcus marched Henry forward.

There were people there, but nobody who Henry could have ever expected

"Timothy?" Henry lunged.

Marcus grabbed him by his shirt and pulled him back. He showed his gun.

"Henry...Plyman? What is this?" Timothy asked, before spotting the man behind Henry.

"Hello, Timothy," Marcus said.

"Marcus? What is this?*"* Henry said.

"Meet our power source," Marcus said, directed at Henry. "There was never any nuclear power. Couldn't pull it off in time. That circular room in the corner is full of useless blinking lights and functionless buttons. All show.

"Timothy, and others like him beyond that door, have been diligently mining coal and running a power station for us. God knows I wasn't going to subject myself to manual labor."

Marcus took a moment to laugh.

"You know what's funny about blueprints? Two bunkers with a hallway between can look like *one* bunker fit for thousands. At least, that's what the government saw in my plans." Marcus pointed at the door to the other bunker. "A residential area over *there*, connected to the mandated recreational area over *here*. Lock a few doors, and voilà, two bunkers!"

The four men stood like statues.

Marcus moved slowly around them, keeping Henry hostage. He put his thumb on the scanner and opened the door to his apartment stairwell.

"Marcus, wait." Timothy kept his hands visible and didn't move forward. "My daughters, they're on the other side of those doors. I need to get back to them."

"Your daughters? Not excited to see the wife? Shelley was always a bit snobbish."

335

"Shelley is dead. She committed suicide."

Marcus's expression remained blank. He turned his attention to Henry.

"Walk forward, five steps."

Henry did so, then turned.

"You'll thank me someday, Henry, you and your friends. After the barbarian hordes pour through those doors and dirty this place up, eat all the food, piss in the pool . . . You'll *wish* I was here to hold the gates."

Tears dripped from his eyes, betraying the blank expression.

"You are going to miss me! Goodbye, Henry."

He shut the door behind him.

Chapter Thirty-Seven

After Marcus disappeared, everyone began to try to decipher the lies and illusions. Henry was caught up on who Marcus shot.

Timothy, Steve, and the two soldiers took in the vast, open space.

They looked up at the high ceiling, the massive pillars, the façade that looked like a street lined with old-fashioned lights and shops. They saw the balcony above, offering a view into the spacious living quarters and fitness facility. To the right, a tennis court, basketball court, and swimming pool.

The rolling power outage subsided.

Mercedes emerged from the theatre, ran up and hugged Steve.

"Thank God. A *brother!*"

Henry was happy to see Steve, too. Confused, but happy.

"I take it we're not under Minnesota," Timothy said.

Henry said: "No. Indiana."

"Marcus must've taken us right off the plane after they drugged us. That clever son of a bitch."

"Let me get this straight – you four, and whoever else is past those doors, have been mining coal to power all of this?"

"Slave labor to uphold your lavish lifestyles, it looks like," Timothy said.

"How many? There are twelve here. Eleven, now that Marcus has left."

Timothy frowned, disgusted with Henry. "Twelve? Henry, there are a thousand people past those doors, and they are starving and living in misery. This . . ." he gestured to the openness around him, ". . . this is gluttony. I think I'm going to be sick."

"Timothy, check this out," Grant said from in front of the hospital. "The tops of the Soylent tanks. The elevator must be through those there."

Timothy tried to explain to Henry. "Seven stories beneath us, there is a cafeteria serving shit. Soylent. It's all we've eaten for weeks. If you want to call it eating."

Henry was perplexed. "Seven stories? Marcus told us those were stored for a few decades from now. We have another couple in that other chamber that we dip into. We replace a meal a day with it, but most of us just skip it."

"Must be nice."

The hospital door opened and Audrey peered out.

Henry told her it was safe. "How are Brad and Jenna?" he asked.

"I think Brad is going to be fine, but Jenna is in bad shape." She started crying. "I'm sorry. I wasn't trained on any of this. I have no experience." She looked at the strangers.

"This is Timothy. That's Steve, and . . ."

The soldiers introduced themselves.

Timothy asked: "Where does Marcus plan on going? Where does that tunnel lead? There is a tunnel in that direction, apart from here. We blasted into it from our coal mine. We didn't explore it much, but it looked far along."

Henry thought about it. "He must have a passageway from his apartment. A crew was heading our way from the Bloomington bunker. Apparently, they've made the connection. There was supposed to be a tunnel boring machine that would break through over there someday." Henry pointed at the blank wall on the other side of the hospital. "Obviously, it's not here, so I don't know where Marcus plans on going."

* * *

Robby took the new visitors to the gardens. They were unimpressed by the weather dome. They went straight for the food, eating everything they could reach.

Timothy satisfied his appetite, then spoke.

"I need to get some of this to my daughters. Hell, I just need to *get* to them. Liza has an allergy to Soylent. She needs real food like this."

He pushed his plate away and looked up at Kent. "Can you get me to a computer?"

339

* * *

Kent led Timothy straight to a terminal in the server room. In a matter of two minutes, he had Marcus's suite door unlocked.

Timothy packed a couple bags of food before they crossed back to Marcus's apartment door. Henry and Kent tagged along.

Now where is this link to the tunnel? Timothy asked himself. It didn't take him long. He walked into the bathroom and noticed the full body mirror. As he did with the panel in the wall hours before, he pushed on it and it opened. *Aha.*

They descended a metal staircase and opened the door at the bottom. They had little light to work with, but it was enough. Henry and Kent stood agape before the massive tunnel.

There were moving lights far off in the distance, perhaps a half-mile away, though it was hard to tell.

"Who do you think that is?" Henry asked.

"Probably the miners coming through the hole we blasted," Timothy said. "It's okay for now, this door locks."

They returned to the suite.

A sofa blocked a set of French doors. They moved it, unlocked the doors and entered.

He showed them the panel, then exposed the trap door. "This leads down to Ashley's office, part of our bunker."

"Ashley?" Henry asked. "That plain, sort of bitchy assistant?"

"She's been a thorn in my side. Anyway, this is a fairly discreet way of passing between the two bunkers."

Timothy crouched to push the staircase down, but quickly stood back up.

"I just thought of something."

"What?"

"I think Ashley is pregnant with Marcus's child."

* * *

Ashley was awakened by the men dropping from her ceiling.

She mumbled.

Timothy grabbed her. "Good morning, Ashley. You are coming with us."

She said nothing. Her one job was to keep the bunkers separate, and she had failed.

The walls were rough-cut in the chamber. There was no polish anywhere, no flair. It was stone, or concrete. It was almost a laughably cliché dystopian aesthetic. Henry could hardly believe Marcus designed such an ugly, utilitarian structure. It looked Cold-War-Soviet, or something out of Pyongyang.

They walked to the hollow atrium.

Timothy pointed out the mine entrance.

Henry looked over the edge. The air was filled with dust. Everything was bland. Above, a giant fan spun.

The elevator stopped on the top floor. Timothy took out his apartment key. "Prepare to be blown away by our luxury." He opened the door.

It was small, and there was next to nothing in it. A couple beds, a few chairs, a countertop and sink.

"Wake up, girls," Timothy said. "We have to go."

"What are we doing?" Henry asked. "I thought we were just delivering food?"

"I'm taking them with us until we figure things out. They're not spending another night here if I can help it."

They all went back down. Henry realized Timothy was right – there was nobody out and about. They returned to Ashley's office.

She sat at the edge of her bed.

"We will be back to sort things out," Timothy said. "Don't try anything stupid."

She waved her hand and hunched over. "Whatever."

* * *

"What do we do now?" Henry asked the group.

"I propose we announce our existence," Mercedes said, "and the existence of this place, to everyone over there before we open the doors. It'll lessen the shock. We'll organize tours and turn the place into a recreational area they can visit. After all, that's what eighty percent of this place is, recreational space."

"But we don't have a way to secure the gardens," Robby said. "They're out in the open and we can't build a wall around them. And that's the major issue for everyone over there, right? Food? They'll march right past all the cool shit like these guys did and go right for the crops."

"What if we start by sending our surplus over every week?" Henry said. "We throw half of it out, anyway."

"I have a question," Kent said. "Why are people hungry over there? We are only six months into something that's supposed to last decades."

"We had a cockroach farm to make a protein paste," Steve said. "Long story short, they got out and attacked the crops. One food source nearly destroyed the other."

Brittney stood as if the bugs were right there. "Okay, my vote is against opening the doors."

"Not opening the doors...is an option." Grant, one of the soldiers who crossed over with Timothy, stood. "I'm confident nobody over there knows yet. We can wall off Marcus's passageway to the train tunnel. We can work with Ashley to explain our disappearances."

"Wait, wait, wait . . . hold up, hold up," Henry said. "Are you suggesting that we *never* open the doors? Just keep it the way Marcus made it?"

Grant shrugged. "Just putting all ideas out there. Mr. Trencher was right about one thing: they'll come over here and they won't be able to contain themselves."

"No way, that's just wrong," Mercedes said as she stood across from the soldier. "We didn't know anything about you guys over there. Now we do. I'm not about to be a slaveowner."

"What do you think, Timothy?" Henry asked.

Timothy leaned forward, both elbows on the table. "My wife died, my kids are starving and sick. All I can think about is pursuing Marcus down that train tunnel and kicking his teeth in."

Henry scratched his head. "I don't think Marcus is our top priority right now. I'm more concerned—"

"I know, I know," Timothy said. "Look, we have to bridge the two sides. Debating not doing so isn't an option. We just have to get our story straight before we open those doors."

"What is our story?" Robby asked.

"The truth," Timothy said. "Marcus played us all, plain and simple. Word has spread about the miners blasting into the train tunnel. I'll talk to Ashley about calling a meeting and breaking the news about the existence of this place. I'll tell the story. We'll send food over first, so they are not starving. That's a good idea."

Nobody objected.

"One this is certain," Timothy said. "All of you will have to make sacrifices. Otherwise, you guys will always be the upper class, and they'll always be the lower class. You won't get to stay in your plush apartments. You all will move over there, in the barebone cells we've had to live in."

The group grew silent.

"I think it's settled then," Henry said. "We will start making preparations tomorrow and we will aim for, say, three days from now?"

"Make it two," Timothy said. "And I will be hunting Marcus down shortly thereafter."

"Two it is."

Chapter Thirty-Eight

"Where have you guys been?" Nora asked.

Timothy and Steve made an early morning return trip to extract Nora and the baby.

"We have to go," Timothy said. "Get Ben and anything else you need. I want to show you what we found."

She grabbed Ben and nothing else. They were out the door in minutes.

They passed a few dozen miners, for once excited about work. News of the mysterious tunnel had spread. There was a buzz in the hazy bunker air.

But, Timothy's hope for not coming across anyone he knew was quickly dashed. Dale waved and approached.

"Timothy! That tunnel is huge! Any idea what it's for?"

"No idea, Dale. Ashley didn't even know about it. My guess is it was an abandoned Cold War project."

Dale nodded. "Makes damn perfect sense now."

Timothy looked around and moved in closer to Dale. "If anything happens to me, I want you to have my apartment." He held out the key. "Those soldiers are free now and I think they might come after me."

Timothy didn't enjoy lying to Dale, but it was a worthwhile rumor to plant.   Timothy and Steve played a vital role at the coal power station.   Their absence was going to be noticed.

"Shit, Tim. Want me to talk to some of the guys? I'm sure they'd help."

"Thanks, Dale. It's okay. Sorry, we've got to run," Timothy and Steve took off, Nora followed with baby Ben in her arms.

After a beat, Dale chastised himself for not telling them about the funny fellow he met in the tunnel after they had left. He thought he recognized the man from somewhere.

* * *

Soon they would open the doors between the bunkers, but for now they still had to be discrete and climb through the trapdoor in Ashley's apartment.

Ashley let them in, resigned. She managed a fake smile for Nora and the baby.

They climbed above to Marcus's old bedroom. Timothy went first, Steve handed the baby up to Timothy.

Nora came up next. She touched the silk sheets. "Oh, wow. I guess some folks had it better than others."

Timothy shook his head. "You ain't seen nothin' yet."

They moved to the living room of Marcus's suite, which overlooked the bunker proper through a long panel of tinted windows. They waited while Nora took it all in.

"What is this?"

"This might come as a shock, but we are actually under Indiana, not far from the airport in Sherman we had to go to all those months ago," Timothy said. "After we took that sedative, they took us right off the plane, and right down to our bunker before we woke up.

"This place belongs to Marcus Trencher. Or, did. Our sole purpose, on the other side, was to mine coal to keep this place running. There was never a Minnesota bunker, at least for us."

"Where is he?"

"Marcus ran off down that tunnel we blasted into. Supposedly, it leads all the way to a bunker in Bloomington. Let's head down and meet the others."

They descended from Marcus's suite to the bunker proper. Henry and Robby came across from the café.

"Hey, what's this?" Henry said, smiling at Baby Ben.

Nora could only manage a meek smile. She turned to show Ben's baby face.

The others came across from the café, where they were gathering to figure out breakfast without Brad and Becky.

"Nora, I'll introduce you to everyone later," Timothy said. "There is something more urgent. Last night, Marcus went crazy just as we arrived. He shot

347

two people, their friends. Do you think you could help?"

"Sure, I can try." Nora looked at Mariya. "Do you mind watching him for me?"

Mariya beamed. "Of course." Nora handed the baby to Mariya. Mariya, baby Ben and the others returned to the café.

Timothy led Nora to the infirmary. Timothy was taken aback by finding Brad, one of the gunshot victims, up walking around. Brad was shirtless, and the myriad of tattoos were as eye-catching as the bloody bandage. The bullet had hit his upper chest near his left shoulder, just under the collar bone. He was in no shape for a handshake, so they gave each other manly nods.

Nora introduced herself to Audrey and Becky. They brought her up to speed as she wasted no time in beginning her patient check. Jenna was in and out of consciousness.

"She's stable now. You ladies took good care of her," Nora said. "But it's still fifty-fifty. We are going to have to feel our way through surgery to get the bullet and any fragments out."

* * *

Henry had stopped halfway to the cafe. "Shit! *Shit!*"

He hadn't told anyone about the asteroid – or rather, the lack of one.

It was an unforgivable omission. He considered the *good news, bad news* approach, but it would sound like he sat on the information. He thought it best to be straightforward.

Aside from those in the infirmary, everyone was hanging around in the café. He clapped his hands to get their attention.

"I need to fill you in on something important. When we scattered from the café last night, I ran into the storage tunnels like an idiot. It didn't take long for Marcus to catch me. When he did, he told me some unbelievable things."

They were sleepy and a little desensitized to crazy news.

"One of the things he told me was there was never any asteroid."

Now the reactions came about – shock, gasps, expletives and dismissals.

"You mean we're down here for no reason? This is all some fucking practical joke?" Robby said.

"Well, no. Marcus said he believes the planet was in danger and is now being induced into an ice age by spraying something into the atmosphere to block out the sun. They want to build up the ice caps, reverse global warming."

"Excuse me," Timothy said, "but who are 'they'?"

"I don't know, but Marcus made it sound like it's people way more powerful than him. He said the science was irrefutable, that we had blown past all sorts of environmental tipping points and drastic measures had to be taken. The asteroid scare was all a ruse to reduce the world population and nullify all the major problems plaguing the planet."

"That's fucked up," Robby said. "And it's also bullshit. The only tipping point we crossed was putting too many fucking unfeeling sociopath assholes in power."

"There's more," Henry said. "Bunker bids were given to everybody, and travel and communications were restricted, remember? According to Marcus, bunkers were made to kill off everyone who didn't get a real bid. Super Holocaust type shit. Like, they built false bunkers all around the world and sent people to them, and these people thought they were lucky, but it was really a massive gas chamber."

More gasps of horror and shock. Ken, normally the quietest of them all, was the first to burst into sobs. Others were taken aback.

"Don't you guys get it? Marcus told me my family was getting real bids," Ken said between sobs. "But there's no way he had them escorted out of Portland. My family is dead. They're all dead!"

The realization set in. They were all promised the same. Marcus assured them all that their families were given bunker bids. They shared no confidence that these bids were for true bunkers. They cried for their parents, their siblings.

Henry felt a pang of guilt. His parents had bids reserved for the Bloomington bunker, unlike everyone else. Were his parents truly still alive in the Bloomington bunker? He had no proof. He had only Marcus's word, same as everyone else. Surely Marcus kept *that* promise.

Henry suppressed his doubts before they could overwhelm him. He let everyone grieve a moment longer, but he had more to tell. He cleared his throat.

"Now, the people who opted out and decided to accept death-by-asteroid, ironically, all might still be alive up there somewhere. But there is a force of drones patrolling to wipe out these remaining people. Between the mini ice age and the machines, bunker life was expected to last 30-40 years, a period which would outlast the straggling humans up on the surface and give the Earth time to heal."

Timothy turned in his seat to face Grant and Blaine. "Any of this drone stuff plausible to you two?"

"Honestly, yeah," Grant said. "Military contractors would show off the latest tech for us. Some of the older guys in my unit went on to be analysts and do consulting work. They saw some crazy shit. Hangars full of drones and kill bots. I can't confirm Marcus was telling the truth, but the tech exists...and not just theoretically, but built and deployment-ready."

"Hold up – what exactly is a 'kill bot'?" Mercedes asked.

"Essentially what it sounds like. A drone, fitted with weapons, programmed to hunt humans. Some models in the air, some on the ground. You know all those sensors we had on our self-driving cars that would spot pedestrians, animals, school buses and stuff? The tech isn't far from that, but instead being used for safety, it's designed to identify and eliminate humans."

"Are they, like, shooting lasers at us?"

Grant half smiled. "Nah, old fashion bullets and bombs. Lasers just for detection."

Blaine nodded. "I talked to guys stationed all around. They couldn't be specific, but they were

351

working closely with Tassor Robotics and other big-time contractors on something very hush-hush. They stole that machine-learning tech from the car companies and weaponized it."

"So a few drones fly over an area, use LIDAR or heat sensors or whatever, spot humans, and either bomb them or deploy ground drones?" Steve asked.

Grant said, "That about sums it up. And, by the way, as lethal as all that shit is, it isn't totally autonomous. If there is an army of machines up there, there is an army of people to do repairs. They aren't advanced enough to fix themselves." He frowned. "There might be whole communities or bases of humans up top running the show."

Wouldn't that be something? Henry thought. The real power players in the world didn't have their own luxury bunkers – they were probably on an island in the Caribbean, lounging about, taking their new CRISPR life-extending drugs.

Robby was still standing, hands on his hips. "What are the odds they are waiting outside our bunker to see if we escape?"

"They could have a sentry bot posted," Grant said.

"Sentry bot?" Mercedes said.

"A stationary kill bot. Kind of stands guard. One that doesn't move much or at all. Outside the bigger government bunkers, I am sure they have several. If they are out to kill everyone, they probably patrol and pass over, clear sector-by-sector, say county-by-county of what was the U.S., like Steve just said. Do they have our place surrounded waiting for someone to step out? I have no idea."

"Remember," Mercedes said, "Marcus went outside for a little while. Came back alive."

"Then it's settled," Robby said. "I'll go out first and make sure it's safe."

Chapter Thirty-Nine

Not everyone wanted to go up.

Nora had to deal with a crying baby. Becky kept by Brad and Jenna. Henry opted to stay down but did see the others off as they crowded onto the elevator platform.

After the long ascent, the platform came to a stop under the concrete dome that acted as a lid on the shaft.

"Hope there's no killer robots out there," Robby said as he cracked open the door.

Timothy moved back. He didn't want to get blasted by a killer robot.

White light beamed through the thin slice between the edge of the door and the wall.

Robby pushed to open it further, but the door stopped.

"What's wrong?" Melonie asked.

"There's several inches of snow on the ground," Robby said.

He put his shoulder into it and cleared an opening.

Robby stepped into fresh snow. Fat flakes floated down from the sky. He closed his eyes and spread his arms and breathed in the cold air. He was once again on the surface of Planet Earth. Who would've ever thought that would be something they took for granted?

The others wandered out; their fear of killer robots alleviated by the moderate snowfall. It looked so *normal*.

The brightness and cold wind made Robby's eyes water until tears streamed down his face. He yelled: *"Wooo!"* to the white landscape.

The others enjoyed their own personal spiritual experience. Some picked up the snow despite being gloveless, others ventured further out.

They stayed out as long as they could bear. Despite being numb nose to nails, they felt more alive than any time in their lives.

* * *

Henry had the bunker to himself.

There was Nora and the baby, but they were nowhere to be seen. He peeked into the infirmary. Becky was reading a book beside Brad. She smiled and nodded. Audrey was asleep on the one open bed. Jenna was hooked up to tubes and machines. It made Henry uncomfortable and he walked away.

Outside the infirmary, he gazed up at the high ceiling not unlike the first time Marcus gave him a tour. He wondered if he would ever see him again.

Did he want to? Marcus shot two of his friends. Marcus enslaved a thousand people to power the bunker. Marcus was complicit in the organized slaughter of billions.

Henry thought Marcus was probably a pawn in the whole scheme, but he couldn't be sure. He was running out of reasons to give Marcus the benefit of the doubt. Marcus kept the truth from them all.

Still, there was an irrational ember of love for who was once his best friend.

Henry lost track of the time. In his wandering and wondering, he found himself in front of the giant, grey door that separated them from a thousand suffering people. He'd seen the other side only briefly, but it was enough to feel the inequality.

Timothy painted a bleak picture of life on the other side. It had the opposite effect of what he intended. The decision to open the door was being put off. Henry could tell when Timothy told them their quality of life would take a dive. They wouldn't look at each other. The thought of living in barren apartments on the other side, and having to rely on Soylent for meals, was depressing. Henry felt horrible that Timothy and so many others had to go through that.

For all the criticism put upon Marcus, when put in the very same position, most of them secretly desired to choose exactly as Marcus did. Henry could sense it. They were the rich living in their gated community away from all the poor service workers.

Maybe that was what Marcus thought he was protecting them from – the uncomfortable decision to put themselves before others. It wasn't their cruelty, it was his! It's amazing what one-step-removed can do to protect one's conscience, he thought.

Henry approached the door. He reached out and touched it.

He turned and looked back across the bunker.

Still empty, still alone.

The thought crept into his mind: the decision could be his. *He* could open the door. Do the deciding for everyone.

Then, he didn't need to.

The door creaked and popped and moved on its own. It was opening.

Tons of slow-moving steel nearly knocked him on his back before he gathered himself. *Who is doing this? Did Marcus set some kind of timer? Ashley? Did Timothy crash the bunker computer? What the hell?*

He pushed at the door, but there was no stopping it. Adrenaline proliferated in his bloodstream. Sweat surfaced from every pore. His stomach dropped. He looked back. Still alone. He swallowed with a dry mouth.

The door came to a halt after what felt like an eternal swing. He felt the air *whoosh* through the dark corridor to equilibrium.

The switch to close the doors was in Marcus's suite. He could get lucky and close it before anyone noticed. And *then* they would open them *back* up in the responsible manner they had voted on earlier.

Before he could take action, he heard a noise in the corridor.

It was the echo of a bouncing basketball – specifically, the cheap rubber kind he played with in the driveway as a kid. It was accompanied by a patter of footsteps. There was no lighting. Out of the void, sure enough, a basketball clipped the wall, bounced, and rolled to Henry's feet.

It was a beat-up old thing, slick and gripless, worn down to black rubber in spots, bulging in others. It'd seen better days. He picked it up as if he wasn't sure it was real.

He looked up to find three grubby little boys in front of him, the oldest no more than ten.

"*Whoah!* I didn't know this was here!" the tallest said, rubbernecking around Henry.

Henry blinked, and after a moment, handed the ball to the smallest child.

"Mister, do you have a basketball court?" the tallest asked.

Henry looked over his shoulder and found himself thumbing back behind him, beyond the tennis court, next to the swimming pool, to the basketball court.

"Can we play on it?" another asked.

Henry shrugged, which was interpreted as "Yes."

They sped around him like he was a rock and they were rapids.

He shook out of his stupor. "Wait, wait, wait – hold up." The three boys stopped and turned around.

"Uh, in there, the court, there is a door to your right. It's a supply closet. There are brand new basketballs in there you can use."

The dirty faces lit up and their sprint resumed. *"This is where the rich people live!"* one shouted to the other two.

Henry found himself alone again. The door still gaping. His friends were still above on the surface. He watched the boys sprint all the way to the court and watched the first shot launched from the corner. It hit the side of the backboard.

When Henry turned back to the open corridor, he met the whites of a dozen angry eyes emerging from the dark.

Chapter Forty

"What is this? Who are you?"

"I recognize him! He's the Plyman's boy. Marcus Trencher's sidekick."

"Where is that prick?"

He put us down in that shithole while this *place was next door?"*

Henry backed up as a growing crowd poured out of the corridor. He found himself putting his hands up in a defensive posture. He looked back to see if the others had come back down from the surface. They were not there.

"Look, everyone, I can explain what this is. Let's just remain calm."

They were anything but. Some pushed past him, gawking at the high ceiling in wonderment and disgust. Others kept their angry coal-smeared faces centered on Henry. All eyes shot daggers.

"We had no idea you were next door to us. Marcus tricked us, too," Henry said.

"How the hell you think you got power? Magic?" a man said, stepping into Henry's personal space.

"Marcus has this whole reactor chamber back here. I'll show you. It looks real. He duped us!"

The man smirked. He didn't buy it.

Henry was about to continue his explanation but was caught off guard by his recognition of the man. A year before, Robby had punched the guy's lights out at Dan-O's Bar and Grill. He hoped the guy didn't remember anything from that night.

"Look, I didn't know anything, I swear. The others here didn't know either. Only Marcus, and he took off down the train tunnel. There is a tunnel that —"

"We know about the tunnel. We blasted into it from the mine."

Henry felt he made a millimeter of progress. "Yes, I think that miner was Timothy Spencer. He lived over there with you guys. He broke through last night. We were trying to figure out how to get these doors open. Honest."

More and more came through. Three dozen? Fifty? Henry couldn't tell. They were spanning out, noticing more and more. Henry was gradually backed up and surrounded by men more interested in the injustice than the newfound amenities.

"You are all welcome—"

The men laughed grimly. A faceless voice in the crowd said, "Don't you worry, buddy! We'll make ourselves right at home."

A woman yelled out from the pantry door. "They have food! Tons of it!" Another had made her way to the gardens, and yelled that there was food there, too. The swelling horde rushed in that direction.

The angriest stayed with Henry.

361

"We are starving over there," a face in the crowd said to Henry. "Starving!"

"My little brother and my best friend both died in that fuckin' mine, while you were over here livin' it up!"

Henry looked back, hoping the others had returned.

"I'm talking to you, boy." The man stepped face to face with Henry.

"I'm sorry. I don't know what to...just...the place is yours. Just please..."

"Let's put him on trial!" a man yelled from the outer edge of the encirclement.

The man in Henry's face said, *"Fuck that."*

The man stepped back and raised his mining pick. He jabbed with it like a spear, connecting the blunt top with the bridge of Henry's nose. Henry was enshrouded in a mist of blood and knocked on his back.

The violence was infectious. Henry was pummeled. Heavy boots stomped and kicked. He was blinded by the blood and tears pooling in his eyes. He covered up as best he could. His mind went blank, defaulted to survival mode.

The frenzy grew more vicious.

Henry was losing consciousness when the sharp end of a pick slipped between two of his ribs. He let out a guttural cry with every bit of air left in his lungs. It shocked the mob into a reprieve. They stepped back.

They looked to the ringleader with the blood-tipped pick, the former drunken yokel other patrons at Dan-O's would goad to do stupid things so they could laugh.

He raised the pick for a finishing blow.

Despite the puncture between his ribs, Henry was able to gasp: "There's no asteroid!"

The crowd let out a chorus of *Huhs?* and *What'd he say?*

"You can go up," Henry said, "to the surface." Doubled over, clutching his side, he pointed toward the door that led to the elevator. He could see its blurry form through the blood and the feet of the mob.

The man lowered his pick, slowly, and thankfully, not into Henry's skull.

"That's where the others are."

It was enough to make the crowd dissipate. The men went to investigate the door.

Hundreds of ragged people now roamed the bunker, ignoring Henry and the pool of blood he lay in. Most went for the food in the pantry and garden. He heard the splashes of people jumping into the pool.

He couldn't be sure, but he thought he may be dying. The hole in his side made it near impossible to move. Another pool of blood was gathered from what he spit from his mouth and poured from his nose.

He kept his bleary eyes on the door. Where were his friends?

His mind escaped the pain and took him up there to them, his friends, on the surface. He held Mariya's hand and ran through the snow he imagined was covering the ground. He saw Robby and felt the urge to laugh, but that hurt too much.

Details fell away and became abstract and senseless. He found himself in the train tunnel with Marcus. Marcus beckoned him to the bright light at the end of it.

It made sense to go.

He was shaken, and the delirium fell away.

"Jesus, those savages," he heard a woman say. "Stay with me." She tapped his cheeks and looked into his bloody eyes.

This flurry of activity around him, unlike the last, seemed to be helping.

* * *

After an indeterminable blink, the same chaos surrounded him, but now he was in a bed. He saw Brad peering from behind the nice women and their hurried movements. He wore a white patch on his breast with a blood-red dot. It looked like a Japanese flag. Henry tried to smile but fell back into a slumber before he could.

When he next opened his eyes, the consciousness felt more sustainable. Nobody hovered above him this time. He noticed his hand was held. It was Mariya, there, crying.

At the foot of the bed, Robby, Timothy, and the others who had went to the surface, were now in a heated debate. Everyone he knew was crowded in the room.

They were looking out the infirmary window, gesturing at the people wandering about. *How did the doors get open?* someone asked. Henry had wondered the same thing.

"Guys," Mariya said.

They turned their attention and gathered around Henry. There were apologies and well-wishing. Henry cleared his throat.

He said, "Is everyone else okay?"

"Yeah, we had a little scuffle by the elevator, but we are fine," Robby said.

"What's going to happen?"

Robby sighed. "I don't know, man. A bunch of them went up to the surface. They have us locked in here while they ransack the place."

"Hopefully they all go to their homes on the surface," Timothy said. "We didn't tell them anything about the squadrons of killer drones that may or may not exist."

"Even if the drones don't exist, they'll be lucky to last the winter..." Steve said.

The conversation swirled above Henry. He was too sedated to keep up, so he contemplated the topic to himself.

If what Marcus said was true, brutal winter weather was to last for a long time. A mini ice age, he had called it. The summer months, if not still freezing cold, was going to be human hunting season for drones. In short, it was the whole reason the bunkers were constructed.

There was no food up there, no logistics chain to fill the grocery. Farmland was tundra. They could go up to hunt deer for old times' sake, but they were going to return to the bunker.

As for their fate, they could only pray for mercy. Maybe there would be a trial. Maybe the former citizenry of Sherman, Indiana would listen to their side of the story and grant clemency. He had hope that they could co-exist. Perhaps they'd be exiled to the Bloomington bunker where they'd see Marcus again.

He squeezed Mariya's hand and looked in her eyes. Whatever may come, he wanted to hold on to his friends.

It was all that mattered.

Epilogue

Marcus Trencher sat atop the skeletal, deconstructed machine that had created the way of his 25-mile trek. His teeth scraped and chattered on gunmetal. A muzzle irritated his soft palate. He flexed every muscle in his body in hopes of it doing the trick, because the muscle in his trigger finger wouldn't. He jabbed the gun inward and tasted blood. Still, he couldn't. He withdrew, again.

So it went, for three days, over and over. Nobody had yet sent a party after him.

He sat on the machine, the machine against a dead end. There was no tunnel breakthrough.

He suspected as much, only after passing the baffled miners and the blasted hole in the tunnel wall. By then, it was too late to turn back. He handed a bottle of whiskey to a guy named Dale and walked past. He deeply regretted it now. He needed liquid courage for such a cowardly act.

The noise of the blast fooled him when he was in a vulnerable state of mind, a poor one; a stupid one. He still was, clearly, but he was well enough to realize

how ignorant it was to mistake a dynamite blast a
mile down tunnel for a boring machine 25 miles
away. Stupid.

He was running out of food and water to keep
him alive long enough to kill himself. The option of
returning to the bunker was no option at all. He felt
he could face up to murder, if he had in fact killed
whoever he shot. He couldn't remember who it was.

What were they going to do, isolate him? Nobody
had the guts to execute him. Nobody, at least, with
Henry around. Maybe exile him to the shit bunker?
He'd take over within a week and lead a revolt. Those
things didn't scare him.

What scared him was the thought of returning a
fool – to look *stupid*. He could barely stand to
consider it. *To look stupid*. Never.

The gun was a better option. He put it back in his
mouth, this time relaxed. There were no protruding
veins this time, no frantic breaths trying to inflate the
gun. Tears dried up days ago.

He imagined his mother and smiled the best he
could with the obstruction. He moved the trigger,
minutely, but it was the furthest he'd made it. His
smile grew. He was ready.

Then, the earth vibrated.

At first, he only felt the metal scaffold rub against
the wall, an annoyance that took him from his
mother's embrace. He opened his eyes and listened.
He put on his headlamp. He set the gun down.

He crawled to the edge of the platform and
looked down. He saw stones hopping. The stagnant

puddles of water, once placid, now danced in rapid, clashing circles.

Is it real? Did he finish the job? Is this is all a figment pieced together by the last synapses firing from his wrecked brain? Was he Peyton Farquhar from the story Henry made him read, rationalizing the irrational passage of death? He waited and wanted to find out.

It grew more convincing. When he struggled to stand, he was sure of it.

He unloaded the gun and put it in his bag. He changed clothes and switched out his now useless bunker smartwatch for a flashier model. He had no mirror, but he fixed his hair the best he could. He moved a safe distance from the wall and waited.

Hours later, the wall blurred and obliterated in his light. The noise pushed him back further. After the dust settled, in its place was the face of a gigantic machine, looking like some parasitic worm under a microscope, with its hooks and blades and hairs.

The machine shut off. Marcus fixed his collar.

After ten minutes, one of the blades wobbled and retreated into the machine. A man stuck his head out, like a munchkin from the gates of Emerald City. He ignored Marcus, disappeared for a second, and yelled, "Guys! We made it!"

Marcus walked up to the machine face. The man now hung out of his window, grinning ear to ear. He finally realized he should say something. "Hello!"

"Greetings. I'm Marcus Trencher."

He removed his watch and tossed it to the man.

"I'd like a ticket for the next trip back to Bloomington, please."

About the Author

Shane Noble is from Sullivan, Indiana. He has lived in Louisville, Kentucky, since 2006, where he attended Bellarmine University to play baseball (and learn stuff).

He hopes to write more books.

Made in the USA
Monee, IL
18 November 2020

48362971R00218